DARK CHOCOLATES

DARK TREATS AND TALES OF MYSTERY AND HORROR

JEREMY BROCK

BLUE WEKA

Published by Blue Weka Publishing

Contact author: https://www.facebook.com/jeremybrockauthor

A catalogue record for this book is available from the National Library of New Zealand.

Photo credit for title page: Blue Weka by R. Shaldrake.

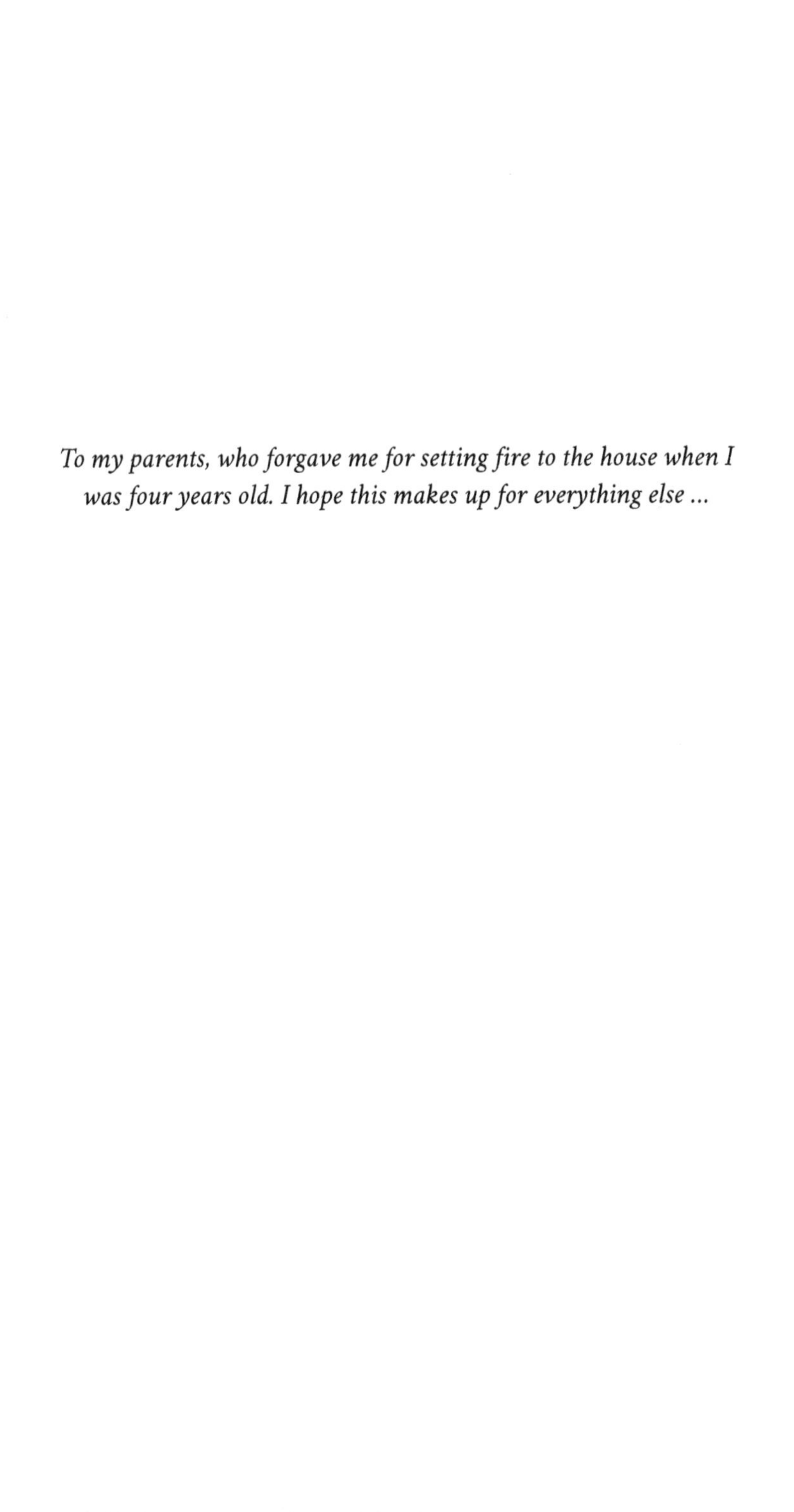

To my parents, who forgave me for setting fire to the house when I was four years old. I hope this makes up for everything else ...

CONTENTS

57 Palm Tree Drive	1
Along Came a Spider …	29
Building Blocks	35
Child-ish	47
Gone Fishing …	53
Young at Heart	63
Hooked	105
Kaleidoscope	125
The Imaginon	147
The Pit	163
Way out	219
About the Author	239

57 PALM TREE DRIVE

THE HOUSE LOOKED IN PERFECT ORDER, SMALL AND WHITE — dainty even. As Detective Jackson looked around he couldn't help noticing every single object on the picturesque property in its proper place, meticulously organised, from the smallest manicured bushes and ball-shaped trees to the fresh garden bag on its stand beside the coiled hose and tap unit. Only the loud screeching of cicadas spoiled the summer morning under the cloudless sky. The sun beat down through the hot, humid air. It felt like time was standing still as he walked up the path, climbed the white steps, stepped past the red wooden door held by the constable, into the cool hallway of 57 Palm Tree Drive.

Sandy, as he was known to his friends, or simply 'Jackson' by his workmates, was thirty-seven years old, but today he felt like fifty. He had been up most of the night with his two-year-old son who wouldn't sleep, so of course sleeping was uppermost on his mind. He knew he wouldn't be getting any of that soon with a murder this morning, an aggravated burglary and an armed hold-up of a service station just added to their job list. It was a fairly normal morning — if anything could be called normal for a detective in Auckland. He spotted his partner, Sam Agraval, standing at the end of the hallway, by the rear door. Sam looked up and caught his eye with a nod, so he ambled down the dim corridor, catching a reflection of his tired face as he passed a mirror on the wall. *Oh God, I actually look worse than I feel!* As he squeezed up beside Sam at the end of the narrow hallway, a blast of her perfume dragged his muted senses awake.

'You look like you've been up all night with Ben again,' said Sam, the clear, green eyes watching him closely.

He just nodded.

Sam's flashy orbs studied him. He knew she was reading him like a book and that just made it worse.

She couldn't help noting his bleak, red-rimmed eyes. They were hidden further than usual inside their crevices. They actually seemed angry above the bloodless cheeks and thin, dry lips. Her eyes dove away smoothly to bury themselves in the paperwork in her hands. He looked past her into the laundry to her left. Everything seemed immaculate in the room, the surfaces gleaming in the sunlight flooding through the window.

'Where's the body?' he asked.

She nodded towards the back of the property, somewhere beyond the rear door.

'Right in the middle of the yard, lying face down,' she replied. Her attention turned back to her notes.

'No witnesses so far,' she added, flicking through the papers. 'The old lady, Mrs … uh Candy found the body first thing, about 8.30. A male, long black hair, lots of tattoos. Upper body is naked. Large wounds to the right side and back of his head, and also to his back and right shoulder. Neighbours heard nothing suspicious, possibly because there was a loud party up the back last night. Mrs Candy claims she went to bed early in the evening and never heard anything.'

They looked up for a moment as they heard the constable at the front door talking to someone. Jackson could see a young boy with a small round face standing outlined in the bright light. In a timid voice, the boy asked the policeman if he could see Mrs Candy. The constable asked him his name.

'Leon,' he answered quickly, sneaking a look round the door and down the hallway. The constable told him to come back later. Jackson turned back to Sam, who continued.

'No suspect. No weapon identified as yet. No obvious motive. Unfortunately, that's really about the guts of it,' said Sam.

Jackson nodded, tilted his head back slowly and wiped his face with his hands. He felt like he could sleep for a week. He motioned towards the back door. She walked over, opened it with a glove-covered hand and they both stepped out into a sun-drenched backyard. It was a decent space, sloping slightly upwards towards a large rock wall at the rear of the property. A couple of garden sheds on little concrete pads stood to their left, with a large vege garden with dark, almost black-coloured soil, tucked behind the sheds. There were citrus trees planted in rows down the property. To their right was a small paved courtyard. Beyond the courtyard stood a revolving clothesline set into the centre of bricks laid in the grass. The circles of red bricks were a sharp contrast to the lush, green grass. In front of them, three forensic experts dressed in white boiler suits and gloves were working on their hands and knees inside a taped-off, roughly square area surrounding the body. It lay there, just beyond the clothesline. They wandered over to the tapes. They stood and looked down at the heavily tattooed corpse sprawled face down on the grass.

Jackson looked around the tidy backyard.

The dead body with long black hair and tattoos sprawled on the grass seemed an abomination.

'So why here?' he wondered aloud.

Sam simply shrugged her shoulders.

He turned and faced the back door for a second. Then he turned towards the sheds, then again to the fence to their right and back to the body.

'Weird …,' he muttered mainly to himself. He walked around the tapes and bent down on the far side of the body.

'Do we have a time on it yet?' he asked, looking up and squinting into the sunlight.

'Basically,' said Sam. 'Gibson did the preliminary, he left about twenty minutes ago. Best guess at this stage is about minus ten or twelve hours. That would make it sometime between 11 pm last night and 1 am this morning.'

'And obvious cause is blunt force trauma to the head — but occurring where, here?' asked Jackson.

Sam shrugged. Jackson straightened and came back round to where she was standing.

'Nowhere near enough bloodstains …,' said Sam. They both looked at each other for a while, not talking.

'Has anyone spoken to the neighbours yet?' he asked, looking across and shielding his eyes with his hand.

'Yes, which gives us something interesting. Apparently the Bentleys, they're on this side here at 55,' she said, pointing out the modern blue, bungalow-styled house. 'They're pretty sure they recognise him. Said the guy had been visiting the old lady on and off for the last twelve months or so. Most of the time he parks his car up the road and sneaks through behind their place, jumps the fence and knocks on her back door. Normally this happens late, about 10 pm to midnight. The husband here, Mr Bentley, has warned him before about going through their backyard at night. With all his tattoos on show, he's pretty sure it's the same guy.'

Jackson absorbed the information with his tired, sluggish mind.

'Where is Mrs Candy?' he enquired, his greyish eyes getting a little sparkle of blue back.

'She's in the sitting room with Humphries,' she said breezily, knowing how much it would aggravate him.

He stopped and looked at her.

'What the hell is Humphries doing here?'

'Apparently they've decided it's better if he's back at work,' she replied.

'Oh great — but why the hell us, for god's sake ...?' Jackson fumed quietly for a few seconds, then decided to let it go. He knew to keep his personal feelings to himself, *but Humphries ...*

They had butted heads for many years in the same department and he knew Humphries had it in for him. The bastard had been promoted to a level higher than Jackson two years ago. Immediately, he had used any opportunity he could to try to get Jackson demoted. He had even cited him for unprofessional conduct. All this because Jackson had abused him on more than one occasion for his stupidity. The last time at a crowded crime scene, full of onlookers. They had developed a hatred for each other, however it had never come to blows, just open hostility towards each other. Jackson had thought he'd got rid of his nemesis three months ago, when Humphries collapsed on a job in Hamilton. Apparently, the office talk was he had some kind of cancer, or terminal illness. Now it was obvious he was back and on the same case as them, just when Jackson thought he had won himself some breathing space. He shook his head to clear his thoughts, but his brain seemed to be made of wool.

'So what was this guy doing visiting the old lady here?' he asked quietly.

Sam waited as one of the forensic team finished up and took some bags and equipment back towards the house.

'No idea. I doubt the old lady's into heavy metal. Long lost grandson maybe?' she offered.

'Do you have any ID yet?' he asked.

'Yep, a wallet in his jeans with about sixty dollars and a few cards in it. The name on the driver's licence is Brendan Jefferies. The photo matches. Age twenty-eight. His address is in Balmoral about five kilometres away. Interestingly, he has a whole lot of previous for mostly minor things — assault, petty theft, burglary. Seems like a classic, small-time all-rounder, pretty much,' she finished.

'You might want to see this,' interrupted one of the forensic team, still at work on their hands and knees. The boiler-suited policewoman carefully shifted the victim's right arm to one side, which revealed some shapes in the grass. Jackson and Sam walked around the tape to look at it closely. It looked like three small symbols cut into the brown dirt. The first symbol looked like it was a capital 'G', or a 'C'. Next to it was a small circular letter like an 'o', or possibly an 'a'. The third shape was just a small bent line. It looked like they had been gouged repeatedly into the grass. The other member of the forensic team began to carefully photograph the marks. Jackson noted the corpse's right index finger was covered in thick brown dirt.

He stood and straightened up.

'What do you think of that?'

Sam shrugged her shoulders.

'The start of the murderer's name maybe? Next week's Lotto numbers?'

He looked around the yard again.

'Have we checked these sheds yet?'

'Yes,' she replied, 'a cursory, for likely weapons.'

They walked over to the first shed and Jackson dragged open the door. Inside, he saw rows of plastic bottles containing chemicals and fertilisers lining the top shelf. The shelves below had a line of neatly stacked packets of assorted plant seeds. In one corner was a bundle of rakes, hoes and other long-handled tools in a wooden rack. Two bags of compost were stacked against the wall. Jackson examined the tools and a pair of dirt-covered gloves on a hook, then dragged the door closed and walked over to the second shed. An unclasped padlock dangled from the bolt on the wooden door. He slid the door open. Parked inside the second shed was a lawn mower beside a sturdy-looking wheelbarrow. On the wall, hanging on a series of wooden pegs, was a weed-eater, a hedge trimmer and a leaf blower. Fuel cans and parts for the weed-eater sat on a pair of narrow shelves. He took a pair of latex gloves from his pocket and pulled the wheelbarrow out into the bright sunlight. He bent over it, examining it closely. Sam waited patiently.

'Has this been done?' he asked.

Sam nodded her head.

'You think it could have been used to shift the body?'

Jackson nodded slowly.

'Get them to examine it again as soon as they're finished on the lawn.'

She made a note in her notebook and asked, 'What about the strange marks cut into the grass, they mean anything to you yet?'

'Mmmm. The first shape might be the letter 'C', or a 'G', or a fish hook, or a badly drawn circle, but whatever it is or means, it was definitely done by the victim.'

She nodded, still writing. The only noise was her pen scratching at the paper.

'Right, well, it's time to talk to the little old lady then,' he said finally. 'Where's her sitting room?'

'Third door on the right, down the hallway. I'll let you know if I find anything else out here.'

Jackson nodded and walked towards the house. He felt so tired. He climbed the steps trying to work out the proper order to ask his questions. He opened the back door and closed it behind him. He made his way down the corridor, turned the handle of the third door on the right and entered. It was a bright room with light-coloured walls and a dark, polished floor. A large cabinet crammed full of fine pieces of china stood against the wall beside the door. Two people sat quietly in the chairs by the table at the far end of the room. Humphries beamed at the sight of him.

'Jackson, I was just telling Mrs Candy, sorry, Edda,' he corrected himself, then carried on, 'how tough you can be on people at crime scenes, so we agreed I'd take her statement to save us both time and trouble. I knew you wouldn't mind, after all we're here to help, aren't we, detective?'

Jackson felt like swearing at him — which was normal. He glanced at the written statement underneath Humphries' hand, then he addressed Mrs Candy, who sat quietly with her hands in her lap.

'Mrs Candy.'

'Please, all my friends call me Edda,' she replied.

He looked closely at her, estimating her age. She looked a fairly fragile old lady, at least seventy, judging by her thin, white hair. She had a tiny wrinkled face and small, nondescript features. A thin mouth sat beneath a button nose amongst a greyish sea of lined skin. A pair of pale blue eyes peered out from the folds and held his gaze steadily.

'Would you like a cup of tea?' she asked politely.

'No, thank you,' replied Jackson.

Humphries beamed again, this time at Mrs Candy. 'I

would love one, Edda, thank you,' he chortled, settling back into his chair.

The old lady got up and shuffled through a doorway to the right, into the small kitchen.

'Thank you, Detective Jackson, that was brilliant. That's all we need for now,' said Humphries.

Humphries smiled in his infuriating way, then turned his back on Jackson, pretending to enjoy the view out the window.

Jackson shook his head slowly as he walked out of the room, but it didn't clear his cloudy mind, or his mounting anger. The man just seemed to rub him up every way possible. He wandered down the hallway, chose the next door to the right for no real reason other than he thought he'd probably be alone with his thoughts. This room was much darker, lined with heavy maroon curtains that were drawn to shut out the sunlight. It was basically a dark, wood-panelled library, with books across the far wall and curios and other items mounted on the wall to the right. In the left corner was a small desk. Beside it was a bare wooden table with two boxes and some wrapped parcels stacked on it. The air was musty in the room, but there was also another smell. He could smell bleach, or cleaning polish, as he stood there. He studied the strange objects and the different feel this room had to the others, then walked back out, quietly closing the door behind him. He tried the last door of the hallway on the right. It opened to reveal a large living room, channelling bright sunlight through the two big bay windows. There weren't many furnishings, just a TV on one side and a large fireplace on the other. There were no paintings on the ornate peach-coloured wallpaper that decorated the walls. As he stood there, he noticed a slight smell of smoke in the room. He walked over to the fireplace. There was a small pile of ash in the grate. He poked the ashes around with his pen absentmindedly, trying to push Humphries from his mind. He wandered over to the windows that looked over the front of the property. The road outside seemed quiet. There were two patrol cars and three plain police cars parked in a row outside the house. He bent down and pulled the edge of the rug up. He studied the back of the rug and the floor beneath. It looked spotless. He stood up as a red sports car drove slowly past the house, with some faces pressed up against the tinted windows. There was a light tap on the door and Sam walked in.

'It's 1.17 already. I've contacted Brendan Jefferies' mother. She lives in Green Bay. Do you want to come?' she asked.

He was looking down at the floor.

'He's got it all … under control here,' she added with a flick of her head towards the other room.

Jackson let out a long, slow breath. He nearly kicked the floor petulantly, then nodded.

'Yep, good idea,' he said disgustedly. 'Let's get out of here.'

* * *

'THAT IDIOT! I should bloody well arrest the prick for obstructing his own investigation,' he ranted, as they sat at a set of lights.

Sam smiled, caught the stony look on his face, then put her hand over her mouth to stop herself laughing openly.

'He really is a bloody idiot!' snapped Jackson, lost in his own little world.

'Been there, done that, remember,' she said to him.

'Got you nowhere too,' she added.

'Well, I smell a bloody rat here, Sam,' said Jackson, the frustration in his voice.

'I agree,' she said nodding, 'there's definitely something weird with this one.'

'Did they check that wheelbarrow?'

'Yes, clean as a whistle, I'm afraid, in fact I'd say too clean.'

'What do you mean?'

'Definite smell of a cleaner — like bleach.'

Jackson glanced over at her quickly as he drove. 'So who cleans their wheelbarrow with bleach, eh?'

Sam nodded. 'Could've been spilled over it, but pretty unlikely.'

They were driving down a street lined with kowhai and cherry blossom trees and he began to slow the car. They pulled up beside an old letter box with the number 159 silhouetted in the faded paint.

'Is this it?' asked Jackson.

'Yep,' replied Sam, as she organised her briefcase.

'You want me to do the talking?' she asked.

Jackson nodded; it was their normal method if they hit trouble. Her talking, him watching.

Brendan's mother had been informed of her son's death only an hour or so before they had arrived. Though she was still upset, she seemed quite willing to talk to them, so the three of them sat together at the kitchen table. She even brought out some of his old photos. There were some shots of a skinny kid in school uniform, a young Brendan covered in mud after a rugby game, and one of him and his mates playing around in the sea. His mother was a large woman with short brunette hair cut in a bowl fashion. Her eyes were red rimmed and tears frequently rolled down her rosy cheeks as she talked about her only child, her beloved twenty-eight-year-old son.

'His father died when he was four years old,' she explained. She told them some details they didn't really need to know. That she would handle the funeral details herself and that she was taking a few days off work. Sam asked her what sort of childhood Brendan had. She detailed how he had been a normal, fairly happy child until about the age of fourteen, when he had become aggressive and withdrawn and how he eventually became intent on self-harm. He had got heavily into drugs at this period and started cutting himself. He literally covered himself in piercings after his seventeenth birthday and began getting tattoos when he was twenty. After surviving an overdose of homebake when he was twenty-four, apparently he had seen the light and, according to her, he had been clean and hadn't done any drugs at all since then. He had been heavily involved with three or four different religions and he had worked as a bouncer in a bar for a short while, about five years ago. Lately however, he had been charged with at least nine burglaries in the last three years and he had been doing community service for some of them. Late last year he committed an assault on an old man in a road rage incident in the middle of Onehunga Town Centre.

Jackson and Sam were surprised how open and honest she was about her son.

'Had you noticed anything recently in his behaviour that had changed?' asked Sam.

'Yes, actually I did,' she answered, looking up at Sam. 'He was very depressed just this last week.'

Her eyes welled up with tears.

'I, I, I thought maybe … I thought he was going to try and … kill himself,' she finished.

Both Sam and Jackson sat up slightly.

'Do you know what was upsetting Brendan so much?' asked Sam.

'No, he wouldn't talk to me about that at all. He's always

been pretty honest with me, but in the last two years, he's kept to himself a lot.'

Jackson's phone rang. He excused himself and walked outside. It was a detective from homicide. The voice on the phone slowly relayed the information to him.

'Are you sure?' he asked quietly into the phone. 'Okay, thanks, Dean.'

He hung up and returned to the kitchen. He wondered if he should let Sam know what he'd heard, then decided to let her continue.

'What did Brendan do to earn his money?' asked Sam.

'I'm not too sure. The last he really told me about anything like that was when he said he had a new business partner and they were doing online deals. That was about two or three years ago. I'm pretty sure that's what he was still doing, because he hasn't had a job or anything since then, but he never really talked about it unless I pushed him and I … I just didn't lately.'

'Did you ever meet his business partner, or did he talk about this person at all?'

'No, he wouldn't talk about it, so … I got the feeling it was a woman.'

'Why do you say that?'

'You know it's strange, it was just a feeling really, when someone gets that much of a hold over someone else … I don't know, but it just felt that way.'

'And you say he was depressed this last week, but you don't know why?'

Jackson moved slightly in his seat as Brendan's mother shook her head slowly, tears rolling down her cheeks again.

'Did he have other interests, something that we wouldn't know about?' asked Sam.

'Well, he read a lot. An awful lot about Normans and

Vikings and their culture, you know, northern mythology or something like that. I remember he used to call himself Thrall when he first started with this partner of his. It's a funny name. I remember that quite clearly, but I haven't heard him say it too much lately. He had the name tattooed across the back of his shoulders. It's some kind of god or Viking figure. It didn't really interest me that much, to be honest.'

Sam nodded and made a note. 'So, any girlfriend or other friends we could follow up on?' asked Sam.

'There was a girl about three years ago now, she used to live up the road in Titirangi, but no … they don't see each other any more.'

There was a small silence.

'Do you know why they broke up?'

Brendan's mother looked up quickly. 'I — I'd rather not say.'

There was a longer silence.

'He — he,' she stammered, 'he apparently attacked her, but … I, I never really believed that … He was never charged and they never saw each other again after that day.'

Sam nodded and made another note.

'Has Brendan had any enemies, anyone who would want to see him hurt badly?'

'Not really, he kept to himself these days. He didn't hang around with his old friends any more and he hasn't talked much lately, so I suppose I wouldn't know about that.'

Sam nodded again. She glanced at Jackson briefly, then closed her notebook.

'Thank you very much for your help, Mrs Jefferies. If there is anything else you remember, you can ring me, or Detective Jackson, on either of these two numbers.'

Sam took a small card from her case and placed it on the table between them. Mrs Jefferies ignored it and saw them to the door.

In the car, Jackson put the keys in the ignition, then stopped.

'That call I got in the kitchen was from Dean Hunter. They're investigating that case where the young girl was attacked in Mt Albert last week.'

'I know the one,' said Sam, 'how's that kid doing?'

'She's still in hospital, they say her physical injuries will eventually heal, but ...' Jackson left the sentence hanging.

'Hunter was going through the snapshots of some known burglars and when she saw a photo of Brendan Jefferies, she broke down. She positively identified him as the attacker.'

They sat there for a few seconds until Jackson spoke first.

'So, if Brendan was heavily depressed about something that happened last week, maybe now we know why.'

'Probably because he knew he'd be caught, sooner or later,' said Sam.

Jackson nodded. 'Interesting that his mother thought his business partner was a woman,' he said, staring out the windscreen.

'You think it's Mrs Candy?' asked Sam.

Jackson nodded again. 'It fits. If so, I think it means they're into the auctions for the addresses and the information, not what they actually buy,' mused Jackson.

'That sounds feasible,' said Sam. 'A lot of the time people put far too much information in the descriptions. Even in the background of some of the auction photos you can make out the style of the house, or the surroundings. You only get the details, however, when you win the auction. So, they buy on specific auctions, which gives them the information they're really after. Brendan burgles the places they select and they split the proceeds. They can always resell the auction goods and hope for a similar amount. All legal and it covers their tracks.'

Jackson nodded. 'Hold that thought,' he said, reaching for his phone.

He pressed a button to return Dean Hunter's call, then put it on speakerphone.

'Hi Dean, can you check something out for me on that Mt Albert case?

'Sure.'

'Find out whether they placed any items on online auctions over the last couple of months.'

'Ok, will do.'

Dean's name disappeared from the screen of the phone, as he hung up. He turned to Sam. 'Right, so now we know he attacked the young girl in the Gordon house and Mrs Candy, his partner in crime, finds out and what ... she kills him?'

Sam looked at him and Jackson shook his head. 'I know — it's a long shot. So let's work it from another angle back towards the murder. Let's say it was some person, or vigilante group, or gang that dumped him in her backyard as some kind of message — a warning to her, after killing him somewhere else. Surely, though, there'd be evidence somewhere of two or three people carrying and dragging a dead body across backyards, lawns and over fences, even while a loud party is going on. It's probably more far-fetched than the idea that he actually died not very far at all from that spot.'

'You mean in the house somewhere, don't you?'

Jackson nodded. 'If they were involved with these burglaries together, then the old lady would know the young girl's attack would come back to her. Maybe she lures him inside when he calls and cracks him over the head with something. It would have to be pretty heavy to stove his head in like that and she's an old lady. I still don't understand how she managed to move him either — his body is way too heavy for a seventy-year-old. I figure that's what the wheelbarrow might have been used for. But why just leave him lying out there in her own backyard? Maybe someone at the party at the back disturbed her. I really don't understand why he was found lying out there.'

The phone buzzed back into life and Jackson answered it.

'Dean.'

'Yeah mate, you were right about that. The family were having a big clear-out and they put about fifteen items online. Hope that helps.'

'Yep. Thanks a lot Dean,' said Jackson.

Sam pulled her iPad out from her briefcase. Jackson's eyes rolled slightly — it was like her little silver shadow. She turned it on and entered a few letters in the search box and waited.

'Thrall,' she spoke out loud. 'He was the dark-haired son of Edda in Norse or Viking mythology, born of a god. Mmmmm … Basically it's just one part of the larger story about fire being given to mankind by the gods. Mmmmm … Weird stuff, eh?'

Jackson had an alarm buzzing away noisily in the back of his head.

'Did you say Edda?' he asked.

She repeated it for him.

'I'm sure that was Mrs Candy's first name,' he said.

'Ah … it's Edwina,' said Sam, flipping open her notebook.

Jackson turned towards her.

'When I introduced myself to her, she said that all her friends call her Edda, even bloody Humphries did it, while I was in the room,' said Jackson.

'Edda — Edda and bloody Thrall!'

They watched each other, carefully searching the other's face to see which one would laugh first, but neither did.

'Strike two for Mrs Candy,' said Sam.

Jackson looked down at the digital clock in the dash. It

was 4.47 pm. He wondered where time actually went some days. He started the car and drove away from the kerb, merging into the traffic.

It was after 5.30 when they finally reached Grey Lynn and turned into Palm Tree Drive. It had been heavy going through the rush-hour traffic. He noticed Brendan's car was gone from where it had been sitting, a hundred metres up the road from Mrs Candy's place.

'They must have finished earlier than we thought,' said Jackson with a slight growl in his voice.

Sam nodded. Her car was still there, parked right behind Humphries' car.

They pulled up and walked to the front door of the house and knocked on the door. Humphries answered.

'Well, if it isn't Hansel and Gretel,' he said sarcastically. 'Just in time to go home — as usual, eh?' He closed the door behind him and began to walk across the front lawn towards his car. Jackson couldn't hold back his anger any longer and strode after him.

'So that's it, Humphries?' he asked incredulously. 'You've wound it up already? You're a bloody idiot! You know there's a connection between the body and the old lady. The bloody murder victim was involved in a sexual assault just last week,' he continued, but Humphries turned away. Jackson followed him. They stood by his car with his driver's door half open.

'Of course I know,' said Humphries, 'and quite frankly and for you, officially, this wasn't done by some seventy-year-old lady, but you know, whoever did do it, certainly did us all a bloody great favour! Trust you to defend a rapist, so who's the fucking idiot now?'

Jackson stood there in disbelief.

'You're not going to sweep a bloody murder under the carpet, just like that?'

Humphries glowered at him. 'You want to investigate that

sick creep's death in your own time, go right ahead — it'll be the end of your broken-arse career, that I guarantee!'

Humphries got in, slammed his door angrily, started his car and drove off, leaving Jackson and Sam standing there.

'Well, that went well,' said Sam.

Jackson grimaced. 'Unbelievable,' he muttered quietly.

Sam looked back at the house. She thought she saw a curtain twitch at the lounge windows.

'So what do you want to do now?' she asked simply.

He grimaced. Why was he was always torn between the devil of knowing and not knowing?

'I'd like to go back in there and …' He let the sentence trail off.

Sam smiled. 'Well, if it helps at all, I can witness that he gave you permission to investigate — in your own time, sort of …'

Jackson turned, admiring her loyalty.

'Well, there's no need to waste your night too,' he said.

She hooked her eyebrows up in mock surprise.

'Sure you're not scared of being all by yourself with the little old lady in the gingerbread house?'

He laughed. 'No, I'm quite prepared to wrestle her into a pair of handcuffs if I need to.'

She smiled at the thought.

'Well, I've got to pick up Gillian from netball at 6 pm. If you promise to treat Mrs Candy nicely, I'll catch you in the morning and hey, get some proper sleep tonight, okay?'

'Yeah, don't worry about that, I'd drop off right now if I sat down and closed my eyes.'

She went to go, then hesitated and he smiled tiredly, putting a hand on her shoulder.

'Thanks for the backup, partner, you get going. I can ruin my career all by myself.'

'I know, but step lightly. Humphries is on the warpath.'

He nodded.

She walked over to her car, started the engine and drove off, giving him a quick wave. He glanced back at his car parked at the kerb, wishing he could just get in and drive away from all of this, then he walked up to the front door for the second time that day. He knocked, but it seemed like no one was at home. He waited for nearly a minute and was about to rap on the door harder when suddenly he heard some footsteps. There was a click, the door swung open and Mrs Candy's wizened face appeared in the gap.

He asked if he could come in and ask her some more questions. Surprisingly, she welcomed him in pleasantly and ushered him down the hall and into the sitting room, where she insisted on a cup of tea again. She promised to answer as many of Jackson's questions as she possibly could as she turned the jug on. She was so friendly, he began to wonder if he was wrong and following a false trail after all.

He declined the cup of tea, then pondered where to start.

'I noticed some boxes and parcels sitting on the table in your library before,' he started.

'Yes ...' she said from the kitchen.

'Do you buy and sell things on the auctions, Mrs Candy?'

'Oh, please, call me Edda,' she said from the doorway.

He smiled wanly. 'Fine ... Edda, so do you buy and sell things on the auctions?'

She smiled at him and a tiny light crept into the small, shrewd eyes.

'Oh yes, I simply love the online auctions, don't you, detective?'

Before he could answer, she carried on in a whirlwind.

'I find them very exciting. It's the waiting, I think, you know – sometimes waiting for the last few minutes to place a bid. Sometimes trying to win something with just one dollar. I think it's very addictive,' she finished.

Jackson nodded, interested to see if she would keep on talking, but now she just looked back at him from the doorway without a touch of fear — almost curiously, he thought.

'Would you like to see the parcels while the jug boils?' she asked pleasantly.

Jackson thought about it; he was sure she knew he wasn't interested in the parcels.

'Yes, that would be very helpful,' he lied. He and Sam practised lying to each other constantly when they were in the car together. It was an intriguing game to them and strangely it was one of the ways they had developed trust with each other. They could certainly pick most of each other's lies. He followed behind the old lady as she led him out of the room, down the hall then into the library.

She turned on the light and a pale, yellow glow illuminated the room from a single bulb. She showed him the parcels and boxes and the little table and desk that she wrapped and unwrapped them on. Slowly, his focus wandered to the bookshelf that covered the whole wall at one end, from floor to ceiling. Mrs Candy's eyes followed his gaze.

'This was Cecil's room, my husband. He called it his library, with his books and his … artefacts. He was very interested in history, ancient cultures, religion, mythology, that sort of thing.'

Jackson nodded as his eyes wandered to the darkest part of the room, where a number of weapons hung gloomily from the pegs in the large display that covered the wall. He stepped forward, a little closer. There were helmets, some shields, two large swords, curved daggers and strange clubs of all shapes and sizes. He noticed a very old, dusty golf club at the bottom, perched on two of the wooden pegs. He picked up the club carefully and weighed it in his hands.

Jackson spotted a small light switch to one side and he leaned forward and flicked it on. It turned on a spotlight that lit up the display. He noticed there was a subtle shape marked against the wood where the golf club had been sitting. The wood had faded and it had left an outline over time. However, now that he noticed it, he saw the shape left on the dark wood panelling didn't look like a golf club. Whatever sat there previously was a long object, with a large, round head-piece at the end. He looked around and Mrs Candy was standing next to him.

'Do you like golf?' she asked.

'I can't stand the game,' he replied.

* * *

THEY WERE both sitting back in the dining room. A column of steam wafted slowly from the teapot as Jackson mulled his next line of questions. She had placed a biscuit tin on the table between them. He decided on a different tack.

'You did know Brendon quite well, didn't you, Edda? That is, as Edda and Thrall, isn't that how it is in Norse mythology?'

She smiled a little smile and took a sip of her tea. 'That's very good, detective. Yes, indeed, Edda and Thrall are two characters in Norse mythology. Help yourself to a handmade biscuit, the chocolate ones are the nicest. He hesitated, looking at the biscuits stacked tidily on each side of the little biscuit tin. He realised he hadn't eaten all day and a gnawing pain in his stomach was now reminding him. He gave in and chose one of the almond shortbread biscuits instead. She smiled again, picked up a chocolate biscuit and bit into it.

'Are you actually a history buff, detective?'

Jackson shook his head.

'No, it's too far away from reality. What is it? The past is another planet to me — something like that.'

Edda laughed. 'Oh no, that won't do,' she said, smiling across at him from the other side of the table. 'It's supposed to be "The past is a foreign country. They do things differently there." Leslie Poles Hartley, I believe,' she added.

He shrugged nonchalantly and took a bite of the shortbread. 'I was never great at quotes in school. So ... Edda ... I'd like to know — did you know Brendan as Brendan Jefferies, or ... as Thrall?'

'Oh, I'll certainly tell you everything you want to know, but please do allow me to do the telling of it. It will be so much more accurate.'

He was feeling quite irritated.

'Please do carry on then,' he said, tersely.

'Well,' she started, her eyes lighting up and her small face creasing into a broken kind of smile. 'I met Brendan about four years ago. He came looking for part-time work and at first he did lots of small jobs I needed help with around the place.'

Jackson nodded, watching her closely. She continued on, her voice animated, but her small, sharp eyes seemed locked on his and never strayed.

'Brendan was a pretty good worker, after a bit of education, that is, and he helped me out with quite a few nasty little problems I had. Well, one day he was talking to me about the online auctions and how vulnerable people were putting their information up there for everyone else to see. I realised he was on to something that I knew nothing about. Modern technology has so much to offer and it was quite beyond me. So I persuaded him to teach me all about it.'

As she continued, he noticed her face seemed to slowly harden into a cold mask, though she carried on talking in that thin, rasping voice.

'Well, after a while, we set about knocking over the best-looking places, one at a time. As I promised you, I'm telling you everything here, detective, so of course, I was the brains behind it and he did most of the other … the physical work. Well, it had to go wrong somewhere in the end and unfortunately it did when Thra—, when that, that disgusting monster attacked that poor little girl in her own bed. It was shocking. Well, I simply couldn't have that, now could I, detective?'

Jackson cleared his throat slowly. 'You realise you may be incriminating yourself?'

'Oh please, detective, you wanted the truth all along and I have promised I would tell you everything I knew and we're so nearly there I'm quite excited, so please don't interrupt me and just listen.'

Jackson harrumphed slightly and sat back in his chair. He finished off the biscuit wondering what might be for dinner that night. She began to speak again.

'So, when Brendan next visited, I made sure I had a parcel for him to see. I deliberately left it sitting on the table in the library. I told him it was some expensive jewellery, but of course there was nothing in the box at all. When he bent over to look at it, I hit him with one of the weapons I chose from the wall display. It was a long club that you noticed was missing when you turned on the display light. It had a ball-shaped striker made of African ironwood with other pieces inserted in the end. I hit him across the head with quite a heavy blow. It was a surprisingly good shot for a seventy-five-year-old lady, I must admit. He went down like a sack of old potatoes. When I struck him again, his head popped just like a balloon. I hit him a few more times to be sure he wouldn't get up again, then I threw the club into the fireplace in the front room and burnt it. I had to get my other little worker, Leon, to help me shift his body from the library, with the help of my wheelbarrow of course. We finally managed to get him past the clothesline and then we dumped him there on the grass.'

Jackson shook his head; he still felt a little fuzzy.

'So why did you just leave him out in the backyard?' he asked. 'And I'll warn you right now, Mrs Candy — I think you've done this before.'

She looked at him with real admiration in her eyes. 'Very, very good, Detective Jackson, I'm impressed with your thinking abilities. You're not nearly as slow as you pretend to be. Well, it's quite true that in fifty-three years of living here in this little house, I have managed to bury five bodies in the garden out there in my backyard. The garden's certainly grown over the years.'

She sat there, beaming like a cat who'd eaten all the cream. He realised suddenly what Brendan had been trying to write in the grass with his finger as he had slowly died. It wasn't 'Candy' like he'd first thought — it was the word 'Garden'.

'So, why didn't you dispose of Brendan in the garden as well?' he asked and instantly knew the answer to his own question.

'Because he was a child molester,' he finished.

'That's correct,' she said, her tone suddenly flat and even. 'I left him there, like the disgusting rubbish that he was. I left that monster for you, the proper people, the police, to clean up. I could never, ever have a creature like that ruin any of my beautiful plants or gardens.' She paused. 'In fact, I only use the very best when it comes to my gardening.' Her face suddenly brightened, her mouth flattened into a sly smile and her small eyes shone like a pair of candles.

'Good people, in fact the very best people are so much better for a real garden — like my husband, or even a policeman, for instance.'

Jackson suddenly felt sick. His head spun as her words swirled inside his head. He realised he'd been feeling strange for a few minutes. He tried to move, but he realised everything had slowed down. His arms didn't seem to work properly and he felt pinned to the chair.

'It's hard to see the wood for the trees sometimes, isn't it? Almonds disguise the cyanide rather well, don't you agree? Mind you, some people can't even smell it, you know. It's just me being careful, really.'

Suddenly, a small boy emerged from the kitchen and darted behind him.

'That's right, Leon,' she said, watching Jackson with a smile, 'bring his things to me.'

She folded her arms as Leon stepped out from behind the chair and his small hands went through Jackson's pockets. His round little face and small dark eyes were locked onto Jackson.

'There's already a policeman lying in my garden,' she gloated quietly, leaning forward, her eyes shining as she watched him struggle to move.

'You detectives, you're so predictable. Once you get a little curious, you're so … sniffy.'

She giggled slightly, enjoying herself. She studied the car keys with its silver fern key ring and the wallet and phone that Leon placed on the table.

'First things first, Leon,' she said, picking up the phone.

She found its power button and turned it off. She handed the phone to Leon who prised open the case and withdrew the SIM card. She nodded approvingly, then her gnarled old fingers picked up the wallet and carefully removed all the cards, laying them down in a row. Jackson desperately tried to speak, but he couldn't get the words out.

'Yes, yes, I know, there's a police car parked outside,' she burbled on, sifting through the different cards.

'Ahh, here we are. The answer to our problems. A gym card. We'll just drop the car off there a bit later tonight, Leon. That should be the perfect place for them to find the car. We'll let them start searching for you there.'

* * *

HIS LEFT EYE blinked by itself very, very slowly. He tried to look to his right, but he couldn't move his head at all now. His eyes began to stare straight ahead and his breathing grew heavy. He knew he was in serious trouble. His limited view went fuzzy at the edges. Mrs Candy got up. The old lady's wizened face loomed into his tunnel vision, her grinning mouth stretching out into a craggy maw of teeth, filling up his slowly fading sight.

'Don't panic now, detective,' she rasped delightedly, a wicked smile dancing across her ancient lines.

'You policemen are just marvellous for my marigolds.'

ALONG CAME A SPIDER ...

When I was born, I knew that I was different from the others ...

It was simple really — just one look at my perfectly formed, long silky legs and you could tell I would be bigger and better than all my other little brothers and sisters. So it proved in the end too, with just the seven of us sisters left alive, the giants of the whole family.

Our mother protected us all carefully from the very beginning, keeping us close, until we finally grew to our full size. Then, sometime shortly after, Mother called us all together with one of her special, high-pitched squeals, which seemed to echo and change us all, deep inside. Suddenly, as one, we chased down and ate the rest. I loved eating up all my little baby brothers and sisters; they were delicious and I think it was the most fun I've ever had. Speaking of eating, we're waiting to eat right now. We are watching each other, quietly reading each other's feelings, from our dark holes. All of us are hungry, waiting for something, anything, to simply arrive, as we try to quiet down the voracious appetites that Mother has given us.

As I look out I can see Sophia's numerous sets of quick darting eyes, flicking backwards and forwards, alert to my every little move as she sits waiting in the web mouth across and closest to me. The smallest of us giants, she is *next*. Mother watches her very closely, so I know … she is next. Behind and slightly above me, Sonya stirs and then retreats back into the densely woven walls of her den and begins feeding noisily on her catch. She is the only one, apart from Mother of course, who has food. I feel the tension building in all of us waiting to eat, our hairs vibrating with the sound of every one of Sonya's loud, crunching bites.

Higher up, I feel Strella rumble bad-temperedly up near Mother, her great feet playing a tune upon the web as she runs stupidly backwards and forwards. Suddenly, Strella ran to the front of her tunnel and for a moment I thought Mother was on the move. Sandila, who built her long, winding passage out on the very edge away from Mother, is hovering just inside the entrance, her dripping fangs twitching angrily to and fro, her front legs arched high. She is angry but still scared. Sandara, with her myriad jet-black eyes watching whenever I leave my den, lives below on the lower side of the web, and great fat Samantha lives at the very bottom, gobbling up nearly everything that falls her way.

I understand virtually all my sisters' thoughts, especially about food. We work together at special times, mostly when building, repairing and adding new lines to the great web. Life is harsh and you must never forget one vital thing — Mother always needs careful watching. Whenever she is really, really hungry, she begins to slowly stamp her great barbed feet and then we all remember what happened to little Stacy and Silla. Stacy and Silla managed to hide in the crack near the window frame when we chased down all the rest. The two of them stayed there, mainly feeding off our scraps, which fell into the crevice from above, until one day when Mother was in a terrible mood, she suddenly rushed down the web in great leaps. Then, with a high-pitched squeal that seemed to go right through me, Mother dragged them wriggling and screaming from their holes and ate them alive.

* * *

I FELT IT FIRST, like a tiny vibration from another place, catching me almost off guard. Then, with a loud and angry snarl, it burst into the web before me, a great, shrieking explosion of movement and energy, its wings tearing at every strand holding them, its great body and legs twisting and fighting for freedom. I leapt across the web without thought as Sandara madly ran for cover, straight down towards big fat Samantha who nearly gobbled her up in sheer delight. I bit and stung, bit and stung, then bit and stung some more, as I had been taught with large prey. Suddenly, before I knew it, Mother was there, watching me.

I had not sensed Mother as I struck and struggled with the creature. Sandara had run away below me and had only just now returned to her lair.

The great entangled butterfly was laid out before me in the silky bed of clinging white strands. It cartwheeled its magnificent, iridescent wings backwards and forwards in vain, frantically hoping for a last-minute reprieve from my deadly toxins. There would be none. I bit and stung and bit and stung again. The great creature's multi-coloured eyes slowly glazed over as my venom shook through its body and after a few spasms from its great wings, it was finally still.

I was very proud of my catch. There was enough for all of us to eat and I had secured it all myself. I never felt Sandara move as my eyes were always fixed on Mother, who simply stared and waited just a few strands away.

I noticed there was something wrong. It was my left rear leg. It wouldn't work; it seemed … caught. I realised then that Sandara had used Mother's presence to approach me from below and had snuck in behind and quietly wrapped my long rear leg tightly into the web. Mother began to stamp her front feet ominously, her fangs began twitching and scratching against each other, making that horrible, grinding noise. Samantha came wobbling up from below, her greedy eyes locked on me, full of black glistening thoughts. The others began to move as one and gather around me. Frantically, I looked around for a way to escape, but there were hungry eyes and mouths everywhere I turned.

In panic, I bit at my beautiful long leg that was trapped behind me. With a few tearing crunches, I bit through the thick cartilage and ligaments. I tore away madly at my own limb. Finally, the crack of bone released the pressure on my leg. I was free — but no! As I looked up, I saw Mother securing my opposite rear leg with a fine and tightly bound wrap right through the sticky strands. I panicked and began to bite at the leg that held me. My jaws were strong and I made quick work of my great, right rear leg but as I turned my head, I saw Mother quickly trapping another leg into the strands of the web. All my sisters and my Mother shrieked at that moment — and I felt devastated. No great cry had issued from me automatically or in perfect synch with my family. I was no longer one of them …

I tore at the leg Mother had just secured, ripping it from my abdomen with a sharp crack and a great jerk of my head. As quickly as I moved, however, Mother was faster. No sooner did I shriek at another bound limb and bite and tear it from my body, I would look up to find Mother had bound the next one fast, through the wall of the web. I would not give in though, not even to Mother. I tore at the next leg pinning me to the web as my sisters began to jump and dart forwards. I knew I had no time left. It seemed pointless though, as Mother wrapped the last of my beautiful, long legs with her sticky, silky steel bindings, securing it firmly into the many woven strands of the web.

My sisters were salivating at the twin prospects lying before them and suddenly Strella and Sonya ran forward in a frenzied rush towards the mayhem, no longer able to control their lust for food. I had no choice ... I bit through the last of my beautiful long legs, crunching through the gristle and bone and then with a sharp snap, my world fell away, just as my mad sisters ran in to devour me. Mother shrieked in anger and leapt right across the web, just missing me as I fell away from them and the whiteness of the great lair. I turned slowly and I briefly saw the great butterfly ensconced in its woven white tomb and all my severed legs still dangling from the web, and then I spun away from the only world I had ever known ...

I felt myself stop with a great jarring motion and I slowly took in the new world on the floor around me. I was quite shocked to find that I could still see and feel everything. I could hear the disappointed shrieks of all my sisters away up on the web and I could still feel Mother's anger, even from here. I could not move properly, as my stumps were bitten off close to my abdomen, so I lay there awkwardly on my side and watched a great world I had never seen. I was mesmerised by the huge spaces around me. It seemed as though I could see forever. To one side of me was a large round object with brightly coloured flowers growing up and out of it. It looked so beautiful and welcoming. Suddenly, one of the large yellow flowers moved. Another feeling came over me. An older, deeper feeling that I didn't like. Something else was moving amongst the flowers and slowly making its way down them. I recognised in horror what it was. I lay there on the floor, unable to move, all my senses working as the large praying mantis clambered slowly off the last hanging leaf and began to move jerkily along the floor towards me. Oh no, I thought – not this, not now. It was a big, long-bodied, ugly creature, with two large eyes on each side of a wide, repulsive-looking head and it had a cavernous mouth, full of great, hideous teeth. I lay there terrified and helpless, my once beautiful legs now just uncontrolled, twitching useless stumps, as it moved gradually and surely towards me. Then very slowly and deliberately, it positioned itself over the top of me. I could imagine the great malignant teeth in its terrifying maw tearing at me, breaking me into edible morsels. I suddenly realised that was not my fate. It was a female creature too and its body had slowly bent down towards mine and now it began carefully injecting me with something. Suddenly, I could feel millions of writhing little forms being steadily pumped into me, until I was near bursting point. Then, finally, she simply walked away …

I lay there waiting, wondering. Slow, tiny, wriggling feelings began to start deep inside me and with a sudden burst the sensations began to increase tenfold, then a hundredfold. A fierce, ugly pain ripped through me, deep inside my abdomen. Her little babies were ravenous, hungry for life and now, they were beginning to eat me …

BUILDING BLOCKS

HEAVY RAIN POURED DOWN OUTSIDE AS DEIRDRE DIALLED THE number from the phone book. It was an absolute shocker out there, but a perfect day to be locked inside, she thought to herself with a little smile. The wind howled against the walls, whistling and moaning under the eaves of the house. Long rivulets ran down the windows, the thin wriggles running the colours together and turning the world outside into strange-shaped blobs.

Suddenly, someone answered at the other end of the line.

'Yes, hello,' she started. 'I was wondering if anyone there does emergency work?'

She could hear the heavy sarcasm in the reply and it struck a nerve deep inside her. She pushed the swelling anger back down. *It sounded just like Sally ...*

'No, it's internal actually, so the weather shouldn't be a problem.'

She waited, listening, then tried again.

'Well, actually all the materials are here, it's just that the other brickie cancelled right at the last minute ... Yes, I understand all that, but the problem is the electrician is coming tomorrow morning and the plasterer tomorrow afternoon, so if I can't get it done today, it's going to be a real problem in lots of ways for everybody, that's all.'

She listened again to the reply.

'Yes, I can pay fifty dollars an hour,' she said, thinking, *You greedy bastard.*

'Yes … all right, I'll pay cash.'

Her eyebrows furrowed in frustration.

'You won't be here for an hour? Mmmm … But will it be finished today? It will. Well, that should be fine then. Yes, all right, see you then,' and she hung up.

You bloody prick, she thought venomously. *Fifty dollars an hour — cash! That's daylight robbery. Well, at least it will get finished today,* she reminded herself. She knew she had enough cash in her bag. *The greedy bastard!*

She walked into the kitchen, put the jug on, then resumed chopping the chicken livers laid out on the wooden board. A heavy rumble of thunder thumped somewhere above the roof. She chopped away at the red livers until they were a slick pile of dark slices on the light-coloured wood. There was a sudden flash of lightning, the bright light illuminating the room. The peal of thunder wasn't very long following it. She poured herself a cup of tea and put a dash of cold water in it. She took a sip, looking around in quiet disgust at her sister's interior design bungles. She quickly grew tired of repainting the horrible colour schemes in her mind and walked over and sat on the sofa. As she sat there, she spotted the pile of bills lying on the coffee table next to her brother's letter. She reached out and pushed them under a magazine out of sight. Her brother's letter from Paremoremo prison still sat there and it just stared back at her, like a corpse. She wondered why he'd written to her. It had sat on the table for a month now. She might open it tomorrow, she decided. She thought of Stephen, probably sitting in his cell in A block.

They'd called him a monster in the papers for beating the men to death with his bare hands, but she knew he wasn't really a bad person. He had killed the two men for money, there'd been nothing personal in it at all. She'd always been close to her brother, but she'd never visited him. Just the thought of the dark, stone walls and clanging steel doors sent a shiver down the back of her neck. She had suffered from claustrophobia ever since she was small, when Mother would lock her inside the hallway cupboard for hours. The sight of the tall, thick walls of the jail were just too much for her — and those old memories. *Memories,* she thought wryly, nearly laughing. Her hand trembled as she held the cup to her lips and took another sip of the reassuring, steaming brew. *Oh, it all feels so good — now ...*

* * *

AFTER FINISHING HER CUPPA, she did the dishes and tidied up around the place. The rain was relentless outside. She was straightening a painting on the wall when the doorbell finally sounded. She opened the door and the wind literally blew him in.

'Hi — Bill,' he said.

'Deirdre,' she replied drily.

He was a small, dark-haired man, with a thin unshaven face and tired-looking eyes, but she noticed he had all his tools with him. The heavy rain had drenched him from the waist up, getting from the car to the front door.

'Are you all set to start?' she asked impatiently, wanting the thing done as quickly as possible.

He looked at her with those sagging, moon-shaped eyes.

'Well, a coffee would be nice,' he tried.

She smirked, annoyed at his attempt.

'Yes, it would, wouldn't it?'

A look of irritation crept across his face and as he took a step, he knocked his bag into the coffee table in frustration. It dislodged the magazine and scattered the envelopes across the floor.

'Oh, sorry 'bout that,' he apologized, and bent down to pick the letters up. A puzzled expression came over him as he stood, holding them in his hand.

'I thought you said your name was Deirdre,' he said, as he handed her the pile of bills.

A look of worry flashed her face.

'It is ... My sister Sally lived here for a while, with her son Jonathan — but they're gone now,' she replied, walking away quickly and placing the letters in a small cubbyhole by the fridge.

He nodded sympathetically.

'So — it's downstairs?' he said, picking up his bag.

'Yes,' she replied, relieved he was finally getting on with it. 'It's this way,' she said crisply and led the way to the staircase.

She clomped noisily down the stairs and opened the door at the bottom. He followed her in and entered the large basement. The far wall was made of plasterboard and it was mouldy and damp in patches. He could see a door roughly nailed up in the centre of it.

'What was in there?' he asked, as he walked over and placed his bag of tools beside the large jumble of concrete blocks sitting in a pile to one side.

'Just an old laundry,' she said, a little huffily. 'I've had a proper one built upstairs by the back door. It's much more practical.'

He nodded, surveying the empty buckets and bags of plaster beside the blocks. He turned to view the tap and basin against the wall at the far side of the room.

'Well, there's everything I need here, I'd better get started then,' he said, turning back to face her.

'Yes, you'd better,' she said frostily, thinking about the fifty dollars an hour he was charging.

What a nasty bitch, he thought, bending down and pulling his trowel from his bag.

He's a lazy little prick, she decided, walking towards the stairs. She climbed the steps, then crossed to the sofa deep in thought. She sat there and began to hope that nothing would go wrong now.

* * *

AFTER FIVE MINUTES, his mortar was fresh and shiny, his string line nice and tight. He put the first block into place with a decent thump and he heard a long, low moan. *What the hell was that? Was that the weather?* he wondered. He trowelled in some mortar, then carefully laid the next block in the line.

Upstairs, the rain and wind beat constantly at the windows as Deirdre sat there slowly getting more worried by her circling thoughts. She had just stood at the top of the stairs. She was sure she'd heard a strange low noise coming from down there. It worried her, but she had an idea. She went to the bathroom, where the builder had removed some rotten floorboards and the old toilet, as it was leaking. She'd had to use the other toilet upstairs for the last two weeks and it was frustrating to have to climb the stairs every single time. There were some open pipes leading through the wall to the basement room downstairs. She took hold of one of the small open pipes.

'Hooooo hooooo,' she moaned down the pipe. 'Hoooo hooooo …'

She stood back up.

That'll keep him guessing, she thought with a grin.

* * *

After two hours, she thought she'd check on his progress, so she descended the internal staircase and opened the door. The block wall was halfway up and for a moment she wasn't sure if she was happy it was half done or angry that the damned thing still wasn't finished. He wiped a bead of sweat from his forehead and looked at her, a smudge of grey mortar smeared across his stubbled chin.

'It's getting there,' he said.

'I can see that. What time will you be finished?' she demanded.

He grimaced.

'Ah … probably another hour or so, then about twenty minutes to tidy it all up,' he replied.

She harrumphed loudly, turned her back and left him to his work again. He turned slowly back to his wall of blocks. As he placed the mortar for the next one, a low noise issued from somewhere deep in the room. This time a small, high-pitched whine accompanied it. It very slowly died away. He stopped for a few seconds, listening.

Halfway up the stairs, Deirdre heard the strange noise. She climbed to the top, then carefully tiptoed into the small bathroom again. Again she placed her lips to the small copper pipe. She moaned down it, trying to copy the sound that she'd heard on the stairs. She repeated it and rather pleased with her efforts, she tiptoed back out again. The wind howled through the trees at the front of the property, throwing the branches around madly in the gusts. She stared out the dining room windows, watching sheets of rain sweep across the yard.

Not long to wait now, Deirdre, just a few more minutes to go, she told herself.

A cascade of water overflowed the guttering and a little silver waterfall began to stream down the side of the house.

* * *

An hour and a half later, as she was sitting waiting nervously on the sofa, she heard the slow, heavy tramp of his shoes coming up the stairs. He emerged from the stairwell just as the jug boiled in the kitchen. The wind still howled against the corners of the house. He walked over to the entrance and laid his bag carefully down beside the door. He turned back to her.

'That'll be two hundred and seventy dollars,' he said.

She looked up at him in shock.

'But that was only four hours' work,' she complained.

'Four and a half,' he corrected her, 'and forty-five for the call-out on a wet day.'

She stood up, fuming at his demand.

'What if I don't think it's worth that much? How about I pay you twenty dollars an hour for the labour and nothing for the callout?' she said, in a threatening voice.

He stood there for a few seconds, looking at her.

'Maybe you're right,' he said finally, in a quiet tone. 'I've changed my mind, it's three hundred and seventy and maybe then I won't tell the police you've buried something suspicious behind that wall.'

She nearly stumbled backwards; his words had struck her like he'd slapped her. *How the hell did he know?* she wondered. She thought desperately for two or three seconds, then her face softened.

'I'm so sorry, Bill, I may have been a bit hasty and I certainly appreciate your … your effort today.'

Lightning suddenly flashed outside the front windows, lighting up one side of her pretty features for a split second.

'Would you like a cup of tea or coffee before you go, then maybe we could discuss the price in ah … more friendly tones?' she offered, with a nervous smile.

In smug satisfaction, he let a victorious grin creep across his face.

What a sick, murdering bitch, he thought to himself.

'Sure, why the heck not?' he said as pleasantly as he could, running his fingers through his dark hair and looking around him.

She walked into the kitchen and began to prepare the tea, taking her time and keeping her back to him.

'Oh, I'm afraid I'm all out of coffee,' she said, looking over her shoulder.

'Tea will be just fine,' he answered.

She poured the tea and turned, then walked over and handed him a cup on a saucer.

'Sugar?' she asked.

'No, thanks,' he said, 'I'm sweet enough.'

She forced herself to smile, then carried her tea over to the coffee table and sat down on the sofa. He took hold of one of the chairs from the dining table. He deliberately slid it roughly across the polished wooden floor, making her cringe. Then he sat across the small coffee table from her, his eyes watching hers. A long rumble of thunder echoed in the distance.

'Nice place you have,' he said.

'Thanks, I decorated it myself,' she lied.

'I really like it,' he returned the lie, with a smile.

This won't take too long, Sally's was less than half that dose, she thought to herself smugly as the rain pelted noisily against the window glass again and obscured the world outside.

'Wow, it's terrible out there, he said, glancing at the window.

'Yes,' she agreed, nodding earnestly, 'horrible weather.'

They both looked at each other for a second, both wondering at the same time if the other person knew what they were up to. Suddenly, the phone rang, disturbing the quiet that had filled the room, and a little nervously, she picked the phone off the coffee table and answered it.

'Yes?'

'Oh, hello.'

She listened again for a few seconds, then interrupted the voice.

'Actually, I'm afraid Sally and Jonathan moved out about two weeks ago.'

'Yes, it really *was* unexpected.'

'No … well, she definitely said she won't be back.' Deirdre spoke the words quickly. Then her small, bright eyes suddenly swivelled towards the kitchen, leaving his for a second. She stood up and walked towards the fridge. As her hand reached into the cubbyhole and fumbled for the right letter, he leaned forward and swapped the two cups of tea on the little table in front of him. She turned back with the envelope in her hand, her sharp eyes watching him like a hawk. He sat there nonchalantly and smiled at her. She tore the end open and pulled out the letter inside.

'I'm afraid I wouldn't know too much about school fees.'

'Oh, I do see, yes, it is a large amount, isn't it?'

'No, she didn't leave any forwarding address at all.'

She motioned in a circle with her finger to him, raising her eyebrows. He smiled back and took a large sip of his tea. She smiled warmly at him from across the room.

'Oh, absolutely, I'll certainly try my best to find her address and if she rings, I'll tell her that Jonathan's school called.'

'Yes, it definitely *is* a shame. Well, she always was unpredictable, my little sister.'

'Okay, yes, I will ... thank you.'

Deirdre hung up the phone.

'What a pain! I'm sorry, where were we?' she asked, picking up her cup from the table.

'Oh, just discussing the weather,' he replied.

She drank some of her tea, her eyes never leaving his. Deliberately, he copied her actions and took a long sip from his own cup. She smiled at him.

He is so gullible, she thought.

She is so brutal, he thought, smiling back at her.

He matched her, sip for sip, until they had both finished the tea.

'Now, Deirdre, that bill of mine,' he finally said, as he put his cup down slowly.

'Oh yes, of course, well, I do think you deserve at least three hundred dollars on such a horrible day. Now where did I put my wallet?' she wondered out loud.

She stood and wobbled slightly on her feet.

'Ooh, I don't feel well,' she said rather slowly, her eyes coming up and meeting his, a slight look of surprise on her face.

He stood and then caught her as she stumbled forwards.

'Don't worry yourself too much about that bill now, Deirdre,' he said, smiling.

Then, he began to slowly drag her backwards, towards the top of the stairwell. Shock was now written across her face, then suddenly a look of complete horror took over her features. She tried to fight him, but she simply couldn't, her limbs wouldn't seem to work properly.

'Come now, Deirdre, it's time to say hello to your sister, Sally — and you remember little Jonathan, I'm sure.'

'Noooo, noooo,' she moaned loudly, her eyes blinking wildly. 'No, not — not behind the wall! Not in there!'

He took a step down the stairwell.

'There, there … it's nothing a little block work won't fix,' he said with a cruel smile.

* * *

Two hours later he returned slowly up the stairs. The storm still raged wildly outside. He looked around at the furnishings and decorations. It really wasn't his style at all. He hoped upstairs was better than this.

Never mind, he smiled to himself, *a coat of paint can hide a multitude of sins.*

A sharp crack of lightning sounded outside and the front windows all went white. He jumped, just a little. He was about to sit down when the doorbell rang. He walked over and looked through the window. There was a tall man with short brown hair, holding a small bag, standing there in the pouring rain. The man had a large, dark tattoo on one side of his neck that crept up over his collar, like some kind of creature trying to get out. He stepped over, then opened the front door.

'And who might you be?' he asked the drenched man with a tight grin, 'the electrician?'

'I'm Stephen,' said the man simply.

They looked at each other.

'I've been away for a while,' the man added as he brushed past and stepped inside.

The tall man simply stood there, the rain dripping from his clothes and forming a large puddle on the wooden floor. He was completely soaked from head to foot. He turned and noted the drying plaster on the other man's face. Then he looked down at his hands and noticed grey smears of cement on his fingers.

'So where have my two sisters got to?' Stephen asked, almost casually.

CHILD-ISH

THERE IT WAS AGAIN — SO I SAT UP IN MY BED IN THE DARK TO listen. Silence … then that low drone again, coming from downstairs, and I swore out loud. I knew Mum and Dad would be far too tired to get up, especially after all Mum's troubles last year. She still wasn't well or happy, or one of those things anyway. Reluctantly, I threw back the covers of my nice warm bed and padded slowly down the stairs. Yep, it was Abigail again. I followed the constant burbling noise coming from the kitchen. Halfway down the hallway, I saw her little pyjama-clad legs sticking out from under the kitchen table. Just as I was about to walk in and go mad at her for dragging me out of my bedroom in the middle of the night once again, she suddenly said in a loud firm voice, 'No, I won't! I won't do it to them!'

I stopped there, a little unsure, waiting in the cold darkness just outside the door. I wasn't really sure why I waited there, to be honest. Then her voice spoke again even louder, 'I won't burn them! I won't!'

I was startled, wondering who she was talking to.

'Abby?' I said tentatively.

There was a long silence for an answer, so I walked in. A triangular slant of light from the moon stole through the window and fled across the sink bench. I bent down to see her angelic face framed in dark curls, looking out at me from underneath the table, caught by a small slice of soft, silver light.

'Who *are* you talking to, Abby?' I asked, studying her small, pretty features.

She looked me dead in the eye, like I was some sort of imbecile.

'My friend, silly.'

Normally Abby carried her horrible little clown doll with her on these late night events. Lately, these wandering episodes had got more and more frequent, but she had nothing in her hands and I couldn't see very well at all in the shadows around her.

'Who's your friend then?' I asked a little cautiously, stopping myself from looking around me in the dark.

'It's Sybil,' she said simply, which made no real sense to me.

'Well, it's late and you need to go to bed. It's 3 am and I'm tired.'

She pouted like a younger sister loves to do when her older sister really wants her to do something.

Then she reluctantly shuffled her thin limbs out from under the table and emerged.

'Are you going to take Sybil with you?' I asked her impatiently.

She looked up at me, her four-year-old eyes scolding me as if my twelve years were so much less than her four. Then she shook her head slowly.

'Well, I'm really tired and I want to go back to bed, so come on,' I said rubbing my eyes.

I knew I shouldn't have, but I added bad-temperedly,

'Sybil can stay down here in the cold, if that's what she wants.'

Suddenly, Abby screamed at the top of her voice. It was so loud I thought she'd wake the dead, let alone Mum and Dad. All the hairs on the back of my neck stood up and my heart nearly burst out of my chest.

'What, Abby?' I asked frantically. 'What's wrong?'

She looked at me, then pointed to the door. 'It's Sybil,' she said.

I forced myself to look at the door, but my feet suddenly seemed stuck to the floor and a feeling of dread began deep in my stomach.

'There's nothing ... th-there's no one there,' I stammered, looking at the dark glass and only seeing our distorted reflections.

'You can't *see* Sybil,' she said quietly, her eyes still fixed on the door.

This worried me, then it made me slightly mad and as my fear changed to anger, a thought came to me. 'Well, then, what does she look like?' I demanded.

Immediately I wished I'd never asked that question.

'She's black all over — even her eyes,' she said quickly. '*That's* why you can't see her.'

I was forced to think about this again for a few seconds.

'Well, then, how do you know she's there?' I asked suspiciously.

'You can smell her,' she said in a tiny whisper.

'What do you mean, you can smell her?' I insisted.

'The burning smell,' she said quickly. 'It's just like burnt toast, or that meat that Dad burnt at dinner — remember?'

I did remember, but my eyes were glued to the back door again. All I could see was blackness beyond the glass.

Then Abby laughed out loud and it gave me such a fright I nearly slapped her.

'What? What?' I said, getting angry again.

'Sybil just said she'd knock on the door if you don't believe me,' she said with a giggle, smiling as though this were some private joke.

'What's so funny about that?' I asked stupidly.

She looked at me strangely, then whispered, 'She hasn't got any hands or feet …'

'What do you mean she hasn't got hands or feet?' I demanded, my head snapping back and forth between the door and her face.

'They got chopped off, because she was bad and she kept touching the darkness.'

She looked up at me and giggled.

Those small, laughing eyes burned through me and I knew I probably wouldn't get much sleep at all now — but I'd had enough and I picked her up by the armpits and ignoring her complaints, I carried her up the stairs to her room.

I put her down on the bed and carefully tucked her in. I gave her a small kiss and her cheek was ice cold — she must have been down there for hours. I was just about to say goodnight when she looked at me curiously and giggled again.

'What now?' I asked, feeling as tired as I'd probably ever been.

'Sybil said to tell you she's right here, in the room,' she said with a small, sly smile.

I couldn't help myself. I turned and looked around the little room, but there was nobody there. I turned back to that impish face. I was thinking about how to answer her when I heard a small whimpering sound coming from under the bed. My heart began to race madly. Then, there came a tiny scratching noise that made me take a step backwards. I steeled myself, took a very large breath, stepped forward and carefully lifted the edge of the bedspread. To my utter horror there was another Abby underneath the bed, curled up on the floor in a tight ball. Her face was pale and white and she was shaking. She looked up at me with terrified eyes and her mouth formed a small hole as she said, 'There's some thing in my bed, Julia.'

GONE FISHING ...

THE SALINE WATER HELD HIM GENTLY, FLOATING HIM ALONG, like a baby in the womb. Thick drops of rain fell all around him like glassy nails ...

* * *

HE WALKED SLOWLY up Grand View Drive in the heat, the blazing sun burning down from above, making the road shimmer up in the distance. It was surreal. You just don't get perfect days like this ever, he thought to himself. He heard a dog barking somewhere. *Where the hell had Boxer got to now?* he wondered, looking all around. He stood there with his gear, waiting for the green light to change. Two red-eyed seagulls landed on the top of the traffic pole with a loud flap of their wings. They both cast their greedy eyes on him from above. The light finally changed and he crossed. He saw way up ahead, from nearly a hundred metres away, that the front door of the fishing shop looked closed, but he figured they must have the door closed because of the wind, or maybe something else. When he finally got there, he was dumbfounded.

Unbelievable!

It *was* closed. The small sign was sitting in the window to make it official. *On a Saturday morning too*, he thought, totally frustrated. He couldn't get any bait at all now. He swore under his breath. It's probably a death in the family or something, he finally decided.

He turned around and began to walk all the way back to the beach. The two fishing rods he was carrying began to weigh his arms down as he slowly walked down the long hill he had only just walked all the way up. The gulls circled high above him in the clear blue sky, screeching forlornly at each other. He looked along Seymour Ave for Boxer. He sometimes went down there to visit another dog, a red kelpie called Cocoa. He scanned the footpaths and checked trees, even the small bushes in the avenue, but there was no sign of him in the quiet street. He passed on and then near the park he heard a dog barking again, but it wasn't Boxer, he could tell. Boxer had a deeper bark.

He crossed the road down at the end as it turned towards Manly itself, then took the winding sandy track through the kikuyu grass that led down to the long, curved beach. It was a truly beautiful day. The quicksilver edge of a glinting turquoise-coloured sea lapped gently, again and again at the golden sands. A majestic, gleaming sun poured down from a heavenly blue vault that stretched above everything. He walked through the soft sand, finally reaching harder sand at the tide mark. He stopped and looked away to his right. There was a couple way off in the distance, further round the long curve of the bay, walking slowly side by side. A family were playing halfway down the beach, where the dunes built up slightly. He saw a little girl chasing a ball across the sand, while her brother laughed at her. He heard a dog bark and suddenly spotted a dog running at the other end of the beach and his heart jumped for a second, then dropped again, as he saw it wasn't Boxer. It was a medium-sized dog, but it wasn't black and white. He turned to the left and trudged off down the beach towards the dark-coloured rocks at the end of the sand. Seagulls squawked and flapped around on the sand noisily, arguing over tiny scraps of food. He reached the end of the beach, crossed the little stream at the corner of the cliffs and began to make his way carefully amongst the large boulders and long, washed-out ridges that ran round the cliff face. He climbed over the large flat ledges, and slowly rounded wave-cut corners of washed-out grey sandstone that the low tide had revealed. He climbed upwards and jumped across a large gap in the rocks. The lapping water below reached into the long, narrow cleft eaten into the rock. He walked along another ledge. Here, the crystalline water was pushing up against a long wall of rock below him. He jumped carefully across another large gap, balancing himself with the two rods. He was nearly at his spot. He climbed up a small bank of rock and loose dirt and suddenly he was there, underneath the branches of a grand old pohutukawa tree. He scrambled down the first ledge. *Perfect,* he thought. There was a little shade amongst the large branches and he could set up his gear here. Down below him was a two-metre-wide ledge for him to fish from, where time, tide and of course other fishermen had created a myriad of small holes in the worn rock. The large pockmarked holes and hollowed-out shelves were perfectly placed to hold your rod, your bait or knife, or even a beer can out of the sun. He opened the bait box. The small tackle box had three plastic baits in it. So — that was all he had for bait. He took the larger rod, which had a trace all set up, and folded a plastic bait carefully over the barb of the hook. Then he scrambled down to the lower ledge.

The sun beat down on the caramel-grey rocks from high in the sky above him. Crystal-green water lapped a metre below the ledge. The sea further out looked darker, cool and inviting. He was sure he could hear a dog barking, but it was too far away to tell if it was Boxer. He walked over to the edge and stood, surveying a black tip of rock poking from the sea out to his left. *Just beyond that rock and right in the middle,* he thought. He stepped back, turned and dropped the rod tip down low, then swivelling, he quickly flicked the rod over and the sinker and baited hook whistled through the air. The line caught the sunlight as it arced away from him. It hung there in the air for a second, then landed with a splash about forty metres out, right in the middle. *Perfect,* he thought happily. He stepped back and selected one of the worn holes in the rock at his feet to wedge the surfcaster's handle in. He stood there, his finger touching the thin green line lightly, just in case a fish happened to be there waiting for his bait. After a minute or two, he decided to get the smaller rod so he could use both at once. He clambered up the rock and carefully threaded a plastic bait onto the line of the smaller rod. He climbed back down and stepping straight over to the edge, he flicked the smaller rod smartly, landing the bait about halfway towards the first one. He smiled, looking further out over the crystalline surface of the water, where a lot of seagulls were swooping around the point. It was a great day to be fishing, he decided. Then he remembered he had only one plastic bait left inside his small tackle box. He couldn't believe the bait shop had been closed on a Saturday morning. That still frustrated him. His mind turned back again to Boxer. If only he hadn't run away two minutes after they'd left for the beach, the little ratbag. *He was probably enjoying himself somewhere,* he thought bitterly. No biscuits for him tonight, that's for sure.

He saw the line on the surfcaster jump twice. *A fish,* he

thought with glee, *a fish.* The rod tip jerked heavily again and he ran forward eagerly, grabbed the handle and began to wind the fish in. He quickly pulled the shining fish up the wall of rock and dropped it carefully on the ledge beside him. It was a perfect golden-coloured snapper, flapping in protest on the wet rocks. He took it up to the higher ledge, underneath the twisting branches of the pohutukawa and placed it carefully in the shade. Then he took the last bait from the box and went back down to the ledge below. He threaded the bait back onto the line of the surfcaster. He flung it out, the hook and bait flying upwards into the air in a high cast, but it plopped into the sea a good distance out. He was enjoying himself immensely. His mind suddenly reminded him of a saying his father had once told him: 'The gods never subtract from one's allotted lifespan the hours spent fishing.'

He really liked the thought of that. He waited for a few minutes by the rods. Everything was quiet, the reel brakes were set lightly, so he left the rods to themselves and leaned his back up against the sun-soaked, warm rocks. Suddenly, he thought he saw something disturb the surface of the water, a long way out. He climbed up the wall to get a better view, but he couldn't see anything out there in the dark, jade-coloured sea. He glanced over at the fish lying in the shade and saw in horror that a couple of seagulls were standing on the fish and tearing great big chunks out of it. They had snuck in under the branches while he wasn't watching. He swore and chased them off and they scrambled away, flapping and squawking into the blue sky. He looked at the fish and realised they had eaten away most of the flesh while he had been busy down below. He turned it over. They had scavenged almost all of it, their sharp beaks going right through its body. It was ruined. Angrily, he grabbed it by the tail and flung it back into the sea, some of the body parts falling to pieces as it hit the water. He thought he heard a bark and looked around, but he couldn't see any sign of a dog, let alone Boxer. He heard a clicking noise below and looked down. The surfcaster was jumping and bucking wildly again, so he scrambled down and raced over to the rod. It nearly leapt out of the hole it was sitting in and jumped straight into his hand as he reached out to grab it. The rod arched over immediately, the tip curving down at the water with the pressure. *It's a decent-size fish,* he thought delightedly. Indeed it was a much larger snapper and this time he worked hard to get the fish to the edge of the rock below him. It fought hard and ran backwards and forwards, fighting him all the way. Finally, he landed it on the rocks beside him and just as he did, he looked up and swore out loud. Boxer was on the ledge standing above him. Boxer's cheeky-looking face, with his black ear and his white ear and one black eye and one white eye, stared down at him, grinning over the edge of the rock.

'You little rascal!' he shouted, but Boxer's head turned and instantly disappeared.

He scrambled up the rock quickly after Boxer. *Damn you, dog, why do you always have to play silly buggers?* he thought.

He had taken Boxer to live with him after he had broken up with Cindy. She'd said to him one day that she couldn't look after him any more and the truth was he hadn't minded at all. He was certainly a bit of an all sorts kind of dog, but he was the friendliest dog he'd ever known. At the top of the rock wall he looked around, but there was no sign of the little bugger anywhere. He climbed along the top of the cliff edge and went as far as he could. Surely he couldn't have come this far. He carefully made his way back again. He glanced down at the ledge below him and saw the seagulls were clambering all over his fish down on the rocks.

Unbelievable!

He swore loudly as he climbed down the rock face and

frantically shooed the squawking birds away. He looked down at the large snapper he'd caught, astonished at the damage the group of birds had caused. They had pecked the thing to pieces with their sharp beaks. The fish was virtually destroyed. They had hacked out large pieces from its frame in only a minute or two. It was totally ruined. Disgusted, he tossed it back into the ocean with a splash. He reeled in the line from the other rod and was distraught to see the bare hook dangling on the end of the line, shining in the sun. The last bait had been picked off clean. Damn it, there's no bait left at all now. Reluctantly, he packed up the two rods and collected the bait box from the upper ledge. He whistled loudly for Boxer, but there was no sign of the little bugger.

Un-bloody-believable ..., he thought to himself angrily as he threw his bag over his shoulder and picked up his rods. He clambered down the rock and made his way along the ledge in the other direction, then took the path up to the dead-end road that ran in behind the cliffs. He whistled loudly again for Boxer. There was still no sign of him anywhere, not even a bark.

His mind wandered back to the day he had picked him up in Ellerslie.

'Why did you call him Boxer?' he had asked Cindy, as she stood in the doorway and scratched one of his ears for the last time. She had looked at him for a few seconds and said, 'I'll let you work that one out yourself.'

He hadn't understood what she had meant, until a few months later, when he'd been looking down at Boxer's left eye, which was the black one. Suddenly, he realised why she had called him Boxer. He had a big, black eye. He had felt a little foolish that it had taken him so long to work the joke out. The realisation he missed Cindy more than he had ever admitted hit him hard as he turned the corner of the street. Now he wished he hadn't broken up with her at all. Maybe he was still too young for real commitment. It was one of those heavy, regretful feelings and he was definitely feeling disappointed with himself as he walked down the road, the rods bouncing lazily on his shoulder. He decided to take the old path from the cliff top. It wound down and eventually came out at the stream that ran to the end of the rocks on the beach. As he stood at the top and looked out over the wide ocean, admiring the superb view in all directions, a small fantail flitted over and landed beside him on the rail. It danced cheekily from foot to foot, flicking and displaying its black and white fan and chirping at him, but then it was chased off by a flock of screeching, squawking gulls from above. Its little striped tail of black and white had reminded him of Boxer.

He wandered down the steep, winding path, driven deep into his own thoughts again. At the bottom, he followed the zigzag path of running water to the beach, then crossed the little stream and began to trek across the sand in the scorching heat. It was hard work under the blazing sun and his mind drifted away to his sister, who was living down in Christchurch. He was worried about all the large earthquakes they were having down there. It just didn't seem fair to the people in the whole area.

An older couple were walking along the water's edge towards him and as they got a bit closer, he called out to them.

'Hello, have you seen my dog? He's black and white and pretty hard to miss.'

* * *

THE OLDER COUPLE kept talking and ignored him, so he walked onwards up the beach.

'Stuck-up toffs,' he muttered to himself, as he plodded

through the thick sand. He carried on, but slowly he began to feel tired. The muscles in his legs burned in protest at the heavy sand as it kept sinking beneath his feet. He decided to have a quick rest amongst the warm, sunny dunes, so he tramped slowly over to a nice-looking spot at the edge of the high-tide mark. He scanned the long crescent of beach for the hundredth time for Boxer, but the black and white spotted bugger was nowhere to be seen. He lay the rods down carefully and sat there on the sand, looking at the magnificent scene spread out before him, like a perfect picture postcard. He'd never seen a more beautiful day in his entire life. Suddenly, he felt incredibly tired and his eyes seemed very heavy, so he decided to lie down in the warm sand for just a few seconds.

Unbelievable!

The very instant his tired eyes had closed, he'd realised with a giant shock that he was actually stone cold … His beautiful dreamy day was simply that — just a dream. The rain fell heavily, tumbling from a lead-grey, overcast sky. The ear-splitting shrieking and squealing of the great horde of gulls, all squabbling as they stood over him, attacking him, was truly deafening. His heart sank. A black and white patched dog ran back and forth, barking frantically, harrying and harassing the large swarm of birds, without any success.

He knew instantly … even before he heard the voice of the young girl running away from him, running in her raincoat through the thick drops of rain, leaving little footprints across the wet sand, crying out in distress to her mother.

'Mummy, Mummy, Muuummmmy! There's a dead man washed up on the beach …'

YOUNG AT HEART

One

She stepped through the doorway and kissed him gently on the cheek. He looked tired and irritable.

'Dearest sister, I hope you're well,' he said, stepping aside and taking her coat.

She smiled wanly; it was his standard greeting, ever since he'd become a doctor.

'I am well, but it looks like you've been burning the oil far too much, Michael,' she replied. She was concerned about his drawn face and tired, red eyes.

'Yes, there's been a troubling development lately. Come in and get warm, I can see the snow falling behind you.'

He hung her coat on a hook and she followed him inside the humble flat. He had been renting it for five years now, from Monsieur Degarde, as it had a large, spare room for seeing his patients.

He began to boil the pot of coffee, as was his habit whenever she visited. She sat in the old frumpy-looking armchair, which boasted a handful of repairs. It sat near the only window in the room. The view was short and sweet, a single tree in the yard, outlined against the unpainted timber wall of the grocer's building next door. She turned back to the inside of his flat. He obviously had only one decent piece of furniture, she decided. His favourite chair, which sat in front of her. It was an ornate-looking oak piece, with a high back. It had nicely carved sections, with the seat and back covered in dark gold and green velour. She knew he escaped to this chair every evening, after his twelve-hour sessions in the 'examination room' next door. He was no longer a barber or surgeon – now, he had become a doctor. The two fields were normally separated, it was rare to be part of both, but he had studied and practised hard for years to merge his skills. The poor people of the town had flocked in numbers to him with their ailments and problems, so the doctor's service had grown naturally from the demand at his door. She knew it was also because he sometimes bartered and exchanged for his fees. His big-hearted demeanour would not allow him to turn people away in need and his knowledge of medicine and a quick, steady hand with a scalpel had aided many locals, including herself.

'What is this latest problem, Michael?' she asked, watching him.

'A horrible abomination and a mystery too, all wrapped in one, sister,' he replied in his slow manner. 'I admit, it certainly consumes me lately,' he added, pouring the hot coffee into a pair of cups.

He spooned two scoops of sugar into hers, knowing she liked three, disagreeing on doctor's principle and also the cost of the luxury, shipped all the way from the West Indies. He carried the steaming cups over to the worn little table standing between the chairs.

She looked up as he placed her cup, unable to ignore the room behind him in its bare, truthful state. Besides the small dresser in the kitchen alcove, a rough bookcase was the only other piece of furniture in this part of the house. Two simple boards held the stacks of his medical books. Not even a solitary rug to cover the worm holes in the floor boards, she noted in silent despair.

He eased into his chair and his thin knees bent at sharp angles. He leaned against the back of his favourite chair and breathed out a long sigh.

After a few seconds of quiet, he asked, 'Anyway, how is this old man of yours coming along?'

Sarah grimaced; she hated the way he put Albert down. He may be older, but he had the vigour and enthusiasm of a man half his age, and she loved his wit and sparkle.

'He is not an old man at all, you rogue, in fact he appears younger than you today,' she quipped, picking up her cup.

He smiled, tiredness melting from his features for a few precious seconds.

'Touché, sister. Tell me something marvellous about him then, apart from his devastating wealth. I am in desperate need of cheering up.'

He eased back and closed his eyes.

'Well,' she started, 'he is the most wonderful speaker, as you know. I think he could make a great singer, or poet. His syntax is near perfect and his grasp of language is quite beyond mine. I find it hypnotic listening to him at times. His knowledge of different subjects is astounding. I have learned so much from him and in such a short time. More than I can remember about wines and plants and food and clothes, or jewels, or any number of different things. But it is the intricate details that speak so well. Did you know that silk takes a little worm years to grow and they keep these worms alive then slowly milk them of their shining harvest? It takes fifty-six yards to make a single scarf, for god's sake — oops, I really must watch myself. My blasphemous outbursts — his religious upbringing frowns upon it.'

He smiled, opened his eyes, then took a sip of strong, black coffee.

'It sounds as if it's going well — you're not only smitten, but also getting rough edges knocked off you too.'

She harrumphed loudly.

'Your fire is going out,' she admonished.

He leaned forward, took a log from the small pile and placed it on the glowing embers. He only had enough wood left for tonight. He'd need to cut some more tomorrow. He tried not to glance at the spindly tree outside the window. He liked the little tree fighting for survival in the yard, but maybe its time was up. He pushed the idea further back in his mind. Tomorrow's problems can be slept on, he decided.

Sarah went to take a sip, then put her cup down.

'I have written a poem, and I would like your thoughts before I present it to him,' she said, a small tremor emerging in her voice.

She pulled a piece of paper from her bosom, unfolded it slowly, then handed it to him. He leaned back. He had always enjoyed her poetry. It was an untitled piece.

What on this wide earth,
Could I possess
Or possibly produce
To define,
And mirror all the thoughts you've stirred,
inside this heart of mine
Then — is my best enough,
to answer such a noble search
To find a thing so real
It hurts,
deep inside this heart of mine

How could you see these things I feel,
How could I ...
bring them to a world that's real
Surely an impossibility!
When suddenly, I realise,
Simplicity is oh — so wise
As my heart does thud,
A sharp pin, with just a prick
That breaks my skin so thick
and brings a dot of blood —
that falls and lands upon the page
True life from throbbing veins
to leave a tiny crimson stain
on folded paper for all time
A precious gift for your old age
From deep within this heart of mine
Finally — a gift to see and hold,
a part that hides — indeed resides
Inside my heart and soul,
It is — simply
the smallest key
that fell with love
and died — for you
this tiny drop
of me

He studied the small blob of blood encrusted on the paper at the end of the poem, slowly taking in her thoughts. It was rather beautiful, he decided, and quite brilliant. Somehow she had managed to give a tiny piece of her heart, and how she had thought of it amazed him. It stirred another idea, hanging further back in his mind, but it stayed there just out of reach.

'I think it's quite brilliant, Sarah,' he said, carefully folding it and handing it back to her.

'I don't know how you think of these things. What will you use for a title?'

She took it carefully and returned the poem to its safe place.

'Thank you, Michael. I—I'm not sure,' she said. 'I was thinking of "Heart and Soul", but it sounds a bit pompous to me.'

'I'm sure you'll find something appropriate.'

They sat there for a moment as small flames began to lick at the log lying on the embers. The sound of hooves clopped steadily past outside as they enjoyed their coffee and talked about Sarah's new love.

'Anyway,' she said, 'enough of me and Albert. What is it that the great doctor of Peat Street finds so mysterious?'

He hesitated, then stood, unsure where to start. He lifted his pipe from the mantelpiece. He packed the briar, his long fingers pressing a small swab into the black bowl.

'It is troubling in a very unique way. It is difficult to explain to anyone, even a lay person.'

She smiled. 'Well, maybe a dullard like me can ease your burden, if nothing else.'

He grimaced slightly. His thin features creased, making him look older in the candlelight. He didn't mean offence and he decided finally, by her teasing, she hadn't taken any.

'Some of the younger boys and girls from the orphanage at St Peters are showing quite distressing signs. I know they are worked very hard at the mill up there, but these symptoms seem completely at odds with normal physiology.'

She frowned, not understanding all he had said. She knew he would elaborate, and so she waited patiently, but instead he grew quiet again, seemingly reluctant to explain further.

Suddenly, she realised she would be late.

'Confound it, I needed to be at Albert's by seven sharp. Whatever will he think of me?' she said, looking alarmed.

'I'm sure he thinks you're the prettiest and sharpest-thinking woman for miles. With a heart and prose to match,' he added.

She stood, straightening her dress, unaware of what he'd just said.

'I must go, I'll see you tomorrow evening, Michael.'

He nodded, quite used to his young sister's impulsive departures. He stood and led the way to the door. He helped her with her coat, then she was gone, a flurry of soft flakes swirling into the room as she left. He closed the door, walked over and stirred the fire with the poker, then he sat back in his chair, deep in thought.

Two

Albert Wilkins stood in the small room downstairs, studying the equipment constructed on the tables and benches before him. His small, wiry frame was attired in the finest clothes Europe could offer. Indeed he looked more like a dandy than the prince himself. His eyes glittered with pride at his latest scientific creation, one that had cost nearly half the price of the average house in London. He examined the copper tubes flowing in long, looping lines from the large brass pumping mechanism standing on a pedestal in the middle of the room. The complex array of valves and small dials littered amongst the equipment shone in the light of the gas lamps. Simon had done well. Everything looked bright and clean and it all seemed in perfect order again.

We're ready to go, he decided. All that's needed is another fresh subject. Somebody with real zest, a real enthusiasm for life. A healthy and happy donor, obviously. He walked across and turned the gas lamps down, then closed the door behind him and took the stairs up to the hallway of the mansion.

* * *

SHE WATCHED OUT THE SMALL, square window in quiet frustration as the horse and carriage rolled down the long, cobbled driveway, drawing her slowly between the avenue of tall trees. A thick carpet of snow covered the gardens and lawns and to her eyes, it looked like a fairy-tale setting. They finally stopped at the steps and the ice-encrusted driver helped her out, then up the grand sweep of stairs. She tried to give him something for his trouble, but he refused, telling her he could not take anything for his work for Albert, then he grunted and hobbled back down the steps to put the horse and carriage away, until the return journey. She pulled the cord beside the large doors. Deep in the mansion, she heard the chime of the bells, followed by the sound of the dogs. Simon answered quickly, opening the door and ushering her in from the cold.

'Miss Maxwell, Albert is in the drawing room,' he said, taking her coat and scarf.

'Thank you, Simon.'

She walked down the mahogany-panelled hallway, a long, handmade Arabian rug softening her footsteps. Large trophy animals stared down at her from high on the dark walls. Dancing candlelight threw leaping shadows across the ceiling as she moved past the heavily framed doorways. She entered the drawing room, where a large fire blazed and cracked in the giant hearth.

'Albert, I'm so sorry, my darling.'

'That's all right, Sarah, but where have you been?' he asked, standing.

He looked very handsome in his dinner jacket, she thought to herself. His graying hair seemed to make him more distinguished than usual tonight, with his face whitened and his dark moustache waxed and shining.

'I was at Michael's.'

He smiled warmly and invited her to sit.

'Ah, the good doctor. Well, that's fine, at least you were safe. Simon is preparing a wonderful meal for us. It's a special surprise. I'm sure you will love it. Would you like a drink before we eat?'

'Yes, please, something to warm my insides would be wonderful.'

'Cognac?'

'That sounds perfect.'

She settled into one of the regal-looking armchairs and he brought over two large round glasses holding a generous measure of golden liquid.

'Well, what have you been up to today, darling? she asked. 'I can't wait to hear more about your research.'

A frown creased his face.

'You know it is to be kept secret, Sarah, you must not talk of my endeavours to others.'

She smiled. 'Of course, darling. Your confidence is kept safely, deep within my heart. It is just my curious mind at work.'

He nodded, swirled his glass and took a sip and she did the same, the fiery liquid filling her with warmth.

'So please tell me what you've been up to?' she pleaded.

'Well, if I really must, but Sarah, if I do let you into my inner sanctum of research, you must prepare to be shocked, or fascinated — or both,' he said, with a smile.

She nodded eagerly.

'I promise.'

He looked at her for a second.

'Cross my heart,' she added, and they both smiled.

He stood, taking his glass with him, and approached the great bookcase. He indicated a large book that was sitting open on a stand.

'I have been studying history today and in particular, the great scientific men and their discoveries. Have you heard of the alchemists, my darling?'

She nodded. She followed him over to the array of shelves and stood near him, her perfume attracting him a little closer.

'I first thought they were practitioners of the occult, but Michael assured me they were studying much more scientific things, like melting metals and ... how to create coloured glass and things.'

He smiled at her warmly, genuinely impressed.

'Very good indeed, Sarah, you possess such a sharp mind, it is a joy to hear you talk. The alchemists indeed studied the art of mixing metals to create different alloys and also adding chemicals to molten glass, to find and manufacture different colours. However, their greatest attempts were focused on transforming simple lead into pure gold. An interesting desire, although that side of science does not attract me at all. I have little need for more wealth, thanks to my connections to the church. In fact, I much prefer to spend money. The subject I am most attracted to, and which is of great importance to my circle of friends, is an older and more arcane belief. The ultimate search to prolong life. The most important of all the great pursuits.'

'You mean the search for the fountain of youth?'

'Yes, though maybe not as you understand it, and why not? It is an honourable pursuit -— after all, why not defeat the greatest enemy known to all mankind — death itself?'

She nodded quietly, it made sense to her. She was sure even Michael would agree.

'Here,' he said, 'look at some of these drawings. As crude as you may find them, they hold some vital information.'

She studied the book displayed on the stand. The open pages revealed a set of drawings that shocked her. There were male and female figures with exposed internal organs, amputated limbs and other grotesque illustrations.

She went quiet and he knew she was slightly alarmed by the images.

'Sarah, there is a method to this science. In fact, history holds many vital clues.'

He pulled a volume from one of the shelves. It was a beautiful-looking leather book, titled *The Greatest Popes of the Catholic Church*. He flicked through the thick vellum, stopping at a chapter on the 16th century.

'Innocent VIII was a magnificent man,' he said, in a hushed tone. 'Highly intelligent, a truly scientific mind of no equal, before or after ... He presided over an immense volume of wondrous intellectual achievements. One of his great quests was the pursuit of life itself. However, he became extremely unwell in his later years and many efforts were made to heal him. Alas, they were unsuccessful.'

A bell sounded in the background.

'Ah, the meal is ready. Maybe afterwards I can show you more research in the smoking room, if you'll grant me that pleasure?'

She nodded. 'I would be delighted. In fact, I have something special for you too, dearest Albert.'

He looked quite surprised. 'Well, now I'm enchanted and cannot wait.'

'It is only a tiny thing,' she said, with a smile.

'We really do make a grand couple, don't we?' he stated.

He put his arm about her waist and they left the drawing room together.

* * *

THE MEAL of marinated venison and quail's eggs in thick, red wine sauce with aubergine and roasted pork croquettes was magnificent. It was followed by a small dish of strawberries and raspberries with a whipped lemon cream topping that was simple, but so delicious, she called Simon into the room to compliment him. Shortly afterwards, they retired to the drawing room, where she presented her poem to Albert.

She had decided on the title 'The Quintessence'. He read it slowly then stopped, examining the drop of blood on the page at the end. He turned and looked at her for some seconds. He was quite stunned, unsure of what to say.

'Please, tell me something,' she pleaded with him.

'I love it,' he finally replied. 'You have no idea how much this means to me, Sarah. Truly, I shall treasure this letter forever.'

She was thrilled with his response.

'I'm so glad you like it. Now, show me what you were so captured by earlier today, Albert.'

'Ah, see here,' he exclaimed, walking to a desk where the green velvet baize displayed a set of five tarot cards laid out in a cross shape. 'These are original cards from the hand-drawn Montecini collection. These cards are over two hundred and sixty years old. They are exquisite examples of her wonderful alchemist series. I must warn you though, Sarah, they are banned by some for their graphic nature.'

She had seen some tarot cards before. She studied these carefully, admiring the exquisite detail and artwork, but the subject matter truly disturbed her. On the card in the centre were two human figures, one male, one female. The figures were naked and entwined together by two great snakes with red and gold scales. Each serpent's head was fully embedded between the legs of one figure and the mouth of the other, while a ghoulish, lion-headed creature watched intently from above. A white griffin stood guard on one side and a dark-faced demon on the other, beneath two strange symbols. The two creatures were waiting for what, she could not tell. Was it a feast of their blood, or innards, or the bodies themselves? Was it to determine a winner and the loser to become the meal? It certainly seemed a grave decision was imminent. The card was titled 'Duality' at the top with the number 2 at the bottom. She compared it to the Death card, numbered 13, that lay on the green cloth, directly above it. The Death card seemed even darker. Below a star-studded sky, a ghostly figure, wearing a dark cape, held a sickle in his left hand. Fire burned freely in his other hand. He was mounted on a silver horse with black wings and he was laughing at a group of children trapped before him, being trampled by the horse's shining hooves. Dark light flew from the devilish creature's eyes and mouth. Demonic beasts of varying kinds sat in the background, devouring half-eaten bodies. The children in the foreground had boils, tumours and large buboes covering their bodies. The basic meaning seemed obvious, but it was incredibly grotesque to her and she wondered what it was in the images that had excited him so. The card on the left of the set of five was labelled the Queen of Vessels. A beautiful woman was pictured with bird legs below her waist. She wore a sickle-shaped moon headdress. It matched the same twin-horned, moon-shaped symbol in her hands, held high above her bare breasts. The twin-horned moon in her hands emptied blood from one end into a large cup at the top of the card. The many cups around her in the background poured the dark-red fluid from one to the other, ending at the last, the largest vessel, which spilled dark blood over her claw-shaped feet. Sarah wasn't an expert on tarot cards, but she thought this card normally symbolised the bloodline, or the renewal of life. The card to the right was the King of Pentacles. A man in fine clothes, wearing a golden crown, held up a twisted snake as a sceptre in one hand and a five-pointed shield hung across his shoulder. A large single star shone in the dark sky above his head. Gold coin-like objects lay discarded about him and a bubbling cauldron of some metallic-looking substance sat on a cross made of large bones at his feet. Skulls bobbed and bubbled at the surface of the large cauldron. She slowly turned her eyes towards the final card of the series. The card lying below the others was another she vaguely recognised. It was labelled The Fool and had the number 0 at its base. A young man was pictured descending a long winding path on a vast snow-covered mountain. A stream made of crimson blood crossed the path behind him. His clothes were tattered, and a stupid smile was etched across his twisted face. He held a single yellow daisy in his right hand. The sun and moon sat each side of the mountain peak. From the rocks on the path behind him, a black cat leapt at him, scratching at the genitals of the dishevelled man as he passed. The path before him was strewn with human body parts.

'I have never seen such strange art. It's wondrous, but deeply worrying at the same time,' she said, looking up at him.

He smiled at her, his waxed moustache lifting up at the ends.

'Exactly,' he said, as he took her hand.

* * *

Three

Michael saw the old lady to the door of the examination room and thanked her for coming. She had brought troubling news from a town further north. She told him many people from the town, old and young, had fallen sick and some had already died. Animals had also died. She had described the bodies. It sounded like an outbreak to him. He made a long note in his journal. His next patient was from the orphanage. He organised his instruments tidily, then turned the journal to a fresh page and nodded to the pair sitting on the stools lined along the wall. A tall woman stood, approaching him, leading a young boy by the hand. The child stumbled and dragged his feet. Michael observed him carefully, the worry lines on his face increasing, as the child finally sat in the chair in front of his desk.

'Charlie, what on earth have you been up to?'

He knew the child well and was surprised by his lacklustre behaviour. The child was normally in good physical condition. In fact, he had won athletic races in the last few years.

'I — I don't know,' the boy mumbled slowly, looking around the room. 'I — I feel tired, Dr Michael.'

Michael looked up at Christina, the matron standing beside Charlie. She looked slightly distressed, but said nothing and shrugged her shoulders slightly. He began his examination, slowly going through his routine. He wondered quietly if surgery might help, but it seemed too far gone now. Finally, after straightening the child's fingers on each hand as gently as he could, he sat back in his chair and began writing.

'Well, young Charlie, it seems you're a little under the weather, aren't you? Have you been doing anything different to normal, playing somewhere maybe you shouldn't?' he asked.

The child looked at him, then looked around the room again, then slowly shook his head. Michael was confused by the young lad's behaviour. Even though Charlie couldn't read or write, he was normally bright and full of energy. The boy turned to the matron and his mouth mumbled something to her.

'Is the washing all goin' on the dinner table for chicken?'

She just shook her head and placed her hand on his shoulder.

Michael stood again and felt the child's forehead, then under his armpit. Strange, he had no temperature. He was quite sure the boy would be suffering from fever. What else would explain his delirium?

He eventually prescribed rest and an alcohol rub. He was at a complete loss what else to do. The small bottle of alcohol he had taken from his cabinet was more than the orphanage could afford, so naturally he waived his fees. The delirium, or was it dementia, seemed very unusual to him, however the severe arthritis in all the young man's joints was deeply concerning.

* * *

SARAH ARRIVED at the mansion early in the afternoon. Yellow light slanted across the fresh snow heaping the ground. The dark trunks of the large trees emerged upwards from the thick, white blanket, their great arms and long, spindly fingers spreading in all directions. The building was formidable in the light of day, the servants' quarters grouped to one side, larger than most homes. The stonework of the main building reached up three levels and looked like some giant, elaborate wedding cake, the dark slate roof dripping at the corners with thick layers of crisp, white snow.

She was shown in by Simon. Albert was in the smoking room, sitting in a large cloud of cigar smoke, studying the pages of a large book.

'Darling Sarah. You appear simply ravishing today. That dress looks magnificent on you.'

She knew it did. He had bought it for her. It was made from the finest silk from Asia in a glorious peach colour that made her face look like fine, white porcelain. It sparkled in the candlelight at night, like nothing she had ever seen before, but even now in the daytime it shone, the richness and depth of colour changing every time she shifted and moved.

'What are you reading?' she asked politely.

'It is the final story of Pope Innocent VIII's demise. A tragic encounter with three young men from the church who volunteered their services and sadly all three of them died, trying to save him. Alas, their brave efforts were in vain, as he too perished shortly afterwards.'

'That sounds very sad, Albert. A terrible tragedy surely.'

'Yes, indeed it was. Please, allow me to finish this page and afterwards we'll have tea and fresh cakes in the dining room.'

'Of course, please finish your reading. I am totally enchanted by these views.'

She stood by the window, gazing across the lawns to the picturesque lake and the thick woods in the distance. She saw a rabbit steal across the snow, leaving tiny paw marks in a long wandering line across the white lawn. It disappeared finally into the hedgerow, behind the garden statues, which were arranged amongst the criss-crosses of the pathways. She turned reluctantly from the tall, sectioned windows and looked around the large, smoking room. The deep-burgundy-coloured curtains beside her were tied back elegantly with golden tassels. The rich burgundy curtains perfectly matched the thick, blood-red carpet. The red carpet was covered haphazardly with so many ornamental rugs, she wondered if Albert could one day spare one for her brother's sparse flat. Everywhere around her stood the finest French cabinetry, ornate chairs and tables. Not a speck of dust was to be seen on any of the dark, polished wood. She began to study the many paintings hung about the walls of the room. They were dark oil paintings and looked very old and the set of portraits seemed morbid and lonely to her eyes.

'My apologies, darling, I have so much to do, I get far too carried away with my work,' said Albert, rising and approaching her as she stood at the window. *He seemed to step so lightly for an older man,* she thought. She looked into his face. If anything, he was becoming more youthful and handsome to her every time she saw him.

'This is such a beautiful place, Albert, you must adore the change of seasons from these windows.'

'Indeed. I can assure you, the autumn colours are to die for, Sarah. There is every shade of gold and red and green and brown, I simply cannot describe it properly. But then you are the poet, darling, I am simply a man of study and learning. However, in appreciation of your fine poem to me yesterday, I have written something special just for you.'

Sarah smiled in delight.

'Well, you must read it to me right now, Albert. You simply must!'

He hesitated.

'It is nothing like your work of art, I assure you,' he replied. 'It is much more mundane and hardly worthy of praise, but it explains my inner thoughts and work. I fear, though, it is far too brutal for your ears.'

Sarah would have none of it and pleaded with him to read it to her.

'All right, my darling, I have memorised it, but prepare for my ugly view, a glimpse of scientific, brutal truth. I have called it 'The Sharpest Edge'.

He started, his chin set high and his voice slightly shrill and demanding.

No time to think
it must be done —
And quick!
Strike brutal cuts
To gash
And slice
And god, the spurt,
the blood, the slick!
Across a face — a smile of ice
cold facts and steel
Join cruel, final eyes
To still my steady hand
The red curtain
will surely rise
What monster lurks?
Behind — Inside?
It's now — I must
cut the quick
without a fuss
pull the tendon
thick and wide
No time to waste
to reach the place
And sip the bloodied wine
Of beating hearts
and turgid slop
of guts
and waste of parts
I take what's owed
To time ...
from this unholy state,
A final breath
that ever slowly, dies
I turn and find

you've closed your eyes
Too late —
The last
your Fate
your life
The thing ...
has passed

She was silent for a few seconds.

'Oh — that was ... it was about death, wasn't it?' she asked.

'Why, yes, of course, there's no fooling your mind, my dear,' he said, looking very pleased.

She looked at him for some time.

'But you wouldn't kill a person would you, Albert?' she asked in a small voice.

He laughed out loud.

'No, of course not, my dear. I could never kill a person, not ever. It is not in my nature, but people die, my dearest, all too often and it is much wiser to study your enemy, so you may beat him. This is my study, my gift for all of mankind. I warned you it was brutal, but so indeed is the great fight. The one between life and death.'

Sarah was shocked, but she slowly realised, she was also impressed. The poem was very dark in its nature, but brutal, just as he'd warned her. He seems so brave to write ... and to feel like that. That must be a good thing, she finally thought. No — a great thing! she decided.

'Oh Albert, that was a magnificent poem. You have such talent with a short phrase. Your control of words and timing is just wonderful. I loved it, and I'm sure Michael too, especially as a doctor, would love that poem.'

'Thank you, dear, you've made an older man younger for just a moment,' he said, and bowed proudly in appreciation.

She had the pleasure of his company for another hour, but then he had business for the evening and she left for her brother's flat.

* * *

ALBERT LAY on the special bed in the downstairs room. He lay there entranced, watching the dark fluid moving slowly through the glass container. The small child was strapped to the bench on the opposite side of the machine. She looked around frantically, but she was secure and the machine between them pumped on, making deep, gurgling noises. Simon was operating the handles and he nodded eagerly across the room to Albert. The older man's hands shook with a great rush of adrenaline. It would be soon, so very soon ... Suddenly, he felt the first tingles of vital fluid reaching his veins. At the exact same time, the young girl began to moan and struggle at the leather belts holding her down. She cried out sharply, in vain.

'Keep pumping, Simon!' Albert instructed him.

He began to breathe slowly, using his regular counting fashion, as the warm, red fluid steadily entered his veins.

* * *

SARAH KNOCKED at the door and Michael greeted her and let her in. Again, his drawn face worried her, but this time she said nothing. As he hung her heavy coat on the old peg, clumps of white snow fell against the stained boards. She moved quickly into the room and stood in front of the fire, warming her hands. He went to the stove and placed the pot of coffee over the glowing hole. After a few minutes, she finally turned away from the welcome heat of the fire, then sat in the old armchair by the window. She noticed the tree was gone from the yard. She turned from the bleak scene outside.

'How have you been, Michael?' she asked.

'I'm fair,' he responded.

'You don't look it, brother. Are you sleeping properly?

'Reasonably,' he replied, turning to face her.

'You worry me, Michael. I don't like to see you so tired every time I visit.'

'Yes, mother,' he replied sarcastically, as he turned back to the stove.

She pouted. He was so stubborn, her elder brother, it must be his greatest flaw. She looked around the room, but there wasn't much to interest her, apart from her tired brother with his back to her.

'How was Albert? Did he like your poem?' he asked her, without turning.

'Yes, he loved it. He said he would treasure it forever.'

He nodded, studying the pot.

'I thought he would. It was very good. You have real talent, Sarah.'

She was slightly embarrassed. He was such an intelligent man, it was high praise to hear him compliment her so openly.

'What did you decide for the title?' he asked, turning to face her again.

'I settled on "The Quintessence".'

'Very interesting,' he said, his eyebrows slightly raised.

He turned and poured hot coffee into the cups.

'Do you like the title?' she asked.

'Yes, it's a little ambiguous, but that's quite a good thing, isn't it?'

'Yes, that was my thought too — something very important, but thought provoking.'

He brought the coffee and placed her cup on the small table. He settled into his chair, holding his cup up to his nose. He savoured the essence of steam pouring from the dark surface.

'Yesterday, you never finished telling me about the problem you had. What is it all about, Michael?'

He sighed. He took a sip of his coffee and placed the cup back down.

'I think there's trouble up at the old orphanage. There's been a procession of the children down here with strange problems that I just can't figure out.'

'You mean St Peters Orphanage?'

He nodded. 'Yes, the conditions of the children are ...'

He searched for the right word. 'They seem anachronistic to me, in a doctor's point of view.'

She put her cup down with a puzzled expression.

'I still don't understand what you mean, Michael. Can't you describe it for me?'

'No, not really. It's very difficult as there's no singular condition. The children are all suffering from different ailments, but they're ailments they shouldn't have at their age. Rheumatism, arthritis, dementia, shingles, neuralgia, to name a few. They're far too young to all be suffering from these diseases.'

'But that could happen at an orphanage, couldn't it, Michael? If there are poor conditions, or the children have been very sick, or malnourished for some time.'

'Possibly, but I know these particular children from this orphanage very well and some of them were healthy only a short time ago.'

'Could there be a sudden shortage of food,' she wondered out loud, 'or something in the water?'

'It's possible, yes,' he agreed. 'I know they work them very hard at the Mill not far from there, with little food or water. However, there's this weird thing that I couldn't put my finger on at first. It's because I knew them. It seems everything they were naturally blessed with — their athleticism, or intelligence, enthusiasm, joy, whatever their greatest attribute was — it has been taken from them. Now, it's as if they've got quite the opposite symptoms — arthritis, dementia, depression, melancholy. It's as if their world has been completely turned upside down at that orphanage. It seems impossible to me that so many different elderly conditions could appear suddenly in young children, all in one place and at one time.

'That sounds terribly sad. I must go up there and visit them.'

'Take care, Sarah. I've had word that there's been an outbreak further north. I fear it's the black plague.'

'God, no! Not the plague, not here.'

'I'm afraid so. It is bubonic, by the reports of the buboes on the bodies of the victims. Those large growths are quite unmistakable. So, if you must go, take Aunt Edwina and if you see any signs of the sickness, return immediately.'

'I will. What is the matron's name at St Peters?'

'Christina, she's a good woman. She brings them here at the drop of a hat if anything is serious. Actually, I think this might be a good idea, Sarah. Anything to lift their spirits might help them and I would love to have a second opinion, even if it's only a poet's opinion, albeit one with a sharp eye,' he added with a smile.

'Oh, you're being a devil this evening, brother. I could throw things at you sometimes.'

'There's not much left to throw,' he replied with a laugh, looking around.

She had to reluctantly agree. She marvelled at her brother's resilience in the face of his difficulties. Soon they were chuckling together in front of the fire, just like old times.

Four

It was a long ride in the carriage out to the orphanage. The weather was mild, but cold, and the views along the river were wonderful. Soon they left the riverbank and headed in towards the mountains and it grew colder still. They had left late that morning and it was early in the evening when they finally arrived at the rough wooden buildings nestled amongst the white hills.

She immediately asked to see the children, but at first, the staff refused her. She didn't understand it. Finally, she pushed past them and climbed the wooden steps to the main room they called the hall, but when she stepped through the doorway, it was so dark in the room, she couldn't see a thing. She asked for some candles, so she could see in the gloom. While she stood there, she heard strange sounds from the room. There were slurping, tearing and crunching sounds in the darkness, like a pack of hungry dogs were being fed in there.

There was some argument amongst the staff outside, but finally three of them brought candles into the room and lit them. Sarah instantly reeled from the terrible sight. The flickering light revealed the forty or fifty children, all sitting at a long table, gobbling dark-coloured morsels before them. Glistening blood ran from their lips and dribbled from their chins. They were unrecognisable to her, as they crouched over the bench, their ghoulish features drenched in crimson gore. They ravenously crammed meat and pieces of offal into their reddened mouths. Many tore at the pieces like animals and the dark, coagulated blood coated their faces. She stepped towards the bench in a trance to examine the food and was shocked. Raw livers, kidneys and other organs lay in a bloody mess, heaped in the wooden platters. She shuddered as one boy bit greedily into a pink and purple sheep's heart, thick, dark blood squirting across the table. A few of the children looked at each other in surprise and shock, the candles now casting enough light for them to see each other. A couple of the younger ones began to cry, seeing the others' gore-slicked faces, but most grunted and slurped loudly, and continued with their feast. It was like a scene from Dante's *Inferno*, she thought. She left, glad to escape the horror of the grim spectacle inside the room.

* * *

THE MATRON STOOD in her office, impassively resolute, as Sarah demanded to know why the children were eating such monstrous things as raw meat and offal.

'Are you out of proper food to feed the children?' she asked.

'Oh no. We have plenty of food at the moment.'

'Then why offal and raw meat? It's disgusting!' Sarah remonstrated.

'It's because we can't feed them blood directly, but they — they need this to re... they need it desperately,' she replied.

It made no sense to Sarah.

'Whatever do you mean?' she asked incredulously.

The matron sighed deeply.

'It has been supplied to us at no cost, by a — a — a generous benefactor. The children are all worn down and they desperately need some ... sustenance. They are quite drained. Many of them are very sick. We are doing all we can to re — re — to rejuvenate them,' she finally finished and let out a long sigh.

'Who is this benefactor?' Sarah asked.

'I — I cannot tell you that,' replied the matron. 'He is wealthy and has donated money for some new buildings here for the children. We cannot possibly upset him.'

Sarah tried to get more information, but for some reason the matron seemed afraid to talk any more. She simply refused to answer her questions. In the end, she had no choice but to return to town in the carriage. The journey back along the roads was troubling and disturbing, every shadow and sudden noise startling her, as they bounced along the cold, dark road. She saw grisly faces in the night and the demons from the tarot cards joined the bloody faces of the children, tormenting her. She made sure her aunt was safely home, then she returned to Michael's to report her visit to him and shelter there for the night. She spent the night in the armchair by the fire, haunted by her grim, frightening visions.

* * *

THE NEXT DAY, she visited Albert again and they had lunch out on one of the small, sheltered balconies, in the warmth of a weak, midday sun. She told him of her travel up to the orphanage, but he seemed consumed by his research and completely uninterested in the problems at St Peters. They spent the rest of the afternoon wandering around the mansion, her interest in the bizarre and strange collections in the rooms jaded by the plight of the children at the orphanage.

* * *

TWO NIGHTS LATER, she dropped in to see Michael. He was tired again, but his spirits were better and she asked him why.

'I have received a letter. It informs me of the great improvement of the children at St Peters.'

'Well, that is wonderful news indeed.'

'Yes, it has been a severe burden on my mind, I must admit, but apparently almost all the children have made a dramatic improvement and not a moment too soon.'

'Oh, I'm so happy for them. It was a worrying sight indeed and I thought it might end up in tragedy, like that Pope that Albert was telling me about. Innocent the something or other.'

Michael looked at her strangely.

'Do you mean Innocent the VIII?'

'Yes, I think that's the one. Apparently three young men tried bravely to save him at the last, but they all lost their lives. I have no idea how, but it was a great tragedy.'

Michael looked at her for a few seconds.

'Those were young boys and the church experimented on them in ghastly fashion. They exchanged the Pope's blood with the boys'. It was one of the first experiments of blood transfer between human beings. It was certainly tragic and yes, they all died, but it was a terrible crime by the church in reality. Those young boys had no choice at all.'

Sarah looked at him in astonishment.

'That's not how Albert told it to me.'

Michael was looking into the fire, ignoring her.

'Parabiosis ... surely not,' he said to himself quietly.

'I don't think you're being fair to Albert,' she said to him. 'I'm sure he wouldn't even think of these terrible things.' Then she grew silent as she remembered some of the words of Albert's poem. Then she recalled the tarot cards he'd shown her and a worried look came over her features.

Michael pushed at the fire with the poker. He refused to look up for a while, then he asked her a question and it hit her out of the blue.

'Does Albert have anything to do with the orphanage? he asked.

'No, he doesn't! In fact, he almost ignored me when I talked about the children just the other day and all their problems. Really, Michael, you've never liked him and now you're accusing him of these terrible things. I can't believe you would suggest ... anything like that!'

'There, there, sister, I'm only asking,' he said, soothingly.

'You are not! I know you. Well, I'm not sitting here listening to you for another minute. You're — you're jealous of Albert and his money, not to mention his success! You're stuck here in this, this hell-hole of a flat with no money and no future. You've wasted your life here and now you just want to ruin mine and Albert's — don't you! Admit it, Michael, you're a poor excuse for a doctor and you were wrong about those children!'

Sarah stood, then stormed to the door, grabbing her coat. He tried to stop her, but she burst into tears and fled past him into the street. She stumbled and a horse and wagon stopped as she picked herself up. She got in and the horse and carriage trotted on, into the snow-driven night, leaving him standing by the door in despair.

Finally, he shut the front door and retreated to his chair, deep in thought. *It* was *ludicrous,* he thought to himself. However, the more he thought about it, the less crazy it seemed. If the blood transfers were short, carefully managed and stopped if they caused Albert any problems at all, it might just work. If they had a machine to keep the blood warm and moving, it was certainly possible. Albert would have been rejuvenated by their blood and probably helped any of the ailments and disabilities he had. It wouldn't be a cure, but it would give him many more years of good health. However, it meant the children got his old blood with all of its problems. No wonder they were showing signs of advanced aging and diseases. He shifted his thoughts back to Sarah. I wonder where she went? The thought nagged at him, until he realised it was most likely she had gone straight to Albert's. And she would have burst into tears and told him all, knowing Sarah. He fetched the letter again and studied it closely. He began to worry. Finally, he stood and took his coat from the hook. He wondered how far it was to Albert's. About five miles, he guessed. He took his walking stick and left the house.

* * *

SARAH STEPPED from the carriage and climbed the stairs at Albert's mansion. The snow fell lightly across her reddened face. Her tears had dried, but she was still upset. How could Michael say those things about her darling Albert? She rang the bell and Simon's face eventually appeared in the doorway.

'Come in, Sarah. What a nice surprise. Come into the drawing room. I will fetch Albert from upstairs. He was planning for an early night, but he has only just retired.'

'Oh, thank you, Simon.'

She followed him into the drawing room and waited by the fireplace, which was still burning fiercely in the grate. A few moments later, Albert appeared. His face was vibrant and his eyes seemed quite alive for the late hour. He strode towards her, a worried look suddenly emerging on his features.

'Why, you've been crying, Sarah. Are you all right?'

'No, I'm not, Albert. I've had a terrible night. It's been quite ghastly and I had to come here. I hope you don't mind.'

'Of course not, darling. Whatever is the matter? Here, sit yourself in this chair and I'll get you a brandy. Then you can tell me all about it. I'm sure we can make it right, whatever it is.'

'Oh, you're wonderful,' she said, settling into one of the high-backed chairs. It felt so comfortable and warm. She suddenly realised how much she missed this place.

He brought them both a brandy, then sat in the chair opposite her.

'Now tell me what the problem is and we'll set it right,' he said, taking a sip of his drink.

'Well, I had a fight with Michael and well, it was awful. He said some terrible things — they were about you, Albert — and I couldn't bear it, so I left and came over here to see you.'

'Naturally, darling, you did the right thing. Whatever is it about? What have I done to your brother that has upset you both so much?'

'He, he accused you of some vile things. Things you can't possibly have done, Albert. I can hardly bear to mention them in your presence.'

'There, there, Sarah, take another sip. Now tell me what it was. I'm sure it's all a great misunderstanding.'

She took a sip and nodded.

'I hate to use the words, but he accused you of using the children in the orphanage horribly and somehow causing them their illnesses.'

Albert smiled, but his eyes narrowed slightly.

'I'm not sure what you mean. Is this the orphanage up in the hills? St Peters, the one you mentioned the other day?'

She hesitated.

'Yes, but he said something about Pope Innocent and how he died. Parabi... it was some strange word he used.'

Albert got up and patted her shoulder gently. He looked into her eyes.

'Now, there's no need to be alarmed, dear. He's just been

working far too hard. You said yourself how tired he's been lately.'

'Yes, that's right. I'm sure you're right.'

'Now listen, Sarah, I think you should stay the night. It's terribly cold out there and you've had a ghastly time. I'll get Simon to prepare a bed for you.'

Sarah looked slightly alarmed.

'I don't — I don't think that would be a good idea, Albert. My aunt will be worried if I'm not home.'

'Oh, I'm sure she'll understand, Sarah,' he said, a gleam in his eyes and the smile on his face growing a little larger.

'No, I really must go, Albert, she will worry all night if I don't arrive back soon.'

'Fine, fine,' he said. 'I'll get Simon to organise the driver. Just stay here a minute, my darling.'

Albert left the room and she sipped at her brandy. Her thoughts began gnawing at her somewhere deep in her mind. Soon he was back.

'Would you like another brandy?' he asked, walking to the drinks cabinet behind her.

'No, I'm fine thanks, Albert. I do have a question though, if you don't mind?'

'Of course, darling, whatever it is, ask away,' he replied lightly, pouring a large tot into his glass.

'Well, I think Michael was being really nasty tonight. He asked if you'd been to St Peters. You haven't been to St Peter's Orphanage, have you, Albert?'

'No, of course not. Why do you ask?'

'Well, he felt you must have some connection to the place, to have access to the children for these terrible things that have occurred to them. I got extremely upset with him for saying such a shocking thing.'

'Of course you did, darling.'

He came and sat down opposite her again.

'You know I would never hurt anyone. I do thank you for standing to my defence,' he said.

He took a generous sip of the brandy and noticed she hadn't touched hers.

'You have no idea at all where the orphanage even is, do you?' Sarah asked.

'Of course not,' he said. 'Drink up, my dear, it will make you feel much better.'

'So, then how did you know that it's up in the hills?' she asked quietly, her eyes watching him like a hawk.

He took another sip of his brandy. His eyes came up to study hers — they were staring at his own.

'You really are a clever little thing, aren't you, Sarah?'

She didn't reply. She watched him, waiting for his answer.

'But not quite clever enough, I think,' he said, putting his drink down. 'You can come in now, Simon. The game is over, at least for our dearest Sarah, anyway.'

The door opened and Simon entered. The burly manservant walked over and stood beside Sarah's chair.

She glanced up at Simon, noticing the look on his face, then looked back at Albert.

'You wouldn't dare,' she said.

Albert laughed. 'Oh, you have no idea, Sarah dearest. No idea at all.'

'I will scream,' she replied, between her clenched teeth.

'No one will hear you here,' he said, then chuckled. 'Take her downstairs, Simon, it's time we introduced her to some real science. I can't wait to feel her beauty and vitality pounding through my limbs. I've spent such a long time thinking about it. All in the name of life — and death, of course.'

Simon grabbed her arm and Sarah screamed, just as she'd promised. Simon's other hand clamped over her mouth and he lifted her from the chair and dragged her kicking and squirming across the room. Albert followed, a look of pure delight on his face. They all descended the stairs at the end of the hallway, then entered the basement room. She saw the array of equipment and a look of horror crossed her face. She realised what Michael had said was right. She couldn't believe it, but here was the final truth.

'Now, don't fight it. It may cause you a lot of pain,' said Albert, as Simon strapped Sarah down against the bench.

Sarah screamed at the top of her lungs.

'Gag her, Simon,' instructed Albert, as he began to ready himself on the bed on the other side of the machine.

Five

Michael walked down the long driveway, his footsteps slowly disappearing in the heavy falling snow behind him. He climbed the sweeping front steps to the large mansion and pulled the rope by the front door. He heard the bells echo through the old building.

'Damn it, who could that be at this hour? said Albert in frustration from the bed. 'Get the door, Simon, and get rid of them. I'll continue setting up here.'

Simon climbed the stairs, shuffled down the hallway and opened the front door.

A tall, snow-covered stranger, stood on the doorstep.

'May I help you?' he asked.

'Of course,' said Michael and he swung the heavy, gnarled end of his stick hard into the servant's face. Simon howled in pain as he fell backwards and Michael followed him in. He immediately struck the man in the knee, exactly where the ligament joins the kneecap. He heard a satisfying pop and the man screamed again in agony.

He knelt down beside Simon.

'There, there, good man. I can understand your pain,' he

spoke calmly. 'Now if you tell me where my sister is, I shall stop this wicked little game of ours, otherwise I shall continue to display my extensive knowledge of the human body and my cold surgical demeanour, which is probably much worse for you.'

'Down — down the stairs at the end of the hallway,' the man gasped between breaths.

'Good man, don't make me come back to remind you of our little game either,' Michael threatened, waving the thick knob in Simon's twisted face, then he strode on. He opened the last door and found the stairwell, then began to make his way down it.

'Hurry up, Simon, hurry!' shouted Albert, as he heard footsteps on the stairs. The adrenaline surges that he so loved were beginning to shake his hands uncontrollably.

The door swung open and Michael entered. He took in the instruments and equipment, Sarah strapped to the far bench and Albert fumbling with his straps on the bed. He leapt across and dealt a savage blow to the old man's head.

Albert crashed to the floor in a heap.

'Oh god!' he cried out. 'Who the hell are you?' His hands were crossed, protecting his face and they shook worse than before.

Michael rounded the equipment and began to undo Sarah's straps. He eased the gag from her mouth.

'Oh Michael, I'm so sorry,' Sarah exclaimed, shocked and relieved to see him. 'You were right! That disgusting old bastard was going to kill me.' She pointed her shaking finger at Albert, who cowered on the floor, a line of blood running down his face.

'I'm an old man,' he cried pathetically. 'Don't hurt me, I'm sick!'

Michael sneered. 'Don't even tempt me. Come on, Sarah, let's go.' Then he hesitated and turning, he swung the walking stick in a great arc and the glass container beside him crashed to a thousand pieces across the floor.

'Noooo!' cried Albert. 'No, you can't! Not my machine!'

Michael struck repeatedly with the stick, crushing and tearing copper lines and smashing valves. He pounded at the dials and levers, destroying everything he could reach. Finally, he grabbed Sarah's hand.

'Come on, let's get out of here.'

They took two steps to the door and Michael put one foot on the stairs, then stopped. Slowly, he stepped down and backed into the room as Simon limped down the last of the stairs and entered the room, hobbling unevenly. He held the shotgun in his hands straight at Michael and a look of thunder was written across his face. His left eye was already closed and his mouth was turned up in a rage.

'Oh thank god!' cried Albert, standing up suddenly. 'Well done, Simon!'

His sharp eyes studied the siblings for a few seconds. 'Ah, the brother. So now we have a real doctor here. I wonder what we should do with you two?'

His face became a gloating, gleeful mask. 'I think we can still get their blood, don't you, Simon? Keep the gun on him, I'll deal with her first.'

He walked quickly over to Sarah and grabbed her by the arm. She tried to fight him but he was surprisingly strong. He pulled her away, towards a chair on the far side of the room. He dragged her over and pushed her roughly into it. Simon grinned at Michael as Michael moved his arm slightly.

'Please do that. Do something, anything at all, please, doctor,' he said in a low, threatening voice, his eyes staring straight at Michael's, willing him to give him an excuse to pull the trigger.

Michael stood quietly where he was. Albert left Sarah in the chair and began to organise some surgical instruments.

As he turned away, Sarah lunged forward. She swung the chair at Albert, striking him across the back of his head with all her strength. The gun suddenly went off and in the small space it was deafening. Sarah looked round for Michael, but all she could see was a cloud of blue smoke. She saw Albert on the ground crawling towards her and she pushed the great brass machine over and onto him. Out of the corner of her eye, she saw Michael and Simon fighting over the gun. She looked around and spotted Michael's walking stick and ran over and grabbed it. She took a step and swung it with both hands at Simon's head and heard a satisfying crack. He fell like a heavy sack of potatoes and stayed down on the floor, motionless.

Michael stepped over and took the stick from her shaking hands.

'I hope I haven't killed him,' she said, horrified at what she'd done.

He smiled at her. 'It's just like old times, sister, but now we fight on the same side.'

She looked up at him in dread. 'I really do hope I haven't killed him,' she said.

He bent down at Simon's still figure and felt carefully for his pulse at his neck.

'Not this one. He'll sleep for a while, that's all. I should have done it myself earlier.'

He stood and his eyes searched the strewn floor. 'But old Albert, well, I'm not so sure.'

There was a moan from the other side of the room and Michael stepped through the litter of broken equipment and shards of glass. He spotted Albert lying half under a piece of the machinery.

'Right, you nasty old bastard. I'm going to inform the church of your affairs at the orphanage. I'm sure you have friends, but I doubt they'll support you and you won't be harming any more of the children. You'll also be sending plenty of money this week to that orphanage, because I truly doubt those children have actually recovered at all. I'm sure you're the one behind that letter. If you don't do all this, then we'll go to the police. In fact, I'm hoping you don't, so they lock you up and you can die slowly in some damp and wet cell of some terrible disease.'

Albert moaned loudly. 'I will, I promise,' he mumbled.

Michael snorted in disgust. 'Let's get out of here. It's time we left — for good.'

They climbed the stairs, found Sarah's coat and scarf and left through the front door, leaving it wide open.

* * *

LATER THAT NIGHT, Michael finished the letter. They both signed it.

'Give this to Aunt Edwina. Tell her to post it in one month, no matter what happens. I can't stand the thought of him getting away with destroying those children's health.'

Sarah nodded. 'Will they be affected forever, Michael?'

'I hope not. They're still young, so their bodies regenerate. Even bones are replaced every seven years or so. I'll help them as much as possible and I'm sure in a few years they'll be healthy again. However, there'll be the odd scar in one way or another.'

She looked at him. 'I got it so wrong. Will they arrest him?'

He sighed. 'I doubt it. He has incredibly rich friends in the church and others in very high places, but they'll be disgusted, I'd imagine, so we'll just have to wait and see.'

* * *

ALBERT SAT in the smoking room, reflecting. They had destroyed his equipment and ruined it for him at the orphanage. It seemed they had cut off all avenues to pursuing his goal. There must be some way, he told himself. He took a sip of his cognac. Suddenly, he had an idea. He got up and walked over to the bookcase. He began searching through a large book of registries. Aha, here it was in the Annual Registry in 1691. Yes, a cat stealing the breath of a young one. It was still possible for him, surely. At least it was another avenue to be pursued, he thought to himself with glee. You cannot stop a scientific mind, he gloated. He rang the small bell on the table.

'Simon, quickly, man, I need you to do an urgent task for me.'

Simon shuffled in stiffly and stood there, his black eye still swollen shut from three nights ago. He nodded finally as Albert gave him the last item on the list of instructions. He left, hobbling down the hallway, then moving slowly out the door on his bad leg. He took the horse and cab. Four hours later, he was back.

'I have found someone perfect for you, master. She is extremely unwell and not expected to last the night. She was young and vibrant, very good looking even, but now it seems she has no chance of surviving.'

Albert nodded eagerly; his squinting eyes shone with mad delight.

'And is she ... is she pure, Simon?'

'Yes, she is definitely a virgin, according to her mother.'

'Good work, Simon, you have done very well. We must prepare for the journey. Is it far?'

'About an hour or so, by carriage.'

'Excellent, you have served me faithfully once again. If I achieve success, I will reward you richly, Simon. Now, prepare my things.'

Simon limped from the room. Albert stood in the smoking room, his eyes staring at his surroundings, but his thoughts were somewhere else. His mind was a turmoil of excitement and delight at the thought of finding a source of such youth and beauty.

* * *

'ARE you sure she is not a local?' he whispered for the fifth time in the tiny hallway.

'Yes, they have just arrived from somewhere further north,' Simon assured him again.

Stealing her last breath will be such a divine pleasure, Albert thought to himself, trying to conceal a wicked, secretive grin. No — it is a divine right, he corrected himself. It would be impossible to stop him now. He was far too clever for the church, or the police, or those two brats, Michael and Sarah. They were petty little fools, just like the illustration on the tarot card. Wandering alone about the great mountain of knowledge, completely lost and picking flowers. Simon returned, then nodded to him. Albert eagerly entered the small room with the young girl laid out on the wooden table. He slowly positioned himself over the dying child. Her ragged breathing excited him, making his heart and mind race with anticipation. The long, irregular gasps began to slow dramatically as he crept forward, his face barely an inch from hers. There was a long pause and he thought he'd missed the vital moment, then her chest heaved one final, agonising time and she breathed out in a great sigh. He drew in her exhalation of air in one long breath, his lips just touching hers as he finished.

* * *

Two days later, Albert woke feeling terribly hungover; his head was heavy and painful to move. He sat up in bed and coughed. It was a hard, racking bark and he felt pain flare deep in his chest. He also felt sharp aches in his armpits and something very uncomfortable … down there. He examined himself slowly, wondering what it was that was bothering him. In shock, he thrust back the sheets and saw the huge, dark-looking lump that had grown in his groin, right beside his manhood. A bubo! A bubo! God — no! It couldn't be! Frantically, he felt under his armpits. Fear rose up in him as he realised several large lumps had grown there as well. *Nooo!* he thought. *No, not buboes!* He coughed heavily again and immediately felt a sharper pain in his chest, and a long dribble of fluid ran down his chin. He wiped it with his hand and saw the dark, clotted blood smeared across his fingers. Suddenly, the horror and sheer terror began to well up inside him. Not the black death! Not like the tarot card! Oh please, please, God, no …

HOOKED

DANNY WAITED INSIDE THE ENTRANCEWAY OF THE OLD market, a dark silhouette amongst the broken shadows. The fish market had closed twelve years ago and had been designated for demolition last year. Every window along the street was smashed, leaving it looking sad-eyed and run-down, and a rusted sign hanging above the doorway had been tagged in bright red spray paint. He couldn't work out whether the graffiti said 'dagger' or 'danger', but the red had dribbled down like blood over the faded black letters. The street light across the road cast a pool of light down onto the footpath in a hazy circle. He glanced up and spotted a couple in the distance, heading slowly towards him. He watched the young couple approach on the other side of the road. They were laughing and holding hands as they wandered down the footpath. He felt angry and he didn't really know why, but all the meth he had been smoking that day fuelled his anger and he could feel its dark energy welling up inside him. The couple stopped, then she reached up and kissed him. They talked for a second or two, then she walked back the way she had come. When she turned the corner and was lost from sight, the young man continued on.

Danny knew this was his moment. He stepped out of the dark and crossed the road. The young man saw him as he approached and attempted to hurry past, but Danny had timed it perfectly and he moved in front of him.

'Hey,' he said smiling widely, showing his hands palm up. 'Do you have a light?'

The man shook his head and went to move on. Danny pulled the small bar he had taken from the dumbbell he used at home and struck at the young man's head as he turned away. The blow was a glancing one. Danny struck again, harder. This time blood flew and the lust grew inside him suddenly as the figure staggered. He bashed him again, the heavy bar crushing the bones in the side of his face with a sharp, ugly crack. The young man fell forwards and lay there, unmoving. He stepped over to the body, thoughts whirling through his mind. He went through his pockets quickly, taking out a wallet and some keys. He stood there worried the victim might remember his face, so he struck him again as hard as he could, venting all his frustrations with the savage blow. Then he looked around quickly, as if he was suddenly aware of what he had done, but the street all around him was quiet. He looked down and noted the dark pool of blood growing outwards from beneath the body of the young man. He put the bar back in his pocket and walked quickly across the road. He took a small side street and moved briskly down it, making sure not to look back. When he got to the tracks, he wandered down the railway lines that ran to the station. He stopped in a dark spot and took the money from the wallet and counted it. It was thirty-seven dollars. He swore, then threw the wallet and keys across the stones of the track. He carried on with his head down, leaving the railway lines before the station. He crossed slowly through town, heading back towards the small flat.

* * *

When he was back and safely behind the front door, he found the little packet he had nearly finished that afternoon and retrieved his pipe. He tore into it, smoking until it was all gone. The euphoria helped calm his nerves. He searched and found half a bottle of whiskey in the kitchen cupboard one of his flatmates had stashed and he drank it in large swigs. In almost no time at all, it seemed finished. He shook out the last drops of the bottle, the sharp taste landing on his tongue, lingering for just a few seconds. He vaguely heard his flatmates come home a few hours later, as he played his music loud in his tiny room. Early in the morning, he fell into a deep and fitful sleep.

When he woke it was evening and everything seemed blurred together, until he remembered his assault of the young man the night before. In the sobering reality of day, he wondered how he had come to such a terrible act. That night he watched the news closely and was shocked to see the young man was in a coma in the hospital. What was really terrible news was he was the son of a local politician. Every time he saw the story come up, cold chills ran down his neck, and his hands would shake uncontrollably. It was reported by some news that the police weren't sure what had happened to the young man who had been found lying on the footpath in central Wellington. He may have suffered an assault, or may have been the victim of a hit-and-run accident. Anyone with any information of the crime was urged to come forward to the police. On the Thursday morning, when the young man died, Danny decided to leave Wellington. He bought a ticket and caught the bus up to Auckland.

All the way up State Highway 1, he kept his face hidden with his hoodie pulled over his head and stared out the window at the sunlit world passing him quickly by. In Auckland, he met up with some old friends who let him stay for a few days, until he'd found a place to live. The first night they went out to a nightclub in Customs Street. He had spent all his money by 10 pm and some of the others bought him drinks until they all left at 2.30 am. He felt relieved, living in a different city from his terrible crime and he noted with satisfaction that the story in Wellington wasn't mentioned much in the Auckland news at all. He thought the nightmare he had created was behind him now. He spent the next day looking for a job, but something stopped him going into any of the businesses he had selected and he simply stood outside them, wondering why he couldn't go inside. That night he took out the last of his money from his savings account. The others were spending the night in and watching a DVD, but he desperately wanted to party and drown his thoughts, which kept slowly turning like a great wheel, back to that moment on the street in Wellington. He decided to go out and with his last two hundred and seventy-four dollars tucked firmly in his wallet, he headed out again, catching a bus into the centre of the city. He found a friendly-looking face in one of the clubs and bought a tiny bag of ice from him. He made a pipe from a glass bulb he took from one of the toilet cubicles and took a few hits. He definitely felt much better. A few drinks later, he was surprised to see his wallet had only a single twenty-dollar note left. A pretty girl caught his eye at the bar, smiled and suddenly, that was gone too. A few minutes later, he was alone outside the bar. He found a quiet place to smoke the remainder of the little bag. The rest of the night faded into a confused blur of over-friendly greetings and manic shouts of abuse and at 5.30 am he found himself broke, drunk and staggering down a deserted street near the waterfront. He didn't know why, but he didn't want to go back to his friends' place. He caught sight of his face in a window reflection and was shocked to see the unfamiliar pale, drawn features, with tears running down his cheeks. He hadn't even realised he'd been crying. Danny staggered onwards, not knowing where he was going. He found an old deserted building down by the docks, clambered in a window at the rear, nestled exhausted into a comfy corner and fell asleep.

He woke in the morning to a terrible stench all around him and realised he had fallen asleep amongst piles of dumped rubbish. The place was full of rotting fish guts and heads, old bait and other unrecognisable, disgusting objects. He found a way out and staggered outside into the bright early sunlight and stood there for a moment looking around. He had no idea where he was. Seagulls circled high above him, cawing in the blue sky. He listened to the early-morning sounds all around him as the city slowly began to wake. Danny walked along the street looking about and he realised the street he had wandered down was actually one of the docks for the fishing fleet. He meandered down the line of fishing boats, stepping over and past thick mooring ropes, large rusty bollards and piles of equipment laid out for the fleet. He stopped and gazed out to sea between two of the trawlers. Mesmerised by the cool, blue waters sparkling and catching the sun in the early-morning light, all his worries sat behind a thin screen as his brain dragged itself awake. A truck drove slowly down the dock towards him and a voice suddenly called out from his left.

'Hey, you better shift, or Jerry will drive right over you, mate! He's half blind.'

Danny looked over. A grizzled-looking man stood on the deck at the bow of one of the trawlers. Long, straggly hair roughly framed the half-bearded face, which was long, creased and thin. The unshaven face couldn't hide a lumpy, bone-white scar on his cheek, which ran nearly to his lip. He grinned over at Danny as Danny stepped clumsily to one side.

'Are you here looking for work?'

Danny stared over the edge of the dock at him, still severely hungover. His badly fogged brain was unsure of which answer to give to the fisherman's question.

'Come on up the gangplank, before Jerry runs you down, mate.'

Danny stood there for a second, then the blast from the horn of the truck startled him and he stepped forward onto the end of the roughly built wooden ramp that lead onto the boat. Something clicked somewhere deep down inside him and he realised it might be a perfect job for him. The chance of the police following his trail all the way from Wellington, then tracking him aboard an old fishing boat here on the docks was highly unlikely. He walked shakily up the gangplank and aboard the boat. The man who had spoken to him stepped across the deck and stuck out a large, hairy hand.

'Rob,' he said simply.

'Da…Darren,' stammered Danny, suddenly deciding to change his name at the last second. He shook the man's hand. Rob gave him a quick, rough shake and his large callous fingers enveloped Danny's in a firm grip that spoke of years of hard, uncompromising work.

'Welcome aboard the *Katie Lee*,' he said with a warm smile. 'You smell like a fisherman. Did that old bugger Geoff send you down?' he asked, smiling at Danny with a slightly lopsided grin that showed two missing teeth.

'Ah, no, actually … I was just looking for any kind of job, that's all,' said Danny, his foggy mind trying to shake off the huge amount of alcohol he had consumed the night before.

'Yeah?' said Rob, a slightly puzzled look on his face. He

hesitated for a second, then turned his head at another blast from the horn of the truck. It had stopped on the dock right beside the boat.

'Well, no matter,' he said, turning back to face Danny. 'The job's yours if you want it, the boat's short-handed this trip.'

Danny nodded slowly, not really understanding. The bright sun hurt his bloodshot eyes as he stared up at the large, burly man standing in front of him.

'Well, if you want the job, you better start unloading that bloody truck,' Rob said roughly, turning away to yell at the man slowly getting out of the truck.

* * *

FINALLY, the *Katie Lee* was fully stocked with fuel, food, bait, water and a ton of other gear and four other men in the crew had all turned up. They threw off the mooring lines and with a small burst of black exhaust from her funnel, the trawler edged away from the dock. They rounded up towards the main channel and began to slowly chug forwards up the busy harbour. They rounded the point at Mt Victoria and turned away from the city to the north, heading past Rangitoto. Rob told Danny they would be heading out past Great Barrier Island. Danny had been out on a fishing boat before, his uncle's little fizzboat, but this was something entirely new. The large volcano of Rangitoto slid by on their right. Danny joined the rest of the deck crew, which consisted of Rob, Josh and Kyle. They were all busy getting different pieces of gear ready and performing tasks around the deck. The day was warm, the sea was flat and calm and as they passed Tiritiri Matangi Island, Danny began to think he had found the perfect place to hide from his problems. What place could be more difficult to find for the police in Wellington than a deckhand aboard a scummy old fishing boat working the seas from the docks of Auckland City? It seemed a million miles away from his last life. He felt the first pangs of nausea growing in him and he asked one of the others, a slim individual with short blond hair called Kyle, if there were any seasickness tablets he could take. Kyle looked at him for a second, then grinned.

'That's a good one, mate. Go and ask Captain Bob for a seasickness pill and we'll all take bets to see if you can swim to the nearest island,' he said.

Then he told the others on the deck in a loud voice and they all began laughing. Danny's face went red with embarrassment. Quickly, he decided to help Josh stack some floats for the nets. They cruised along at a steady five or six knots, motoring out through the gulf towards Great Barrier Island, which was finally emerging from the horizon at the bows of the boat. There was a yell behind Danny and for a few seconds he completely forgot the name he had given Rob when he'd introduced himself.

'Darren!' The others turned as one and Danny saw the fear in the faces of the deckhands around him. He suddenly realised it was his name being called out and he quickly turned. It was too late. A large, meaty hand struck him in the face and he staggered backwards, his feet stumbling amongst the gear on the deck. He fell amongst the nets and floats they'd just stacked. He looked up into the red, angry face of the man standing above him.

'Ya little turd, don't ya know your own fucking name?'

'Or are you fucking deaf?'

Danny was shocked. He had thought Rob was a big man. The man who stood before him was at least six foot four and built like a brick shithouse. He had a pair of bunched shoulders like rocks, with thick sinewy arms bulging with muscles. His face was stubbled and blotchy with large red and white spots. But the most unnerving things were the thin, dark slits for eyes. They were burning with a furious intensity. 'Where's ya fucking voice, ya skinny little mongrel, are you a mute too?' he roared, the spittle from his mouth flying across the deck and hitting Danny in the face.

Danny didn't know which question to answer first.

'N-no, I was just concentrating on my job,' he stammered in defence, completely shocked by the blow and reeling at the sight of the huge, angry man standing above him.

'I was just concentrating on my job,' the man mimicked in a high-pitched voice. 'Get your shit together and stop fucking snivelling around on my deck, you cretin-faced little poofter, or I'll dangle you off the stern as fucking shark bait.'

The man's eyes burned malignantly down at Danny, but there was also a touch of delight in his angry features. Then he simply turned and strode away and his hulking frame disappeared up the stairs into the wheelhouse. Danny half-crawled, half-slid to one side of the boat, his face red and his ears burning from the shame and abuse. Josh was standing there with a broad smile on his face.

'Well, now you've met Captain Bob,' he said. 'Whaddya think? He's a bit of a handful, eh Darren?'

Danny grimaced. He wondered why he'd ever thought it might be a good idea to come on board the fishing boat.

'Is he always like this?' Danny asked.

The smile dropped from Josh's face, like a glass hitting the floor.

'Just get on with your work, Darren. Don't drag me into any shit about the skipper.'

Danny tried to lose himself in any job needed on the deck over the next couple of hours. There were a few northerly swells now, gently rolling under the boat, and he began feeling queasy again. He wondered what he had got himself into.

Over the next twelve hours they fished for fresh bait, mainly mullet, then snapper, or kingfish, taking kahawai and anything else as a by-catch. They were now fishing about forty miles past Great Barrier Island and the sea around them was a deep inky-blue colour. Apparently they were fishing for hapuka, but he hadn't even seen one yet. There wasn't a speck of land in sight, no matter what direction he looked, and the swells had steadily grown until the boat was dipping and diving around in a great lumpy ocean. The day seemed like it would never end and even when night came and darkness fell, the work went on and on. He slowly got used to everyone calling him Darren instead of Danny and he kept as far away from the skipper as he could at all times. There were four of them working the foredeck under lights in the dark night and the other three men were working below in the freezers and fish holds. Finally, sometime after five o'clock in the morning, the skipper called a halt as the sea went strangely quiet and the fish became hard to find. The crew assembled in the tiny saloon for some food from the galley and a few drinks. They would take a break for four or five hours and then resume again. Apparently, they weren't supposed to be drinking on board the boat, but as the men joked easily amongst themselves, it became obvious from the stories being told that these weren't the only rules that were constantly broken on the *Katie Lee*. The skipper stayed in the wheelhouse and Danny felt very relieved. He had been dreading their next meeting. The boat had seemed large when he had come aboard, but now it seemed very small indeed, especially way out here with a great big angry skipper prowling around. Rob, the first mate, called a halt to their drinking about 7 am and told them all to get some sleep. Danny chose a bunk not being used by the others and was asleep within minutes of laying his head down.

* * *

THE NEXT DAY was almost identical to the first and Danny felt completely dead on his feet by midnight, but still there was no relief once again until five in the morning. By then he was completely exhausted.

'So, Darren, you enjoying your first trip yet?' asked Gary, in the cramped seats of the saloon. They had just eaten a large meal and were all drinking straight rum from their coffee mugs. Danny greedily gulped his down like it was water. Suddenly, the skipper walked in. He had another bottle of rum with him and he banged it down on the table in front of them. There was a short silence. The skipper nodded to Rob and the first mate got up to take over the wheelhouse. Danny saw mixed emotions around the table — there was everything from fear, amusement, to sadistic joy written amongst the faces of the crew. The skipper unscrewed the top of the rum bottle and poured himself a large drink into an oversized mug.

'Help yourselves, ya mongrels,' he said, leaning back in his chair and taking a large swig.

The others needed no second invitation and poured liberal amounts into their mugs. Danny hesitated for a second, then reached for the bottle.

'Not you, ya little creep!' yelled the captain.

Danny froze in his seat, a great wave of fear rising inside him. He looked anywhere but towards the eyes of the skipper. Unbeknown to him, two hours ago the captain had received a call from the company enquiring whether they had taken on a new crew member for the trip. It was unusual for the company to request details of a crew member over the VHF and Captain Bob wondered just who this Darren was. Maybe he was the son of someone inside the company's head office or something. Whichever, he was going to bloody well find out … especially after their last trip.

'So, Darren, where do you come from mate, Queersville?'

A couple of the others sniggered and he saw Gary and one of the other men, Trevor, squirm in their seats.

'I'm from Whanganui,' he said, as evenly as possible.

He had an aunt living there and had spent his holidays in his youth in the river city and he knew it well enough to lie, or so he hoped. The skipper looked at him for a few long seconds.

'What are you doing up here in Auckland then?' he demanded.

'Just looking for work,' said Danny.

'The Bendover bar was probably full of trannies,' snorted Kyle. A couple of the others laughed.

'When did you get to Auckland?' asked Captain Bob, his narrow eyes probing Danny like a pair of searchlights.

'A few days ago,' said Danny. He figured he should keep to the truth as much as possible, but he felt indescribable fear building steadily inside him. He didn't like the way the skipper was looking at him, or singling him out.

Captain Bob looked at him again for a few seconds. It certainly didn't sound like he was some company director's sprog to him, but he could still be some sort of spy. He figured he would make sure, one way or another. He reached over and unscrewed the lid of the rum, then slowly filled Danny's mug to the very top.

'Drink up,' he said simply.

Danny hesitated, then reached over and pulled the mug to his lips and took a large mouthful. He was so tired and thirsty, it tasted like strong honey to him now, *nectar of the gods,* he thought to himself. Maybe the skipper had finally accepted him. The men poured rum into their mugs again and the large bottle was going down quickly.

'So, Darren, do you think you're man enough to handle the life of a fisherman?' asked the skipper, pouring himself another mugful of rum. He drained almost all of the mug in one go.

Danny nodded carefully; he knew he couldn't say anything else. 'Absolutely,' he added.

The skipper got up. 'I'll get some more piss,' he said, 'nobody leaves.'

He had to bend his head going out the small doorway, turning his shoulders slightly to get through the door frame. There was quiet for a few seconds. Then Dave spoke up.

'You should be careful, mate,' he said quietly to Danny.

'*You* should shut your mouth,' said Kyle from across the table.

'He needs to know,' said Dave, his eyes meeting Kyle's.

'Know about what?' asked Danny, looking around the faces at the table.

'About the last trip,' said Gary evenly.

'You guys should shut your mouths,' said Kyle, his voice becoming low and threatening.

'Well, it was the last trip for somebody, put it that way,' said Dave.

There was an ominous silence in the room. Danny felt a cold prickle slowly creep up from the bottom of his back.

Did that comment really mean what I thought it did? he wondered, as the boat rocked from a decent wave.

Suddenly the skipper was back, another full bottle of rum in his hand. Again he banged it down on the table.

'Drink up, or drop your pants,' he said with a smirk.

Kyle laughed loudly.

'Maybe we should put the fruit here in a bowl on the table,' he said.

Josh sniggered, as they all started on the next bottle.

Danny had nearly drained his first mug, so he finished it,

then refilled it, a warm glow growing inside him. They all began to get completely drunk. After a while, Danny realised he needed a leak. He got up. The skipper's eyes were like twin lasers locked onto his.

'Where are you going?' he growled.

'Whaddya think? I need to piss,' said Danny, swaying slightly. He realised he was now very drunk.

'You should take some care,' said the skipper, his eyes never leaving Danny's. 'A fishing boat is a very dangerous place to be. People die at sea all the time.'

The room was quiet. His eyes were venomous and locked on Danny's. Danny wasn't sure what to say.

'Everyone dies, even you, mate,' he replied evenly.

Danny was shocked. He had no idea where those words had come from inside him and he quickly staggered out of the saloon and towards the rough little head by the companionway entrance. He squeezed in and relieved himself, the sway of the boat making him clutch the walls beside him. As he opened the door to return, he saw Trevor standing outside the doorway of the tiny cubicle. As Danny went to go by, Trevor stopped him. He put his face right beside Danny's and whispered slowly to him.

'Be very, very careful, mate. On our last trip the skipper killed one of the deckhands after a bad argument. He cut him up in a fight. They gutted him and threw him over the side.'

Danny went to move off, but Trevor gripped his shoulder, stopping him again.

'I mean it,' he said, more forcefully.

'He carries a large knife with him at all times. We think he's completely crazy, a real psycho. He made everyone aboard say the guy had fallen over the side and was lost at sea. And watch out for Kyle, he's in deep with him.'

Danny looked up and saw an image that froze him to the spot. The skipper was standing there, only a few feet away, filling the opening in the narrow hallway. He had heard everything Trevor had said and he stood staring at both of them with a look of pure venom. Hate and drunken fury poured from the small, dark eyes set deep in the blotchy, red face. Trevor glanced up and pushed past Danny quickly and slammed the door closed to the toilet. Danny stood there, a cold sweat forming at the back of his neck. The crewman's words had chilled him to his core, but the sight of the skipper standing there was the worst thing he could ever think of. The skipper took a small step forwards, reaching down to his boot with his right hand. Danny knew there was nowhere to run on the boat, but he did it anyway. He tore down the steps to the deck, looking frantically for any place to hide. He heard the demented laugh from somewhere behind him.

'Yeah, run, ya little fucker. I'm going to find you and when I do, I'm going to chop your bits off and feed you to the fish!'

Danny heard his boots coming down the companionway and he fled into the darkness of the foredeck. Captain Bob emerged from the doorway a few seconds behind him and stepped out onto the deck. He held a large, shiny knife in his right hand. He smiled at the thought of hunting this little prick down. It would be even more fun than killing the loser deckhand on the last trip.

'Skipper!'

He turned and looked up. Rob was standing above him at the top of the outer stairwell. The door was open and light spilled from the wheelhouse.

'What the hell are you doing?' asked Rob, looking down at him.

'Mind your own fucking business and get back to the wheel, before I come up there,' he snarled at his first mate. Then he turned away and Rob reluctantly returned to the wheelhouse.

'Kyle!' he yelled at the top of his voice. There was a short silence, then Kyle appeared behind him.

'Yes, Skip,' he said warily, his bloodshot eyes squinting to see in the darkness.

'I heard our new deckhand and Trevor talking about our last trip. Get below and check the holds and the engine room. I'm gonna find that little fucker. He knows too much now, for both our sakes. Make sure you flush him out this way.'

'I'm on my way, Skip,' said Kyle, and he disappeared again.

Captain Bob began to move through the equipment on the foredeck, the long, razor edge of his knife glinting softly in the darkness. He thrust it down a number of times amongst the fish in the bait bin. Nothing there … He moved on quietly, his large frame padding along the deck softly. He slowly checked the area around the fuel drums. Again, there was nothing he could see. He slashed at one of the bulwarks in frustration and a spark flew from the edge of the knife. He crept on silently towards the bow, every nerve in his body tingling in excitement at the pending moment of the kill.

From where he was hiding amongst the large coils of nets, Danny had watched as Captain Bob's hulking figure thrust his knife deep into the bait bin. He knew he couldn't hide forever. He was terrified and he was sick of hiding. Sick of sleeping in cramped places and sick of stinking like fish guts — but then … Suddenly, he had an idea. He carefully untied a piece of polyurethane pipe from the rope on a float. After the skipper had moved forward in the darkness, he eased out from under the nets and climbed carefully and as quietly as he could into the bin, sinking slowly down into the foul sludge of stinking squid and pilchards.

* * *

The *Deodar III* was streaking through the dark water at full speed, its twin engines burning fuel furiously as it tried to keep up with the police helicopter somewhere up ahead in the night. Occasionally, they caught a glimpse of its navigation lights as they followed along searching for the *Katie Lee* somewhere up ahead of them. In the main cabin, Detective Inspector John Francis from Wellington folded the warrant in his hand and slid it back into his pocket.

Daniel Stenhouse, you can run, but you can't hide, he thought with grim satisfaction.

One of his officers had identified Daniel Stenhouse in an image from a remote camera located at the railway station. The young man had walked through there early on the morning of the incident. It was not far from the scene of the crime and just fourteen minutes after the victim had said goodbye to his girlfriend. They had found an address for Daniel Stenhouse. When they had visited the flat, a searching constable had found a bloodstained shirt in a laundry basket and a steel bar in the closet with blood splatters on it. The blood on the bar and the shirt had both been matched to the victim. The detective inspector had then followed steadily along the trail of the young man's desperate run to Auckland. Finally, he had tracked him down to the fishing boat *Katie Lee* after they had got a lucky break when they received a complaint from a security firm. They had observed a young man leaving an old warehouse down on the waterfront. Another camera on the docks had showed the same young man walking away from the building. He had immediately recognised Daniel Stenhouse from the images. He hadn't appeared on any cameras down at the end of the docks and a simple call to the fishing companies had finally confirmed that a young man had boarded one of the fishing boats as a casual worker early that morning. He had his man in his sights and he was simply reeling the line in. There was nowhere to hide out here. A burst of radio jargon erupted from the VHF on the console. They had spotted the fishing boat up ahead in the darkness. Then another burst came from the VHF. He almost couldn't believe the message. It was from the *Katie Lee*. He nodded to the armed officer beside him. The *Deodar III* swept up behind the fishing boat in the darkness, then in unison, both the helicopter and the police boat turned their spotlights on the vessel and hailed the *Katie Lee* to stand to. They informed them they would be boarding the vessel. The detective knew there was no escape for Daniel now.

* * *

DANNY EMERGED from the stinking bait in the large bait bin where he had been hiding. The searchlight from the *Deodar III* lighting up the foredeck was blinding, but to Danny it was as welcome a saviour from the darkness and terror of hiding and fearing for his life as he could imagine. Strangely, he welcomed the police. He was quite happy to go to jail now, quite happy for the police to charge him with the murder of the young man in Wellington. He felt pure relief surging through his mind. As he walked forward into the beam of bright light, he heard a bellow of rage erupt from somewhere behind him. Out of the gloom, a large shadow lunged forward and he saw a flash of silver from the corner of his eye. Too late, he tried to move; suddenly he seemed frozen to the spot and a red-hot pain burst in his side. In disbelief, he stared at the small, bloody tip of the great knife in Captain Bob's hand, sticking right through the skin of his stomach. With a wrench that caused him to gasp, the knife ripped upwards, then turned. He was caught, stuck on the great silver blade with the bloody point that now protruded from his rib cage. He felt some of his guts sliding softly out and slippery, warm blood run freely down his legs. There was a sharp crack, then three or four more in quick succession. He felt Captain Bob's body behind him writhe in response to the gunshots, then fall away. Danny slowly fell to the deck beside him and stared up at the bright light as it grew and seemed to steadily envelop his vision. The sounds of the helicopter, the voices and all the shouting began to slowly diminish. He touched the sharp tip of the blade that was still jutting from his chest. Slowly, he realised what a fish felt like to be hooked on a point of steel. He wished he'd never killed that man in Wellington and he realised he'd done it because he was weak — so terribly weak. The bright lights faded away and a great cold darkness grew from the steel point in his chest, steadily creeping right through him. He tried to say sorry, but his lips wouldn't say it, it was too late …

KALEIDOSCOPE

GINA MOVED THROUGH THE SPOTLIT, GOLD-CURTAINED doorway, stepped into the theatre, then stopped. The sound of people talking, the rustle of programmes, the gentle clink of wine glasses, all a warm faithful memory to her ears. Soft, tinkling noises echoing across the room perfectly matched the sparkling visuals of opening night extravagance. She simply loved the theatre! The flash of fine jewellery, the stunning evening clothes all vividly and proudly on display, it made her feel so at home. She studied the bright, eager faces, sitting there expectantly in great rows of plush red seats laid out in a giant semicircle before her. Even the gallery upstairs was full. Gina had been waiting for this opportunity for so long now, it made her breath catch in her throat. She quickly pulled out her phone and snapped a shot. The tiny click etched the glittering memory in her mind. She slipped the phone back into her black, silk purse. A man hurried past, knocking into her and clumsily spilling one of his drinks down the side of her stunning new dress. The red wine left a long dark stain on the beautiful turquoise material.

'I'm so sorry,' he apologised, as he stopped at the next step down and turned back.

'It's not right,' she said, her thin features caught on an angle in the bright lights.

He apologised again and his youthful face crinkled with a deep frown. He looked genuinely remorseful.

'It's all wrong,' she said impatiently, looking past him, up at the stage.

He realised she wasn't speaking to him any more. He slowly wandered away looking slightly sheepish and carrying his glasses more carefully. She walked carefully down the plush red carpet, knowing her row and seat number off by heart. She stepped into the long line of seats, slid past the elderly man with his young companion with her programme curled in her lap, past the gay couple in their matching yet unmatching suits and sneakers, then finally the elderly lady dressed in black, her diamond-encrusted silver brooch matching her flowing silver hair. Gina carefully picked up the small card that stated 'RESERVED' with her name 'Gina Fleming' typed in small black font underneath. She looked around for a few seconds, taking in the atmosphere of the theatre, before she finally took her seat. She had been here so many times she knew the lights would dim, the curtain would be raised very slowly and the opera *Carmen,* would soon be under way.

* * *

THE FLAMENCO DANCER was dressed in a blood-red dress, her matching shoes decorated with tiny, iridescent sequins that flashed in all directions from the rows of lights. At the moment, she stood statuesque, caught motionless in the spotlight on the left side of the stage. Another spotlight emerged in the middle of the stage. Then it suddenly narrowed to a tiny beam, quickly turned in small circles, then widened out into a larger beam that swept slowly across to the right, finally revealing a guitarist sitting on a simple wooden chair near the side curtain. He sat there quietly, his guitar in position, his hands lightly touching the strings. He waited for the correct moment of silence to unfold, then he played two simple notes. Simultaneously, the dancer came to life; her body began moving slowly, her feet a little quicker, rapping out a sharp clickety, click, click, clickety click as she began to spin very slowly on the spot. The guitarist repeated the two notes faster, waited, then played them quicker again, as she spiralled around, building her rhythms with her feet. He filled in a small piece of the melody, as if asking her a gentle but probing question. The dancer's arms began to sweep up and down her body in long, flowing lines. Her fingers extended outwards and flew dramatically all about her body, then gently slowed until her hands seemed like two pink butterflies floating curiously about her. The guitarist moved smoothly into the song itself, his dexterous fingers adding a synchopatic bass line and willing her on as she began to move around the stage. The flamenco dancer's feet suddenly changed timing dramatically; her toes and heels began slapping aggressively at the hard wooden floor, adding a new complex rhythm to the beat of the notes. She bent her upper body down dramatically towards the floor, then quickly flung her face back and stared at a point at the back of the concert hall, well beyond anyone sitting in the theatre. Her face was suddenly a stone mask of pain — of death. She suddenly swooped and began to spin her own story out with her feet belting out staccato rhythms, her long crimson skirt hiding the incredible effort of her legs as the many frilled layers swirled in and out, erupting in showers as she and the guitarist kept the audience spellbound. Gina straightened up in her seat slightly, leaning forward, her soft brown eyes intense. She absolutely loved this part — but she knew she had to leave …

Gina walked from the theatre and made her way quickly along Queen Street towards the Town Hall, where her car was parked. She saw the clock was reading 10.56 pm, both hands on the face angling upwards into the black night. She frowned and her pretty face looked annoyed. She had left ten minutes early on purpose, but somehow she had already lost two whole minutes. Maybe the clock was fast. All around her, the hustle and bustle and bright lights of Friday night in the big city beckoned and called, but she wasn't interested in being delayed, even for a moment. She looked back and saw the minute hand move to 10.57 and she began to run the last few metres. Unlocking her car door, she jumped into the driver's seat and quickly started the engine. With just the barest of looks, she accelerated out of the parking place and pulled an instant U-turn, leaving a taxi blaring its horn at her reckless manoeuvre. She straightened up, poured on the speed and just made the lights, going through the intersection as the LED lamps turned orange, then red. Her nervous eyes checked the rear-view mirror as she accelerated up Queen Street. She let out a small breath that no police car was in sight. At the top, she turned left onto Karangahape Road, her heart beating a little quicker. She should make it easily this time, she told herself. The lights at Symonds Street held her up though and as she drove onto the motorway and gunned the little Mazda into the evening traffic, she glanced down and checked her watch for the hundredth time that night. It was going to be a tight call, she realised. She should have left even earlier. *If only that damn show wasn't so beautiful,* she thought, as she swung into the outside lane and floored it. The Mazda jumped forward and raced down the fast lane, then she cut across three lanes to make the Market Road turnoff. She made it down Market Road without trouble, then tried to drive quickly through Cornwall Park, but all the speed bumps in Puriri Drive slowed her down. Finally, she turned left onto Greenlane Road, accelerating away before the light even turned green, turned quickly right into Whetu-rangi Road and right again onto Campbell Road, her tyres squealing as she made the corner. *Not this time,* she thought to herself — not this time …

As she reached the roundabout at the top of the mall in Onehunga, some large roadwork signs and flashing orange lights lit up the road ahead. They threw long flashes of orange colour across the darkened road.

She swore loudly at the roadworks, as she was forced to make a decision and her mind raced madly, but she knew there simply wasn't time to go any other way. With a sinking feeling, she turned left into the mall and made her way down through the twin line of shops in the shopping centre itself. She knew this area very well. Onehunga and the Manukau Harbour was the original town centre of Auckland back in the 19th century, when big sailing ships called into the harbour. She knew all this because her mother had lived here all her life and had told her many tales of its history since Gina was a young girl. It was Queen Street she was driving down, named after Queen Victoria, however now it had lost its former glory and it was simply called 'The Mall'. However, it was still a special part of history she held dear to her heart. One of her mother's favourite stories was how in 1893, when New Zealand women were the first in the world to be given the right to vote, Elizabeth Yates had been elected to the position of the Mayor of Onehunga. She was the first woman in the entire British Empire to hold the office of Mayor. It made her feel quite proud thinking about Elizabeth Yates as she drove down 'Queen Street'. She loved Onehunga because it still had that old-time feeling about its streets and buildings. She was approaching the old Hard to Find Bookshop.

Now the building was empty, all the signs gone from the windows. It still reminded her of the day she had wandered in and bought her first book from the weird little shop, with its funny old stairs and eccentric maze of rooms, all wandering off into so many different corners of the building. The book she'd bought was a William Burroughs novel, called *The Place of Dead Roads*. A good friend had suggested it to her. It was dark and moody, a broken-up, kaleidoscopic view of life from a supposedly great author and it was a brilliant piece of literature, using a technique of rearranged cut-ups of words, but she hadn't really enjoyed it much at all. She had a sudden idea and without braking, she checked to the right, then dived hard left at the Church Street roundabout. She spun away from the old church, then almost immediately turned hard right into little Waller Street, a small business lane which ran along behind the shops on Mainstreet. Her car raced down the small lane at high speed. As she came up towards the railway station entrance at the end, she flung the little Mazda left around the corner. Her tyres squealed and she gritted her teeth, holding on to the wheel. Her zigzag course took her into Princes Street and then right again over the railway lines into Galway. She was nearly there. She approached Neilson Street. She knew she was panicking, going far too fast, but she simply turned the corner with just a glance to the right. She flew out of the side street and careered straight across both lanes of Neilson Street. A motorcyclist swerved away as the little red Mazda seemed to come from nowhere at high speed. The rider swerved hard right and flew across the grass median strip, somehow missing two small trees and bouncing crazily onto the other side of the road before he regained control. Fortunately, there was no one coming the other way and he straightened, then swerved back onto the correct side of the road. He accelerated up behind her and blasted the horn in frustration at the idiotic driver of the red Mazda. Gina laughed. She couldn't help herself and put her finger out the driver's window as he flashed his headlights at her. As she came up to the corner, she glanced down at her watch. At that moment, a carload of youths who'd been drinking in the turnaround by the waterfront near the cemetery accelerated in front of her, their wheels spinning wildly against the bitumen. She never even saw them. Her Mazda clipped the back of the car with her head still down. Her car leapt to the right, out of control. She never even saw the bus coming the other way. It caught the little Mazda almost head on. The large bus travelling with much greater momentum leapt upwards and forwards as they collided, its giant wheels running up the small bonnet of the car. Everything suddenly burst into thousands of pieces, like a bomb going off. The bus driver was flung from his seat as glass and metal exploded in every direction. The Mazda was driven like a wedge beneath the bus, crushing the passenger and driver's area of the small car as the large, heavy axles of the bus crunched through the cabin roof. There was a horrible grinding noise as both vehicles still vainly tried to continue onwards. The bus shook with the terrible impact, driving the car backwards with a horrendous screeching noise down the road, then finally everything came to a shuddering stop. Smoke and fumes from hot brake fluid, oil, fuel and battery acid filled the air. Almost immediately, the screaming of people on the bus began. It had happened so fast that few of the passengers on the bus could explain to the policeman and the two ambulance officers who arrived first on the scene what had actually occurred. A young motorcyclist helped with some details of the Mazda's erratic driving prior to the accident and even described the other car, a Subaru Legacy, which had sped away into the night. They had all watched helplessly as the fire crew arrived and two firemen began frantically trying to cut the wreckage apart. Tragically, they could hear the heart-rending cries from the occupant. She was trapped deep inside the tangled mess as the men peered and crawled underneath the bus to try to locate the driver. Suddenly, a loud thump split the night as the deadly mixture of oil, diesel, petrol and other fluids burst into flame. The fire took hold instantly and although other firemen ran forward trying to douse the leaping flames, they were beaten back by the scorching heat of the blaze. There was simply no way to save the person trapped inside the wreck as the hungry, fuel-fed flames roared higher and higher into the smoke-filled, black night.

* * *

GINA WALKED through the large doorway framed in deep midnight-blue drapes and stepped into the grand old theatre. She stopped, the soft patter of people talking, the rustle of programmes and the gentle clink of glasses like a warm, faithful memory to her ears. The sounds tinkling through the theatre perfectly matched the glitter of opening night. She loved the theatre! The sparkling flashes of jewellery adorning the finest evening clothes in the vast rows of plush seats before her made her feel so at home. She had been waiting for this version of *Romeo and Juliet* for so long now, her breath caught in her throat. She took out her little camera and squinted through the viewfinder, but before she could take a shot, someone brushed past her from behind. The woman who bumped her stumbled backwards, then spilled half the the drink she was carrying down the side of Gina's new shimmering purple dress.

'I'm so sorry,' the woman apologised, stopping and turning around.

'It's not right,' Gina said impatiently.

The woman apologised again; her face went red with embarrassment.

'It's wrong,' Gina stated, as she looked up to the stage.

The woman realised Gina was seeing past her and she slowly wandered off, carrying her drink with some care. Gina took a few steps across the lush green carpet. Knowing her row and seat number off by heart, she stepped in and slid past the man with the programme folded in his lap and his young companion, the two elderly businessmen and the middle-aged woman dressed in a green silk dress with a matching emerald-jewelled brooch. Gina picked up the small white card stating 'RESERVED' with her name 'Gina Fleming' written in small black letters underneath. She slowly looked around the old theatre, drinking in the atmosphere for a few seconds, then took her seat. She knew in a short time the lights would dim, the curtain would be raised and the ballet she'd been waiting for would soon be under way.

* * *

WHEN SHE LEFT THE SHOW, she turned right and made her way quickly down Wellesley Street, to the large underground car park. She had left nearly fifteen minutes earlier, well before the final act. That was her favourite part and it tore at her heart to leave so early, but she was sure she had left the theatre in time — this time. She gunned the motor of the dark blue Corolla twice, accelerated up the ramp and turned onto Queen Street. She drove past the brightly lit theatre entrance and turned left up Airedale Street, past the pub where she'd had her infamous post-degree party only three years before. Three of her friends had been arrested in the drunken mayhem. On Symonds Street, almost on cue, a police car pulled up beside her and when the two policemen turned and looked at her, she gave a short, nervous smile.

They stayed beside her until the Karangahape Road lights and again they waited there as the slow-changing lights seemed to take her whole lifetime to finally go green. She edged forward at the same rate as the police car, then slowly sliding off to the left, she dove onto the motorway ramp and away from the eyes of the policemen, hoping to put her foot down. However, the traffic was heavy tonight and she had to fight her way over to the second lane, her indicator flashing for an age before anyone would let her in. She checked her watch for the hundredth time. Where does time go? Finally, a space opened up in the third lane and she put her foot down to make the gap. An old van moved over in front of her slowing her down, blocking her sight almost completely, and together they followed the closely packed cars steadily across the Newmarket Viaduct. She looked over the edge, down to the houses, where her old flat had been in St Andrews Road, as they slowly crawled across the long concrete span stretching above Newmarket. The old van finally moved over and she pushed forward as the motorway opened up slightly. She couldn't help but give the driver the finger as she went by. She flew past the Market Road offramp as the traffic eased on the left and without indicating, she rocketed down the inside lane and took the offramp at Greenlane. She shot round the roundabout and the little Toyota's tyres squealed against the new asphalt. At Great South Road she was caught in the queue turning left and waited there while a group of teenagers sauntered across the road, laughing. She glared at them as they meandered slowly towards the footpath. The cars finally moved in front of her and she only just made the lights as it turned far too quickly from orange to red. At Campbell Road there was another wait. A white Mercedes in front of her dawdled up Campbell Road and stopped maddeningly when the lights went orange at Wheturangi Road. She pulled out and roared past the

Mercedes up the hill and ran the red. She flew along Campbell Road, where she used to walk Cocoa, her dog, a chocolate-coloured kelpie. Just thinking about Cocoa made her eyes well up, as she saw all the brake lights suddenly coming on ahead. There was a long line of traffic banked all the way back from the Royal Oak roundabout and she swore loudly as she was forced to turn down into the Mall leading into Onehunga. This time she turned right at the lights at Trafalgar Street, where she'd gone to the party where she'd first met Andrew. Then she turned left into Selwyn Street, racing madly down the hill, the little Corolla's wheels nearly leaving the ground. She flew past the old pub on the left and the older church and cemetery located behind it. The cars were streaming from the motorway onto Orpheus Drive. She knew it was named after New Zealand's worst shipwreck in 1863, when 189 men were lost at the entrance to the Manukau Harbour. She'd seen some of the graves at the back of the little church with her father. Then the light changed in front of her and heavy traffic poured straight into Neilson Street. A motorcyclist sat ahead of her, hesitant to enter the heavy flow at the free left turn. She swore at him and hit her horn impatiently. Finally, they turned into Neilson Street and she roared past him, nearly driving across the road onto the wrong side. She swerved back into the lane and made the next set of lights and accelerated over the railway bridge. Not far now, Gina thought desperately. As she came up to the corner, a carload of youths heading to the cemetery, where they regularly stopped to smoke on a Friday night, accelerated across the road in front of her. She braked hard to miss the Nissan Skyline. The motorcyclist suddenly appeared from nowhere, roaring past her on the right, as they both flew into the corner slightly out of control. Both vehicles reacted, the motorcyclist swerving left, leaving her one place to go as she swung the wheel. The Toyota Corolla slid to the right, the tyres screaming at the bitumen as the car slewed sideways across the road. The truck driver saw the blue Toyota at the last minute and tried to avoid the oncoming car, but he had no chance. The car simply smashed into the front of his truck, still sliding sideways, with a sickening, crunching explosion of metal and glass. He was flung from the driver's seat as the momentum of the truck drove forward and over the smaller vehicle, its large wheels running up and over the bonnet, wedging the little Corolla hard underneath. The speed of the car drove it under the truck, the heavy axles crunching through the roof, destroying it in a burst of shrieking metal. The large front right wheel drove into the door frame, crushing the metal with a horrible, grinding crunch as it sliced through the light steel. The truck seemed to jump in the air, pushing the car backwards with a horrible grinding, scraping noise down the road. Finally, it lurched to a shuddering halt with the little Toyota wedged underneath. Steam, smoke, fuel and hot brake fluid poured from the vehicles welded together by the sickening collision. The smell of destroyed parts and various leaking fluids rose up in a sickening plume as the passenger in the car began to scream.

It took only a few minutes for the police to get there, as the police station was only a short distance away, located in the town centre. The fire emergency crew arrived a few minutes after them. The firemen worked frantically, trying to find a way in towards the screaming occupant trapped deep inside the tangled wreckage. A large tongue of red flame erupted suddenly from one side of the car and a firefighter rushed forward with his extinguisher, blasting at the flames to starve them of oxygen, but it was too late. With a loud thump, more flames burst through and in an instant, a great fire took hold of the wreckage. The firemen rushed forward, but the flames beat them back. Bystanders and witnesses alike stood helpless as petrol and diesel fuelled the fire, which roared higher and higher into the dark, smoke-filled night.

* * *

GINA WALKED SLOWLY through the main entrance, studying the beautiful ornate doorways and intricate panels of the corbelled ceiling inside the foyer of the old theatre. She showed her ticket, then stepped through the plush curtained doorway and into the auditorium. She stopped and drank in the sound of the people talking, the rustle of programmes, the delicate clinking of wine glasses that echoed around the large space. The sharp, little tinkle of noises perfectly matched the sparkle of a typical opening night spectacle. She'd always loved the theatre! The display of fine jewellery and stunning evening clothes, with so many bright, eager faces sitting expectantly, row after row before her, simply filled her with excitement. She was slightly late and the rest of the audience had almost filled the golden, velvet-covered seats. Even the dress circle was already full. She had been waiting for this special moment for so long, it nearly caught in her throat. She quickly pulled her iPhone from her Gucci purse. The tiny click of the shutter etched the shot of the waiting audience deep into her memory. Someone rushed past and brushed her arm. It was a young girl, catching up with her parents. She caused Gina to stumble backwards, then down a step. She bumped into a man already standing there, spilling the drink he was holding down the side of his suit.

'I'm so sorry,' she apologised.

'You should be,' he snapped nastily. 'Take some damn care for god's sake. It's not a nightclub!'

'No, that's not right,' she said impatiently, looking past him.

He nodded, then looked at her, the frustration etched deeply on his face.

'It's all wrong,' she stated again, as she looked over the top of his head to the stage.

He wandered off, still angry, brushing at his suit with his free hand. She took a few steps across the lush, black and silver flecked carpet, knowing her row and seat number off by heart. She stepped in past the man reading his programme, his elderly companion, two very large men in jet-black tuxedos, and slid past the young lady in the long, midnight-blue dress who wore a large, lapis lazuli encrusted brooch that caught the light. Gina picked up the small card stating 'RESERVED' in large black letters with her name 'Gina Fleming' written in a flowing silver script beneath. She stood, slowly looking around her for a long, treasured moment before she took her seat. She knew the curtain would be raised soon, the lights would dim and the opera *La Traviata*, the one she'd been waiting an age for, would soon be under way.

This time, she waited for the final act to be completed. The finish to the magnificently choreographed show involved the whole cast. They were gradually merged onstage throughout the long piece as they approached the grand finale. The tension built as the number of performers steadily grew on stage. The conductor's arms were a whirl of motion, continuously directing the female lead, the baritone quartet, the chorus group and the orchestra, all from his small, raised platform. The exquisitely dressed performers interacted in a presentation of their combined skills as the final act began to steadily unfold. She would never get tired of this, she realised, as it all built to a magnificent, synchronised crescendo. As the last bar of the orchestra slowly faded away, the audience stood as one. They clapped and cheered and the large theatre shook with noise.

'Magnifico!' shouted the woman standing beside her.

Gina walked slowly past the fallen programmes and empty wine glasses and made her way leisurely through the buzzing crowd at the entranceway. She stepped out onto Queen Street, the bright lights of the buildings and the sparkle of night like a small piece of heaven locked securely away in her mind. The crowd leaving the theatre swept her along past the old Civic picture theatre, where she'd been to see *Goodbye Pork Pie* as a five-year-old. Then she finally peeled away from the people filling the sidewalk and walked to the small, square building over to her left. She entered and took the elevator down to the car park underneath the Aotea Centre. As she rode down she realised it was the same one they'd used when she and Andrew had seen *Phantom of the Opera* all those times ago. She remembered him kissing the tickets and putting them in his top pocket as they stood together, riding down the lift. He had kept those tickets in an old jewellery box in the top drawer of his dresser. The little Honda Jazz sat silently beneath a pair of fluorescent tubes and she walked up to it, trying not to rush, opened the door and got in. She checked her watch for the hundredth time out of habit, then started the engine, gunning the little motor. She reversed out and headed for the exit. Leaving the car park, she drove up Greys Ave, to the lights at the top of the road, which had a green arrow to turn left. She pulled on the leather-covered steering wheel, and swung left onto Pitt Street. She drove on up to K' Road, caught the lights perfectly, shot over the steep, little hill and down the other side, then stopped at the traffic lights to Upper Queen Street for only a few seconds. She turned right, followed it to Newton Road and stopped at the corner, opposite where her father had worked. He was a hard-working man, but she couldn't help remembering he had abandoned them all for a pretty blonde lady from England; an English woman he met in a bar down on the waterfront. It still upset her deeply, especially thinking about how it had hurt her mother. She turned up Newton Road and fell in behind a police patrol car and they made another set of lights together and then both turned onto Khyber Pass Road. The police car carried on down to Newmarket as she waited for the arrow at the entrance to the motorway, beside the Thai restaurant with the life-size elephant statue outside. The one where she and Andrew had dinner that night, so long ago. The night they'd first slept together. The light went green and she accelerated onto the motorway, first indicating right to get to the outside lane, then changing her mind suddenly, she hugged the left lane and immediately got off, taking the Gillies Ave offramp. Gina came to a stop behind a van. She backed up, changed lanes and took the outside lane. The light turned green and she beat the van off the mark, accelerated down Gillies Ave and caught three sets of lights in a row. She waited, then followed the left-turn arrows to Greenlane East highway. As she came up to the highway she decided to turn left again as a Mercedes-Benz was going straight ahead in the other lane. She drove the short distance to the next set of lights at the Manukau Road intersection. She waited there, looking across the road at the old antique shop that she loved to fossick around in, hunting for bargains. As the light turned green she put her foot down on the pedal and flew past the shop, the tyres of the silver Honda squealing in protest. It was the shop where she'd bought her two favourite items in their old flat — an old kauri dressing table and a thick, deep-piled Egyptian rug, which Cocoa had slept on and left her chocolate-coloured hairs on. The ones she had refused to clean off the carpet for a year and a half, long after Cocoa had been buried under the peach tree at her mum's place. She drove straight ahead at Greenwoods Corner, on to Pah Road, eventually stopping at the red light at Mt Albert Road. She sat there, outside the pink leadlight shop, 'A Touch of Glass'. She looked over at the sparkly coloured windows where she'd stood at the counter and picked out pieces of pretty glass for the stained window in her mother's front door. She had studied the glass samples and held them all up to her eye, one by one, choosing each piece so carefully for her mother; looking through those tiny pieces of glass, comparing all the colours and textures against each other in the bright sunlight. The light suddenly flashed green and her instinct kicked the accelerator pedal and the little Honda roared away. Frustratingly, she had to stop again at the Trafalgar Street lights, beside the sprawling Masonic Village, where Andrew's grandparents had stayed and spent their last few years. She loved the memory of sitting outside on the little porch in the sun and drinking countless cups of tea. The light turned green quickly and she accelerated away down the steep hill, her wheels hardly touching the ground. At the bottom, she turned left at the first roundabout, her tyres complaining again on the tight corner. She wound along the road beside the little man-made lake, where she used to take Cocoa for a run, a play and a pee in the long grass, before she drove to her mother's place, where her dog would be spoilt like a favourite child. She took the right at the roundabout and drove past the Mitre 10 building, where she'd regretted not taking that job the kind old lady had offered her. Unfortunately, working in the garden department amongst the little plants and trees and spectacle of seasonal flowers didn't pay that well. But she'd always thought it would have been a dream first job. She took the short side street that led to the Neilson Street lights and waited while the flow of cars from the motorway filed steadily by. She didn't mind waiting here for the long line of cars. She knew she must be late. The light finally changed and she turned onto Neilson Street and made the next set of lights, where they'd removed the little railway bridge for the new train station. With a slight start, she saw a motorcycle in the distance, disappearing fast around the corner far ahead. She kept her foot down on the pedal gathering speed, knowing the motorcycle was gone and thinking surely the kids in the car would all be down at the waterfront by now. The Honda was moving quickly now. She didn't need to check her watch to know how late she was, but the impulse was so strong, she did it anyway. A flash of red inside her car made her look up. An ambulance with its flashing lights had pulled out in front of her from a side street and it was accelerating across the road, heading to the cemetery and the harbour edge. At the last moment, she thought she'd make it and turned the wheel to the right slightly as the ambulance sped away. The ambulance just clipped her bumper. Her right-hand tyre touched the side of the kerb of the traffic island and the tread on the new tyre grabbed the stone kerb and wrenched the steering wheel in her hands to the right. She saw the approaching concrete truck at the very last second. The driver was watching the flashing red lights of the ambulance. He had no chance to avoid the little silver Honda as it appeared from right behind the ambulance and smashed into the front of the truck. The impact drove the smaller car under the steel bumper and threw the truck driver violently from his seat. There was a horrific, tearing noise that filled the night air as the momentum of the heavy concrete truck drove it forward and up into the air, its large tyres rolling up the bonnet of the car, the heavy steel axles crunching through the thin roof, crushing the passenger and driver's compartment. The massive weight of the truck forced the car under its chassis, then pushed it backwards down the road with a terrible, grinding screech.

* * *

Gina walked slowly through the ink-blue curtain-lined doorway of the new theatre and stopped …

* * *

Not far away from the scene of Gina's accident, parked in the Waikaraka Park Cemetery and only a short distance from Gina's gravesite, Andrew sat quietly in his car with his new girlfriend sitting in the passenger seat beside him.

'So, she was beautiful,' said the girl looking over towards Gina's grave in the soft moonlight.

Drifting clouds threw shifting patterns of silver light across the little geometric shapes in the graveyard. They were all lined up in long rows, spreading out and away from them. The older part of the cemetery to their left was fairly run-down and the graves and stones all lay jumbled together at various angles. It was a lonely view.

'Yes,' said Andrew, 'Gina could be a little impatient from time to time, but she was clever and yes, she was beautiful.'

'It's so incredibly sad,' she said with a tiny sigh from the passenger seat.

'How did you cope with it?'

There was a silence, then Andrew spoke again.

'Not very well at first, to be honest, but eventually you have to deal with the reality. Then when you simply can't grieve any more, I suppose you have to move on,' said Andrew, watching her eyes and the unsure expression etched across her face.

'What do you mean?' she asked.

She turned towards him, her eyes catching the light emanating from a pole only a few metres away.

'Well, fate is a pretty strange thing,' said Andrew slowly.

'Sometimes I don't think you can change it at all, no matter how hard you try, or which way you turn.'

'Do you really believe that?' she asked, her face suddenly unsure again.

Andrew looked her squarely in the eyes, noticing the tiny reflections of light and colour dancing against the deep black of her pupils and his voice caught in his throat.

'Yes, I'm sure,' he said.

'Like Gina said once: Life is harsh. Time is luck. Use it well, because no matter what you do, when your number's up, your number's up.'

As he finished his words, he looked into the mirror and froze in his seat.

* * *

GINA PULLED herself from the wreck with one last magnificent effort. The tangled glass and metal cut at her body again, taking some of her hair and giving her even more terrible injuries. Her shockingly burnt flesh and badly broken limbs only half supported her, as she squeezed from a jagged gap in the wreckage on the far side of the burning pile-up. The larger vehicle and the thick clouds of smoke and raging fire hid her from the crowd standing shocked and helpless on the other side. She dragged herself away from the terrible scene in a Herculean effort. She'd had enough of trying to undo things over and over again — a thing she'd done once and couldn't ever undo, no matter how she tried. She'd decided it was time to break free completely — to use the last of her reserves in one huge effort to let go of this world, forever.

Much further down in the dark gaps between the street lights, Gina slowly staggered across the road, dragging her injured limb behind her. That strange feeling inside her strengthened again, pulling her broken body forwards. Gina turned into the lane that led down to the cemetery and grinned.

* * *

ANDREW'S HEART leapt in his chest when he glanced up and saw the creature approaching from behind. At first he had no real idea what the zombie-like soul staggering slowly up to the car was but as it got close, somehow he recognized Gina's features. Then a deep uncontrollable terror swelled up inside him, overwhelming him. He heard a talking sound inside the car, but he couldn't hear the words properly and he found he couldn't speak either. The whole time his disbelieving eyes were riveted to the burnt and broken creature steadily growing bigger — in his little silver mirror. Finally she reached the back of the car, hesitated, then chose his side. His ex-girlfriend, he reminded himself with difficulty, as he watched her haul herself toward his driver's window. He slowly turned to look in his side mirror and realised with horror that the window was half open. The girl beside him began to scream loudly, as Gina gripped the edge of the glass with a blackened and bloody three fingered hand, her shattered face rising slowly into the gap between them. She turned and stopped and held her eyes just inches from his. After a few long seconds Gina finally looked past him. She let out a broken sigh into the car. The shocking smell of burnt skin and flesh was overwhelming, as her hand reached in toward him. Andrew heard another scream from beside him. Gina's broken hand brushed his cheek. The burnt and badly damaged face studied Andrew, then slowly she grinned again.

He was petrified and couldn't move a muscle in his seat, as her broken fingers scraped softly across his face.

'Be brave,' Gina rasped, then straightened. Her mangled hand let go of his window. She turned away and slid off, making her strange, broken way along the pathway, eventually disappearing among the dark tombs and statues near the middle, in the older part of the graveyard.

Gina had no idea she had so many relatives here. Many more than she'd ever known about — and they were all calling to her right now. Calling her home. That was the strange feeling constantly pulling her forwards and it grew stronger with her every step. She smiled broadly and a flock of birds scattered upwards into the night. Finally, Gina knew she was ready.

THE IMAGINON

HARRY HAD A TRULY GREAT IMAGINATION. HE HAD THE KNACK of telling tall stories, or highly imaginative tales, to anyone, young or old. They were often great woven fantasies that seemed to go on forever if you let him and he could spellbind kids for hours. The youngsters would be lost to the outside world and would even want to stay, living in that special world that Harry had created and painstakingly built for them, even long after his ideas had stopped flowing from his creased, old lips. He dreamt many times that one day he would create a machine that would spit out these phantasmagorical stories that children would listen to for hours on end. It would be his 'Imaginon' and it would make him rich and wealthy beyond his wildest dreams. As I've already mentioned, Harry's normal dreams were amazing, so his wildest dreams were very wild indeed.

Harry worked in the maintenance department for the council. His area was mainly plumbing, but as a repair expert you simply needed to be half plumber, half builder, half electrician, half tiler, half courier driver and occasionally a bit of security, so it wasn't really that simple at all.

He parked his car at the back of the pump shed, which was tucked into the side of the hill, about halfway down Onetangi Beach. He walked around and opened the boot of the station wagon. Then he walked back and unlocked the door to the pump shed, dragging the old wooden door open on its broken hinge. Inside, he could immediately see the leak. It was a fine jet of silvery water, curving out of one of the reducers. He turned off the main valve and waited for the leak to slow as the pressure dropped. He opened another valve and released any water in the line. It took him about twenty minutes to retrieve another reducer, the tools from the back of his wagon, then replace the faulty reducer in the shed. Harry finally turned the two valves back on and checked with some satisfaction that the new reducer wasn't leaking, then he slid the door closed and locked the shed.

He drove slowly down the road along the beach to the large toilet block, near the pub. He parked outside, then approached the building. He called out hello a couple of times and not getting an answer, he walked into the women's toilet block to test that the pressure had returned to normal. There, lying on the bench before him in the changing area, was a young woman. She was laid out on the teak rails as if she was a tourist sleeping, but he realised this young woman definitely wasn't sleeping. She had a stark white, bloodless face and her eyes stared straight up at Harry like she was watching him. There was a red pool of blood beneath her, so he stepped closer to see where the blood had come from. She had three large wounds to her torso. Her sleeveless arms dangled from the bench slats and one bloodied hand was resting carelessly on the floor. He noticed she had a tattoo on her shoulder. It was a spider holding a small pink rose and the name Deborah was written underneath it in bright red ink. Suddenly, Harry felt like he was having a heart attack. He felt his pulse racing wildly and that familiar throb of veins in his head when his blood pressure rose out of control. He had to walk out as the air became thick and unbreathable in the changing rooms.

Just outside, he stopped and leaned against the wall in the pale, wintery sunshine, taking in a few breaths of the cold sou'wester until his pulse came back to some kind of normality. He stepped over towards the station wagon to reach for his cellphone sitting on the console. A young girl seemed to appear out of nowhere. She ran towards the toilet block as he looked up. Thirty metres away a woman who was walking stiffly down the road with a pushchair called out to her.

'Wait, Charlene, wait!'

Before Harry could yell out 'No! Stop!', the girl had suddenly run inside and disappeared. He waited for the scream with a heavy ache in the pit of his stomach, but strangely it never came. Instead, the small girl darted out the door just as her mother reached the pathway and with a large smile towards her mother, she held up both her hands. Clear water dripped from her small fingers. They both ignored Harry and carried on down the road towards the end of the beach. Harry watched them as they walked away, his mind steadily working a full circle. His movements seemed to require a huge amount of energy as he took the five or six steps to the toilet block doorway. Then he entered the shower block, just as the hordes of cicadas began their shrill, screeching cries. He stood in the middle of the room and his head turned slowly from one side to the other, but there was no dead body lying on the bench any more. He shook his head with his eyes closed and then opened them again, slowly, twice. There was nothing there at all …

* * *

Later that night, a half moon hung in the black sky over Onetangi. Wisps of dark clouds slid across the sky. Lines of dark swells reared up like clockwork from the sea, ran towards the beach, then ended themselves upon the sands in great shivering, white crashes in the moonlight. Near the edge of the beach, a couple were enjoying the live entertainment just inside the Onetangi Tavern. They had moved to the rear of the bar and were sitting near the exit. Where the woman was sitting on one of the tall stools, she could see out to the edge of the wide wooden staircase that led down to the dark sands on the beach. She was quite pretty, in that lovely girl-next-door kind of way. Her blonde hair was up in a bob, which showed off her jawline and the curve of her neck. She wore a short, blue sleeveless dress, which revealed a distinctive tattoo on her shoulder. It was a black spider, holding a small pink rose. Underneath, red script elaborately spelled the name, Deborah. She took a sip of her drink and laughed, her eyes catching the lights. She put her bourbon and Coke back down on the table with a thump, which brought little caramel-coloured bubbles erupting to the surface.

'Come on then, show me that special island adventure,' she said to him loudly, a little drunk.

'Unless you haven't got the guts now?'

He smiled.

'I will, if you will,' he said.

His eyes were locked on her large, black pupils.

She nodded, smiling, and they left together, slipping out the door. She took his hand in the darkness as they went down the steps and onto the beach.

* * *

Harry was down at the depot first thing in the morning, getting his jobs lined up, when the call came through. Sarah had walked in and found a dead body inside the Onetangi toilet block. It put all the hairs up on the back of his neck. As he went about his various jobs, the image he'd seen the day before kept haunting him and interrupting his thoughts. Later on, he deliberately caught up with Sarah at Little Oneroa. Some of the things Sarah had told him on the small hill in the late afternoon, looking out over a flat, blue sea that stretched away to the horizon, made his skin crawl. It was a young woman with terrible wounds to her stomach and chest, Sarah had said quietly. She was just lying there on the bench, exactly like Harry had seen. It was towards the end, when Sarah mentioned the tattoo that he felt sick. A tattoo on her shoulder. It was a spider, holding a rose, with a name written in red underneath it. Deborah, he said to himself before she told him, the red writing said Deborah …

* * *

A WEEK later Harry was repairing some broken tiles in the showers of the changing sheds up at the Onetangi Sports Park. He was mixing some grout on a copy of the local paper when the headline broke through the dark mess and he suddenly realised he had covered most of the front-page article about the murder with the thick, sandy mix. A few words leaked out at the bottom and he didn't have to put his reading glasses on to see the name at the end of the article. It described the murder victim as a young English tourist, named Deborah Stevens.

He checked his watch. It was getting late. 4.47 pm. He'd have to make this the last job of the day. He pushed in some fresh grout with his old putty knife, working his way along one line at a time. The sound of his small, sharp movements echoed around the empty toilet block. Finally, he finished the last piece. He tested the first section of grouting. It was still a bit wet. He'd let it dry for a few more minutes, he decided. He walked out and stood outside, looking over the grass fields. A man away to his left picked up a tennis ball with one of those curved ball-throwers that could pick the ball up and throw it for a dog without bending down. The old man hurled it across the grass. A small bitser of at least four completely different species of canine took off after the tennis ball, its legs going in different directions and its eager bark echoing off the large banking around the sports ground. The little dog brought a smile to Harry's face. It charged straight past the ball on the ground and once it realised it had missed, it turned and tripped over its clumsy legs, tumbling wildly across the ground. It was back up in a flash and searching. When it finally found it, the dog scolded the ball loudly, then faithfully began to wobble back towards its master with the tennis ball clamped proudly between its jaws.

Harry decided it was time to go back to check the grout. He turned away from the scene on the fields and entered the toilet area again. As he rounded the corner, he stopped in his tracks. Before him, stretched out on the concrete floor, was an injured young man. He'd had his head smashed in. His injuries looked horrific and pools of dark, sticky blood covered the floor all about him. Harry's mind reeled. He had walked out of here only a minute or two ago. How could this have happened? He studied the body, hoping for some detail, something that would explain the shocking act in some logical way to him. There was nothing, no explanation he could see, or even find in his thoughts. If anything, it looked as though the body had been there for quite a while; the dark pools of blood were congealed, the face or what was left of it was greyish blue, with blotchy patches and bloodless white gums.

He walked out quickly, just as the cicadas all rushed in,

singing in their thousands, drowning out everything else in his ears.

Outside, he took some deep breaths. His mind swam madly about and he felt like running away. The big blue sky opened up right above him and he could see the shapes of birds circling away, incredibly high up in the thermals coming off the freshly mown fields on the golf course next door. He knew deep down he had to, so he forced himself to walk back inside the building again. He told himself he wasn't mad, wasn't going mad, wasn't ever going to be mad, but it really didn't help him very much. His pulse fluttered like a schoolgirl in true first love, his head floated like the lightest of clouds, spiralling high up into the blue heavens with the birds. Every footstep through the changing sheds took his full effort. Finally, he rounded the last corner. He looked down. The body was still lying there … He didn't know whether he was relieved or not now, but he rang the police this time. They were there in only ten minutes, swirling down the gravel road that led to the playing fields, the police car throwing up a great cloud of pinky brown dust. Shrapnel-like gravel flew from the wheels of the car as it took the last curve, turned into the car park to one side of the building and parked. Harry took them to the entrance.

'He's in there,' he said and stood there quietly. He could physically go no further than the door. The two young constables hitched up their thick leather belts with all their paraphernalia attached, then disappeared inside. He waited … he could hear the tramp of their boots.

'Uh, Harry,' said one of them as he suddenly came back out.

Harry looked up, the terror written across his face.

'You'd better come in, Harry.'

Harry followed the young man in and although the cicadas began madly screaming at him as he walked around the corner, their screeching cries slowly died away into a soft warble in the background. He saw there was nothing lying there on the floor, nothing there at all on the benches. He looked around the room, almost desperately, for a body. The two young policemen looked at him, but Harry didn't say anything at all. The bloody corpse was gone — again.

The two policemen looked a little surprised as they drove off down the long dirt driveway, unsure what to make of Harry's story of a young man with severe face and head injuries lying there in the toilets, when in fact there was nothing at all to be seen. However, they were even more surprised the very next morning when they got the call — again. They were definitely very shocked and very surprised when they found the young man exactly as Harry had described him to them, lying there, exactly where Harry had said he'd seen him on the concrete floor, surrounded by large pools of dark, congealed blood. And just as he had described to them, the injuries to the man's face and head were truly horrific.

* * *

THEY WERE SITTING in the smoko room. Harry had spent nearly four hours at the police station.

'I hear you've been down the cop shop,' said Joseph, with a smile.

Harry didn't understand why people said 'down the cop shop'. It was near the top of a hill, so surely it had to be up, not down. He studied his milky brown tea and nodded.

'Yeah, they just wanted to talk about the kid they found at the sports fields.'

Joseph grinned.

'Been doin' away with some more dead bodies again, eh, Harry?'

Harry smiled tiredly back at him. Joseph was a big guy and a hard worker and they got along very well. He shook his head slowly.

'Nope, I've given that up, Joe. Every time we bury one of the neighbours, the smell just drives Mavis mad.'

Joseph laughed as he picked up his cup.

'Aw, stop it, Harry, you're scaring me now.'

Harry snorted. It would take something pretty big to scare Joseph.

Joseph had been Harry's friend for some time. Probably ever since he'd shown him the Magic Moonlight Box. It was one of Harry's special inventions. Joseph had looked at Harry very sceptically when he showed it to him one day.

'It's just a cardboard box with a hole in it, Harry,' he'd pointed out.

'Yes, but have you ever held a moonbeam in your hand, Joe?' Harry had asked him.

'No, I've never done that,' admitted Joe.

'Well, it's a full moon tonight, so try it out and tell me what you really think tomorrow,' and he'd handed the cardboard box over to Joe.

Joe and his daughter Makama had taken it out later that night and held it up. They had opened the side like it was a little door. They had positioned the hole just right and Makama had put her hand inside and lo and behold, a little beam of silver moonlight had appeared through the hole and Makama had let it dance there on her hand for over an hour. It was spellbinding. Joe had thought Harry was a misunderstood genius ever since and they'd become close friends.

'Hey, I hear the kid they found was another tourist, the young brother of the woman who got killed last week.'

Harry just nodded, not wanting to pass on gossip. He'd also heard the same thing from the police. Harry had been thinking about it in the back of his mind ever since they'd mentioned it to him.

'Where are you off to? I've got the council office job,' said Joseph, taking a last sip from his cup.

'Ah, the rotten floor,' said Harry. 'I've got another leaker at the library.'

Joseph nodded as he stood up, washed his cup and placed it upside down by the sink, then wandered out the door.

* * *

HARRY WALKED OVER, climbed the steps to the library toilet and as he approached the small doorway, the cicadas all began to screech in deafening unison. He felt his heart begin to race and though he told himself sternly it was just a leaking tap, his body began to protest at the mere thought of entering the small toilet. He went back and sat in the car for five minutes trying to get the screeching in his ears to quieten back down again. Janine from the library wandered past and waved to him in greeting. Harry smiled and waved back, hoping she wouldn't stop. She didn't and disappeared around the side of the building, towards the art gallery.

God Almighty, Harry, just get in there and fix the damn tap, he told himself.

He opened the door of the car and stepped out, the cicadas greeting him instantly with a loud chorus. He forced his shaking legs slowly up the stairs and wrestled weakly with the door handle. He opened the outer door and the cicadas were like an eruption, shrieking at him in their thousands again as he stepped in and stopped. He'd known it, way before he'd seen it. Here he was, once again facing another dead body. A man sat awkwardly on the first toilet in the stalls, his bearded mouth hung wide open. He was slumped half against the wall and half up against the cistern. His arms were both sliced open in a long line from the bloodied hand almost to the elbow and thick crimson fluid lay everywhere, down the sides of the toilet bowl, sprayed on the walls and splashed across the lino flooring. It had pooled and spread right across the floor of all three stalls, like the blood had actually tried to get away from itself. Harry could see a note lying in the thick blood on the floor, with a little silver blood-covered razor blade beside it. He didn't bother with the leaking tap. A million shrieking cicadas drove him out and all the way to his house. He rang the police station from there, before Mavis could get back from work.

'No, I know you'll probably find nothing now,' he told the same detective that had spoken to him at the station.

'Well, tomorrow sometime, it will likely be. Yes, that's right, tomorrow sometime — I'm feeling quite sure you'll see it tomorrow,' then he hung up.

He stood there. He thought it was all over, but he didn't know why he thought that. He really hoped it was all over.

When the policemen checked and found the bloody corpse of a middle-aged male in the library toilet the next morning at 11.36 am, they at first thought it was another unsolved murder for them to deal with. Once they read the suicide note sitting on the blood-covered floor beside the razor blade however, they realised what had happened.

The man's name was Anthony Jenkins. He had owned and run a small eco backpackers, where there were solar panels and wind generators for power, thermal panels to heat water collected from the rainwater tanks and even sawdust for the toilets when you pressed the flush button on the cistern. Times had been hard lately and although it was a popular place, it hadn't made much money for a very long time. He had gradually drained his savings, then the bank had foreclosed on him, taking everything he owned just last month. Somehow after a night of binge drinking at the local bar with one of the backpackers that was staying with him, something had happened to him. He had been with the young woman at the bar at Onetangi late at night and they had wandered off down the beach for some drunken fun. Unfortunately, the extreme stress of his personal and financial situation meant he had failed miserably to perform for the very first time in his life. She had laughed at him and something inside him snapped. He had chased her to the nearby toilets, then in a panic, he had stabbed the young English tourist called Deborah Stevens to death in a drunken, psychotic rage. He had written it all down in his suicide letter, to the very last detail. Deborah was travelling with her younger brother Allan. He had caught up with Jenkins and confronted him down at the sports fields six days after his sister had died, and things had gotten out of hand, again. Jenkins had taken a piece of galvanised pipe lying on the grass and beaten the poor young man to death with it, then he had dragged him back inside the building, leaving him there in the changing sheds. Once the gravity of his monstrous crimes had sunk in, it had become too much for him. He had finally gone to the library to find Janine. He had always liked Janine. He wanted to say goodbye to someone that he knew, but she had already left by the time he arrived late that morning. So he wrote the final part of the suicide note while he sat there in the toilet. He knew he couldn't live with what he'd done. He had taken the bottle of sleeping pills and emptied them into his palm, then swallowed them, then he slit both his wrists to make absolutely sure. So, it was definitely over, just like Harry had said …

* * *

THE POLICEMAN LOOKED Mavis carefully in the eyes. Her

rheumy blue irises seemed sensible enough, but he had so many doubts about everything today.

'Are you sure about this Mavis?' he asked again, just to make sure.

'Yes, John, I'm quite sure. I know you said he had nothing to do with these murders and I do believe you, but he hasn't been very well for quite some time now. I should know. You've been dealing with him — can you explain it?'

He shook his head. 'No, no, I can't.'

'They're calling them the toilet murders. It has really upset me and everyone on the island is talking about him. He really does need some proper help, that's all.'

Detective Sergeant Mathews stood there, then nodded sadly. He turned and waved the car on from where he stood at the door. The police car, with Harry sitting quietly in the back seat, drove slowly away from the house.

* * *

'AND SO YOU'RE not seeing dead people in the toilets any more, Harry?'

Harry shook his head slowly. Not in the toilets, no — but he saw dead people everywhere else throughout the hospital. In fact, it seemed like there were more dead people here than live ones.

'That's good, that's excellent,' said the doctor nodding as he sat behind his desk.

Harry looked at him despairingly. The little boy with the pale blue, eager face was sitting right there on the doc's knee and the poor kid was trying so hard to get the man's attention.

How stupid are these medical people? Harry thought incredulously.

He stood up, stepped forward quickly and slapped the doctor hard across the cheek.

'Wake up,' he said simply.

The doctor blinked, both his eyes opened wider and his cheek began to go red.

'Don't tell me you can't see him. He's trying to talk to you right now,' said Harry, in a monotone.

An orderly rushed into the room and grabbed Harry.

'No, don't hurt him,' said the doctor anxiously, standing up.

Harry didn't struggle, or fight.

'Take Mr Bander back to his room for now,' said the doctor, straightening up some papers on his desk.

The orderly nodded and led Harry out, holding his arm firmly. They walked down the long, lonely corridors and the little boy with the pale blue face swung his pallid, bloodless arms as he skipped alongside Harry and the orderly. He laughed cheekily at Harry as the orderly hurried Harry along. The little boy called out and waved to all the people sitting in the TV room as they went by. Suddenly, it hit Harry. He couldn't explain anything at all to adults because they were really hopeless at understanding almost everything. But children, they were something else entirely. He had always been able to speak to kids, all his life. Suddenly, he knew exactly what to do. And in that instant, he also knew exactly how to build his Imaginon machine. It would be a small round-shaped box, he decided. It was all beautifully simple, really.

They walked down the last corridor to his room, which was located in the south wing of the hospital. All the wings had painted stripes of different colours down the middle of their floors. The patients all called the south wing the Tiger Wing, because the orange-coloured walls and the black band on the floors gave the wing its 'tiger' stripes. Harry suddenly had a kind of premonition. He tried to push all the horrible feelings back. They were suddenly welling up from somewhere really deep inside him. They were far too strong for his mind and they surrounded him, like a bunch of ghouls circling someone at a party for the dead. Then the cicadas started. Their screeching steadily grew louder. When they reached the door to his room, the little boy hung back and hid behind the orderly. He hung on to the back of the man's leg.

'See you soon, Harry,' he whispered, then he ran down the corridor, his little legs going like pistons.

Harry didn't want to go into his room. He knew something waited for him in there. The orderly got rough with him and they struggled briefly. Harry was a big man, but he was no match for the younger man's strength and eventually he was bustled and pushed into the room. The large, thick door was slammed shut after Harry, then the lock closed with a heavy *ka-chunk* and he heard the orderly's footsteps slowly fade down the corridor. Harry stood just inside the door, his eyes locked and staring up in horror. There, in front of him, dangling from the ceiling was a body turning slowly on the strips of woven sheets tied securely around the light fitting. The cicadas began to scream in his ears. Though the face and hands were terribly swollen, blue and grotesque, he recognised his own features as they slowly turned to greet him. He began to scream. Finally, the shrill screeching of the cicadas and his scream merged together into one long, eternal note.

THE PIT

Dearest Edgar,

My friend, I pray this letter retains its seal and finds you in good health. The time has come to leave the comfort of Sydney for the rugged islands of New Zealand.

Travel to Wellington city any way you can. This is deadly urgent! Get a boat across Cook Strait, in fair or better weather, then turn west when you reach southern lands. Head over and through the great mountain passes and down to the West Coast, to sleepy, old Karamea.

From Karamea, leave the town and roads behind and strike directly inland, east against the river, past Mt Stormy, wet days and nights of wonder, beyond the Falls of Heaven, past even Mt Luna, still drive on and on, towards the lonely Twins. Finally, find the Roaring Lion River, it is hidden deep in the bush, waiting to pounce — maybe then, you'll be nearly halfway home.

When the first branch and the Lion's elbow line up and Betelgeuse is caught between the Twins, north will open the serpent lair's door. The last canyon leads down the stairs to the hidden forks. You will see it in the evening, when the moon is full, hunting in the east. From these forks, seven turns of a rope to the northwest will find a large grotto, hidden deep inside the face of the cliff. Within this great cavern and located in the centre of it, is the great pit, where I have found many wondrous, glowing stones. They are rubies, Edgar! Rubies! Sitting there smouldering, like raw specks of fire in the damp and gloomy shadows!

I have included a map to assist you. But, you must beware! The end of March closes the door and the Roaring Lion will guard it for another year and I too will be gone.

I will also tell you a truth here ...

A deadly glitter of dark things I have discovered, deep in that grotto, will call out my name — forever!

Take care, but make haste at once, my dearest Edgar. Your wildest dreams of riches are here, at hand!

Your closest friend and partner always,

Allan Poe.

He stopped at the top of the moss-covered bank, dropped his pack and pulled the paper from his pocket. He rested his boot against a boulder and unfolded the yellowy old map for the hundredth time that day. He squinted down at it, his mind trying to imagine the real world within all the squiggles marked on the old paper. High above, the wind keened through the silver branches, stretched thin against the steel-blue sky. The great beech trees stood majestically all about him, the thick, lower limbs slumping their long, twisting arms in all directions. Here, down at ground level, the sou'wester was unpredictable — wild and gusty one moment, then somehow gone the next. He stood studying the old map, when his papers flapped slightly, then spilled from the opening of his pack. The wild gust of wind flung them away, to be caught amongst the underbrush, leathery hornwarts and thick silvery ferns that grew all around. A small fern with its long, curved arm of spiral fronds had caught a letter. It was the old letter he'd found with the map, hidden inside the back of the timeworn, antique desk. The frond held vainly to the letter as the wind threatened to wrestle it from its curled, silver fingers.

'Shit!' he swore loudly, as he grasped and missed, slipping on some devilish moss beneath his boots.

He grabbed the letter on his second attempt, then scrambled about quickly, retrieving the rest of his papers. He picked up another letter from the mud … It was *that* letter, addressed to:

Colin Davies,
22 Durham St,
Karamea.

HAYLEY'S LETTER, from the little house in Granity. The letter where she'd told him he was only really half a person and not worth the time she'd wasted on him. Thick mud smeared the front of the envelope, but he could still see the loopy 'l' and 't' of Hayley's careful prose in the lines of the address. It was so different from his own slanted, left-handed scrawl. He wiped most of the mud off with his hand and placed everything back into his bag, then closed the zipper tightly.

He felt so tired deep down. Everything seemed to take a huge amount of energy and effort and he knew he needed to eat again, because his energy levels were so low.

He had originally thought it would take him a couple of days to find the grotto on the little map and now, here he was with basically a week gone by and he still hadn't found it. The upper branch of the tributary he was standing beside was hidden amongst the endless twists and folds of the Roaring Lion River. What he had thought should be simple to find, while he was sitting in the cafe at Karamea, or walking the endless sands of the great ocean beach, with a dying red sun falling into the sea beside him, now seemed nearly impossible. The problem was, he was fighting a great monster. The endless, glittering, jungle-like green bush. He couldn't describe it as anything but jungle-like, because it was so heavily strewn with aggressive plants and insects, all perfectly designed to embed themselves, hack, poison, sting and generally suck blood from anything that moved. He was thankful knowing there were no highly dangerous or lethal creatures to come across in New Zealand native bush. Apart from, of course, the odd poisonous spider, or a wild pig, both of whom were generally secretive creatures and kept their own company, but everything else here simply attacked him at the first opportunity, stung him, clung to him, sucked his blood, or just constantly flew about his face and drove him mad. All the while, the rugged terrain endlessly held him back. Thick, constantly dripping foliage pushed against him, misled and defied him, indeed it even cut and injured him. It had poisoned him as much as the insects did and after an exhausting week of battling almost every step, it seemed to have totally and finally surrounded him.

He turned and studied the dancing compass needle against the backdrop of the endlessly twisting, churning river. He had watched the stunning sight of Betelgeuse, the red star at Orion's shoulder, rise late last night, right between the two peaks of the Twins, against a backdrop of a billion shining stars in crystal-clear mountain air. He was positive the location of the cave must be very close to him. He looked away to his left and studied the large boulders he could see around the next bend, a little upriver. Somewhere, very close up ahead … he told himself, possibly only a few bends of the river away, was a dark grotto hidden beneath these huge, granite cliffs. He stood, exhausted, in beaten awe of the brutal surroundings, the river thundering in his ears, the majestic snowcapped peaks towering high into the sky around him. He was cold and shattered, but his light blue eyes burned with a fever that the coldest South Island river could never cool. It simply had to be here, he told himself — again.

He battled his way around five, then six more bends of the river in the fading light, counting them off excitedly in his mind and searching the cliff-like walls at each bend, one by one. Finally, the inevitable night fell. It fell so fast out here in the mountains, in fact it swooped down on him, throwing the whole valley into a sudden shadow, as if one of the world's greatest birds, the largest of all the eagles, that used to soar amongst these same peaks so many thousands of years ago, had flown silently, right above him.

* * *

THE NEXT MORNING he woke and scrambled about in the cold, rekindling the remains of his fire. The filtered light began to creep into the darker corners of the bush around him and catch speckled colours of lichen covering the rocks and banks beside the river. The yellowy light somehow enhanced the olives and browns and golds at his feet, a stark contrast to the glistening forest all around him, which consisted of a million different shades of green. Often, it was like being in an enchanted world, but it was certainly a cold one, too. He cooked one of his last freeze-dried meals and washed it down with a mug of hot coffee. The sun began to warm the valley about eight o'clock, so he hastily broke camp and continued up the boulder-strewn banks of the Roaring Lion River.

He stopped an hour later, the sun climbing into the sky above. He stood on a small bank with gigantic, grey-blue boulders jutting from the silted earth around him. The largest boulders were enormous near the edge of the frothing river, but here, they stood only as tall as he was. They were covered in thick manuka scrub and rambling bushes on both sides of the river. He looked around the scene a few times. He felt there was something weird or familiar about it. He searched fairly slowly amongst some tangled gorse, tearing and scratching his hands and arms, as he looked for possible entrances under the bedrock, but he found nothing. He moved further along the bank and fought some more with the twisted branches covered in thick little spines. After a while, he found crawling underneath the gorse was easier than fighting his way through it. He scratched at the roots with his fingers, but the plant was growing from a tiny crack in the rock. He crawled out from under the bush and stood up. There was certainly no cave entrance to be found here. He looked up and saw a jagged seam running in the dark rock, high above him. He looked further up the formidable river, then up at the jagged seam again. He decided it might be worth it, so he scrambled upwards, clambering slowly over some large, mossy boulders, being careful not to slip and fall. He climbed twenty metres, almost straight up. He reached a small ledge, then stopped and looked around carefully. There was a level area in front of him covered in a few ferns, some gorse and a single manuka bush. He began to search amidst the bushes that grew from any crack in the rocks these hardy plants could get a root into. He stopped suddenly, crouching and squinting at the ground in front of him, hunched over under the gorse. He could see a very small, dark hole at the base of one of the large boulders. The dark gap was too small though, about the size of his fist. *Probably a water rat's hole,* he thought to himself. Mainly out of days of utter frustration, he brushed at the edge of the gap with his hand. The dirt, stones and pebbles fell away easily and a larger hole instantly began to open up. Working quickly, in just a few minutes he created a large, round hole, almost half a metre wide. It led further downwards, beneath the boulder above him. He looked at the large boulder closely. If it caved in while he was in there, the hole he'd just dug would be his resting place. Satisfied the huge boulders were firmly wedged against each other and could not move, he crawled back out from the bushes again. He threw off his pack excitedly, took out a torch and his small prospecting hammer. Then he quickly tunnelled back under the gorse and began to carefully worm his way down the hole he had just created. It was dark and murky and after a while he had to brush lots of spider webs away. The torch beam displayed dry, dirt walls beside him as he worked his way downwards and along. Suddenly, the hole began to open up wider, he heard some echoes and he realised he had indeed found some sort of cave, or a larger opening. But was it the right one? He finally reached the end where a lip formed and he slowly pulled himself into a chamber, which sounded quite large from all the sounds around him. Very carefully, he stood and shone the torch about in the darkness. He was standing in a large space, about half the size of a tennis court. Water glistened from all the limestone and granite walls and it dripped steadily from the ceiling, which was mostly three or four metres above him. He moved around the chamber, shining his torch at the walls, searching for any other openings. Two passages seemed to lead off in different directions, so he explored them both. The first was a small tunnel that led nowhere, closing off into a blank wall after about five or six metres. The second one narrowed for a while, then opened up into another larger chamber. He saw there was another chamber beyond it and as he moved forward, he noticed a dark depression in the very middle of the last chamber. His heart rate increased in anticipation and his racing pulse began banging in his ears as he stepped slowly across the wet rock. It certainly appeared to him to be a largish hole, right in the centre of the chamber. He shone the torch at it. It took a few seconds, then to his delight, he saw it was indeed full of dark, wet gravel and stones. Was it his imagination, or could he actually see fiery little pricks of red in the gloom? He stepped a little closer. He turned the torch off and then switched it back on. He did it again. A first he saw nothing, but then suddenly — it was true, the light of the torch beam was glinting and catching specks of red from some tiny stones scattered amongst the rubble. He carefully stepped down, testing his weight on the heap, then scooped up a handful of gravel. He scooped up another. A tiny little speck of dull red glowed in the beam of his torch light. He pulled a plastic bag from his pocket, poured the handful in and plunged his hand back in again, deep into the myriad of dark, wet stones. He filled the plastic bag to the top, then climbed slowly back out. He looked carefully around, in case there was another entrance or exit to this chamber, but he couldn't find one, so he made his way back to the first chamber and the little tunnel he'd opened up. He squirmed back up the long entrance and finally emerged like a demon of the night from the gorse bushes, his eyes blinking in the bright sunlight. He pulled a grading plate from his backpack and almost in a trance, made his way carefully down to the river.

He sat at a small side stream, where a gentle pool of crystal water had formed and he slowly began to wash the stones from his bag. As he tipped the waste carefully from his plate, he watched in growing delight as a few dark-coloured blobs emerged from the dirt and gravel. After ten minutes, he stopped and looked down at a small group of tiny dark beads in the fine dirt, sitting in the cleft of the plate. He carefully picked up one of the largest pieces and held it to the light. As it caught the sunlight, it sparkled quite brightly, emitting a bloody colour in a fiery little dance. He felt the feeling of joy and success welling up inside him. He thought back over the last two months, since he'd found the letter and the little map. He had bought the old desk in a night auction at Stevenson's Household Auctions, then driven back and lugged it up the steps of his flat. He had found the letter and map inside a compartment in the back of the desk after he had removed the drawer to clean it and it had made a strange click. When he had turned the desk over he could see through a tiny gap into the area behind the drawer. His fingers had found the small panel that slid open and suddenly the letter and map had fallen out. He hardly believed the story in the letter when he first read it, but he'd followed all the details. Now he actually stood here, in the middle of nowhere, the glint and promise of rubies mesmerising him in the pure golden sunlight of day. It *was* real! He wanted to go straight back down into the grotto and fill everything he carried with the rough gravel containing the magical little stones. Instead, he began to set up his camp. He had only enough food left for his meal tonight. He figured he would need to leave sometime tomorrow, so he had a hell of a lot of work to do.

After quickly setting up his camp on the ledge not far from the entrance to the grotto and gathering firewood, he took his small, fold-up spade, both torches and some plastic bags and wormed back down the entranceway again. The grotto below was dank, dark and uninviting, but his eyes sparkled with excitement. He made his way through the dripping chambers, following his wandering beam, towards the pit. This time he shone his torch carefully into the pit before he started. There seemed to be more little points of light flashing at one end of the pit than the other. He walked over to that end and stepped onto the pile carefully.

He began to dig earnestly, shovelling large amounts of gravel into one of the larger bags. His spade hit something hard and he stopped, sweat dripping from his brow. His eyes burned with excitement. He wondered what it could be. He felt around with the little spade, then gently began levering the object up to the surface. He grew more and more excited as he slowly levered a large round object out of the dark, wet gravel. His pulse raced. Suddenly, it came free and with a flash of white, he dropped it, yelled and scrambled backwards, all at the same time. His heart pounded in his chest and he tried to calm his frightened nerves in the gloom of the chamber. The human skull grinned mischievously up at him from near his foot. He picked it up gingerly and climbed back out of the pit. He carefully placed it on the damp rocks beside the wall. He studied it for a few seconds, then he went back over to the pit, looking around for the little spade and finally found it again with the help of the torch. He moved across to a spot a few metres further down the pit and decided to dig again, his heart still beating quickly in his chest. He set the torch down carefully beside him and began working quickly with the spade with both hands in the dim light. He filled the other large bag he had brought in, then picked up the torches and carefully carried the bags through the two dark chambers. He shoved them into the entranceway, pushing them upwards as he worked himself laboriously out of the dark hole. Then he took them down to the river bank. The sun was low in the west, just behind the mountains, and light was fading steadily. He had been down there much longer than he realised. He set to work quickly, washing and sifting the contents of the two large bags of gravel, with the help of torch light. It was almost dark when he had finally finished. He had quickly found that most of the tiny stones were much darker than the rest of the gravel. They sat near the bottom of his pans like little black seeds, rolling slowly backwards and forwards. There weren't as many of them as he had hoped out of all the gravel in the two bags, but it was certainly something. With the help of the torch, he climbed back up to the ledge, carefully emptied them into his first bag, lit his fire and made himself some coffee. After he'd finished, he finally turned to the bag he had placed in the pocket of his rucksack. The bundle of little stones in the bag was only enough to fill a small matchbox, but even in the dim light of the fading torch, he saw the glow and sparkle of fire jumping from the tiny stones.

He slept fitfully that night — any loud noise or crack of a branch had him sitting bolt upright, his eyes searching the gloom and his ears straining in the darkness.

At first light the next morning, he carefully covered all signs of his camp, then dragged some large stones over and placed them over the entranceway to the chamber. He covered the stones with dead fern fronds and edged back out of the small bushes and stood there studying his work. It looked quite normal. Then he hoisted his pack onto his shoulders, climbed carefully down from the ledge and began to fight his way back along the river again.

He pushed through the thick bush as fantails danced busily about him, cheeping away in constant cheeky conversation as they happily gobbled up the tiny insects he disturbed. Occasionally he would catch sight of a plump, brown weka darting through the undergrowth, just like a cartoon roadrunner. Kaka and tui patrolled the branches above him. Every possible colour of the spectrum seemed represented by the pouring river and its edge of bush and it was wondrous in the early-morning rays. Here and there, leaves and plants caught the angled light. There were rings of bright yellow mushrooms, neon-coloured moss and liverworts, red and purple lichens. Even the great trees beside the river, their huge, steel-grey trunks and thick, tangled branches, drank in the splendour of the day. A faint, pinkish mist hung lightly in the air in the bush sections and birds high in the trees greeted the sun with a thousand different songs. His day was similar to a hundred others he had enjoyed before, but he found he recorded every scene, noticed the tiniest of details and saw great wonder in the things all around him. The sharp glisten of red light tinted his every thought, image, or feeling as he pushed onwards through the bush.

He spent the night near the top of the valley, a soft roar of a waterfall in the distance. His sleep was interlaced with vivid dreams of glorious, red fires and ghostly images of grinning white skulls.

The next morning, he woke cold under the clear skies. After a basic breakfast of his last muesli bar and some black, sweet coffee, he set off again. He was hoping to skirt the Twins by eleven o'clock. As he climbed higher, the environment around him steadily changed. The wet, glittering plants of emerald-coloured forest thinned away and were finally left behind. Now, the grey boulders emerged from grey, red and brown grasses, amongst the dirt and raupo and flax bushes, which began to dominate the mountainous environment. Even the air became colder and drier in his throat. He reached a long ridge and began to follow it. He carefully stepped past small windswept manuka trees, frozen upwards in strange, twisted poses, on the rocky side of the narrow path and a steep drop of nothingness, which fell away for a thousand metres on the other side. He stopped for a second or two, caught by the views. He could see all the way to Mt Luna to the southwest and Mt Stormy to the northwest and a thin swathe of deep, blue sea stretched out between the two peaks. The views everywhere were magnificent, from ever darker rows of snow-covered ranges all the way to the horizon, to the silvery churn of the rivers far below, catching the light in the bottom of the valleys. He continued on and passed over the ridge, down the other side and began to descend steadily, soon emerging back into lush green bush again. *Nearly there*, he thought to himself wearily. He made it to the swinging bridge that crossed the river, then finally up the hill to the rest area, where he had parked the car. It was just after 2 pm. He drove quickly back down to Karamea and parked his car outside Greenstone Heaven. He felt the weight of the small bag of stones in his hand a couple of times, then got out, walked through the front doors and wandered nervously up to the counter. He could see Garth Casey busy at one of the desks out the back.

Colin waited patiently. Finally Garth looked up, removed his thick black spectacles and approached the window. Colin couldn't help the small grin that came creeping out of nowhere to spread across his face.

'Well, if it isn't the famous, young gold prospector. How did you go? Find any big nuggets in them thar hills?'

Colin shook his head. The old bugger who ran the shop was a curmudgeonly old fossil. He was over eighty, with a shining, bald pate, and only a few long wisps of white hair left behind both ears, that reached down to nearly touch his shoulders. He was a rough but friendly old soul and someone Colin had grown used to, especially after his many fruitless attempts at discovering his 'fortune' in the rivers above the town.

'Nothing like that, mate, just some old stones that might be rubies.'

The old man smiled wanly. 'Rubies? You won't find them round here, mate. Wrong conditions for 'em, though there's an old legend about some old duff back in the 1900s claiming he'd found some. Can't remember his name, but like I said, no chance of rubies here. Garnets maybe, but more likely some coloured gemstones, or bits of old glass you've found, but let's have a look.'

Colin handed the bag through the gap and watched as the old man tipped them carefully onto a square of paper and placed them on the tray of some digital scales.

'Twelve grams — agreed?'

Colin nodded, his eyes watching the old man's movements like a hawk.

'Take a seat over there, kid, this won't take long,' said the old man gruffly.

Colin sat down on a thick bench seat made from rough slabs of swamp kauri. The top was sanded smooth to reveal the honey-coloured timber laced with a few chocolatey swirls. He couldn't help thinking of the river and its hidden chambers and caves up there, beyond the walls and the hills of the town. Garth Casey's old lined face suddenly appeared in the window. His demeanour held the same battered old expression, but his small eyes now sparkled with life.

'Where did you find these?' he asked coyly.

'Oh, somewhere up the main river,' Colin replied evasively. 'What are they?'

'I'm not actually sure,' said the old man, 'they're pretty small pieces and I'll have to check properly before I can tell you what you have. If you feel like maybe having something to eat, I can probably give you a definite answer in about an hour. I'll give you the receipt.'

Colin looked at the old man carefully as he scribbled something in his receipt book. He tore the page off and handed it through the window to him. It simply said '12 grams of small stones for evaluation — received by Greenstone Heaven'.

He trusted old Garth, but he felt uneasy at leaving the shop without the stones. Hunger and tiredness pushed him and he simply nodded, then reluctantly turned and left the shop.

* * *

After an hour sitting in the River View coffee shop and enjoying a giant breakfast of bacon, eggs, hash browns, fried tomatoes with sausages and mushrooms and washing it all down with two large cups of coffee, he felt much better than before. He made his way back to Greenstone Heaven and walked up to the window again. Garth was waiting for him and the look on his face was as inscrutable as ever.

'Well, were they garnets after all?' asked Colin.

The old man looked at him for a second then shook his head. 'No,' he said, 'you'll be rapt to know they are in fact rubies, but you couldn't have got them from round here. It's impossible. Where did you say you found them?'

Colin's face stretched into a grin and he had to stop himself from thumping his fist on the counter in delight. They *were* rubies!

'Oh, straight up the Karamea, about forty or fifty miles, right on the river bank itself.'

The old man looked at him shrewdly. 'You know, you need very specific conditions for rubies. They don't just tumble down a river. They grow from a substance called corundum and also need a bit of chromium. You would need a limestone cave system, or some kind of river system. You know like an old river bed, or maybe an ancient waterfall that has long dried up. Occasionally you find them high above the river up in the cliff walls. You'd need those kind of conditions anyway.'

Colin looked at Garth curiously through the window.

'How does an old river bed get up into the cliff walls?'

He could feel the old man's eyes boring into him, like a pair of drills.

'Well, when water comes into contact with limestone it simply eats it away, son, just dissolves it basically. You're then left with a hollowed-out area inside. It's also how you get all your other shapes, like stalagmites and stalactites, all forming from the running water. Often these old caves are really ancient river bed systems, or waterfalls, like I said. They're normally found in mountain systems close to or even directly over an alpine fault. The plates push up one side of the system over the other and over a few million years these river beds are actually raised high above their ancient sites, sometimes by hundreds of metres up a cliff wall.'

Colin nodded; it sounded very much like the cave he had found.

'So, how valuable are these, Garth?'

The old man looked at him shrewdly. 'These are very small and they're pretty rough. They can be used in commercial situations, so obviously nowhere near as much as larger rubies that we use in jewellery. Large, raw rubies are priced just over two thousand dollars a carat at the moment, I think. The twelve grams of rough little stones you have might be worth nearly two thousand dollars at the most, I suppose — to someone else, of course.'

'What would they be worth to you, Garth? Would you buy them?'

The old man nodded slowly.

'Sure, but it wouldn't be anywhere near that much. Hang on a second. He picked up a calculator and stabbed at the buttons with a gnarled finger.

'Eight fifty is all I could give you for them.'

Colin thought for a while, then he nodded again. His bank account was just about empty and he needed the money.

'Okay, that sounds fair enough. Have you got cash?'

The old man shook his head.

'We never carry cash here. I can give you a cheque though and the bank's open.'

'Sounds good to me.'

The old man wrote the cheque out and handed it to him. He passed it through the small gap.

'One more thing, son. You say you found them on the Karamea, on the river bank?'

Colin slid the cheque into his wallet.

'Yes, that's right,' he said, avoiding eye contact with the old man.

'Well, that's good luck to you there, son. Many a man has passed away never seeing a cent from that river. You've stumbled on something pretty rare. I take it you were in your licence area?'

Colin nodded without saying a word. It was nowhere near the area that his prospecting licence covered.

'Y-yep,' he stammered. 'I thought it was a waste of money finding no gold there, but now, it seems as though it's actually paid itself back, eh?'

The old man grinned and his face creased.

'Good for you, kid — hey, go get some more and make us both rich, okay?'

Colin laughed.

'You betcha. Catch you on the next trip, Garth.'

The old man watched him turn and walk out of the shop. The door shut behind him with a bang. The old man picked up the phone sitting on the counter and his crinkled fingers tapped away at the buttons.

* * *

THE LAUGHTER in the pub that night was perfect medicine for

the lonely days of bashing bush and freezing streams, and with a thick wad of money in his pocket, Colin felt happier than he'd been for years. He was even happier than he had been in Granity with Hayley and Danielle, in the little house in Granite Creek Drive. The thought of Hayley turned his warm, drunken mind inwards, to the darker areas, the places where he had hidden his demons. She had berated him at the end, calling him a coward and only half a man, because he couldn't love her like they both wanted him to. It brought up all the dangerous memories again, flooding his mind with the dark, heavy thoughts of the abuse and his helplessness in the brother's house. He could suddenly feel the rough hands of Brother Simon on his body, the smell — no, the stench — of the man's breath on the side of his face. The animal-like sounds that disgusted him to the core of his soul, that had taken something from him that could never be returned. The abuse had started when he was eleven, with a trip to Dunedin, with the church. It had continued until a month before he turned eighteen, when he'd run away from the home in Greymouth and never returned. He had seen a psychologist just once, after his doctor had recommended it, saying he needed to deal with his issues, or the risk was, it could do him a great deal of damage and probably destroy any chance of a relationship with Hayley. It had been so traumatic for him, going the first time to the Finlayson Clinic, that he had never returned. Worse still, Hayley had been suspicious of him suddenly visiting a 'shrink'. She had no idea it was so he could simply try to talk to her about his problems. She probably would have gone mad if she had realised he'd also visited the police without mentioning it to her. He had driven over to the Karamea police station from Granity and laid an official complaint about his abuse at the home. Sergeant Ratherty was the officer handling his case. He had first recommended Colin not to lay any charges at all for various reasons, but in the end he had relented and agreed to file them. That was nearly two years ago now. He hadn't heard much more about it, even though he'd been to visit Sergeant Ratherty three times. Apparently it was a 'slow legal process' and had to be done properly through 'official' channels. After Hayley had found the appointment card for the Finlayson Clinic they'd had a pretty severe fight, which ended with her slapping him across the face. She told him to 'get some balls'. He had retaliated, pushing her backwards to land on the sofa. Then in frustration and shame he had walked out of the little house in Granity. After a week of silence, she had needlessly asked him to shift out. He was ashamed he hadn't spoken to Hayley or little Danielle for nearly two years.

He wandered away from the crowd in the pub, lost in his reverie of maudlin thoughts, and was now sitting morosely in a corner, out on the deck, contemplating the quiet street. He realised that he had to get back to the cave and work the pit again. It was the answer to his problems. It was the only good thing that had happened to him for as long as he could remember. He stumbled home, pouring himself in the door to his flat. He threw his clothes on a chair and was asleep in minutes, the dark night folding around him. The alcohol he'd consumed was like an old friend, protecting him from the twisted memories, vulgar visions and nightmares that had haunted him for the last ten years.

He woke groggily, his head pounding. He dragged himself awake, then sat on the chair by the window with a coffee in his hand, thinking. He knew what he needed to do. He began to plan his second trip much better than the first. It had been a long journey finding the cave, but now he knew the location, he could go straight in and out. He knew what he needed for supplies. He would travel very light, with two days' food, and he didn't even need the map or letter this time. Where to hide them? he wondered. He took his Bible down from the second shelf of the bookcase. The one Hayley had given him for his birthday in Granity. It was a present he hadn't wanted at the time, a trigger he didn't need, but it was the only thing she had ever given him and he didn't have the heart to throw it away. It was beautifully embossed with thick, dark leather. He didn't know whether he believed in God now, in fact he didn't know whether he had ever believed in God. How could he have believed in something that had turned monstrous so quickly and used him so wickedly? It had also turned him into a pathetic creature that seemed completely helpless at times. That was what hurt him the most. He had loved being with Hayley and her daughter Danielle, and the Bible was the only thing he had to remind him of the days in Granity. He opened the thick book, slid the folded papers inside the back cover and returned it to the bookcase. He spent the rest of the morning organising food supplies, then went into Karamea and bought a new stove to cook on, complete with two little square pans that nested inside each other. He packed his rucksack carefully and added two canvas sacks and a small, lined bag that he bought from the hardware store. It was nylon on the inside and leather on the outside and he imagined it full of glistening, fat rubies. He bought an expensive LED flashlight with rechargeable batteries. That night, he had sausages and baked potatoes cooked in foil from the fireplace, as his mind was already in the bush. He sat there deep into the night, the wondrous feeling of being rich running playfully around in his head. Should he go back and see Hayley once he had sold the stones? Would she be with someone else by now? Probably. Would she want him, now that he simply had money and would he really want her, knowing it was money that possibly brought them back together? He sat before the fire, watching the flames dance and leap before him, but all his mind saw were red sparks of fire, burning and glowing in a dark, damp and gloomy cave, far off at the bottom of a distant mountain.

When he finally dropped off to sleep, he was still there, inside his cave.

* * *

HE PACKED the car straight after breakfast, then warmed the tired old Mitsubishi up. He had been driving it for nearly five years now and he certainly liked the idea of buying a newer car. He drove out of town onto the main road, heading up into the first of the hills. There was hardly anyone about on such a beautiful day. Out of town, a lone motorcyclist wound around the curves behind him as he began to climb steadily up through the ranges. He drove past snowcapped Mt Kendall, then Mt Luna, both their peaks wreathed in wispy clouds. Near the top of the range, the lone biker whipped past him on a long stretch and disappeared with a roar through the curves up ahead. He thought he might catch a glimpse of the old bike again when the road straightened out, but instead the road was empty, except for the odd campervan trundling towards him in the opposite direction.

He carried on towards Motueka, until he could see the Twins breaking the skyline to his left, then he turned down the road into the small settlement of Kaituna. He wound further in towards the Twins, then finally into the side road that led down to the little rest area. He drove in, parked the car under the stand of totara and locked it. Hefting his back-pack across his shoulders, he took the track that led into the bush, with nothing but the birds for company and some annoying clouds of hungry sandflies. He climbed upwards, heading towards the Twins' jagged peaks high on the skyline. He made good time and stopped for a bite about 1 pm, enjoying the breathtaking views, just short of the ridge. It was early afternoon when he finally left the snowline behind him and descended down amongst the dry, brown grasses and dusty scrub. He camped the first night near the river, amongst a large stand of giant nikau. He cooked a basic meal from the dried packets and drank black coffee sitting beside the fire, as the night fell around him and the moon and stars appeared. They began to slide across the sky on their seemingly endless journey from horizon to horizon. He drank in the glorious image of endless, brilliant stars, wheeling slowly through the night. He loved being out in the bush.

He woke in the morning and the excitement began to well up inside him. The river coursed and jumped beside him. Here the water showed every hue, from beautiful greens to deep blues, dark and startling reds and oranges, even silver colours, with always the purest froth of white bursting forth amongst the rocks. Deeper stretches like the one in front of him were so clear, the water seemed colourless, like thick, molten glass pouring past. Long, triangular spears of light stabbed through the surface, like yellow daggers reaching right to the bottom, as the river poured through the bush and over the endless, jumbled rocks.

He was so enthusiastic that morning, he set off without breakfast. Only half an hour later though, he slipped on a large rock while crossing a stream and fell head first into the cold water. He pulled himself up and admonished himself for being so stupid. He rolled his jeans up his right leg and with some alarm, he saw an ugly gash above his red, swelling ankle. *Goddammit,* he thought to himself, *not now!* He couldn't afford to make stupid mistakes out here in the rugged landscape. He tore one of his spare T-shirts into long pieces and wrapped two of the strips tightly around his ankle and then hobbled about, regretting his childish enthusiasm. He decided to have something to eat and rest his foot for a while.

After an hour or so and feeling much better, he set off again and this time he set himself a slow, steady pace. It was getting quite late in the day when he finally spotted the bend of the river he was looking for. The cave wasn't very far from here. He made a camp site as the darkness was falling. He heard the tui and weka calling to each other throughout the valley, as they seemed to do every night after the last glimpse of sunlight. He made a small camp fire in case anyone was around. That night he slept fitfully, imagining images of grinning skulls all around him.

The morning broke with a light rain falling from an overcast sky. He quickly packed up his camp and set off. He rounded the few bends in the river, climbed up to the small ledge and moved his gear under the gorse bushes, near the stones covering his hole. He examined the entrance carefully. The light rain was still falling like a fine mist and dusting his shoulders and hair with tiny, silver drops. To his eye, the entrance looked exactly as he had left it. There was no shelter in the gorse bushes, so he cleared away the hole, then dragged all his gear down the tunnel and stowed it in the driest part of the first chamber. Excitedly, he entered the second chamber, the torch beam bouncing round the walls. He made his way over to the pit and quickly got to work. He filled the first thick sack nearly full with a muddy stone mixture, then dragged it over to the entranceway, by his gear. He went back to the pit and continued.

Shortly after 2 pm, he stopped and wormed his way up the small shaft three times, pushing and cajoling his gear and the heavy bags of wet stones up and into the light. It had stopped raining, but the sky was full of leaden clouds, hanging low over the mountain tops. He made a coffee, then took one of the bags down to the river, found his favourite spot near the little stream and began to carefully wash some of the gravel. He concentrated on his pan in the slowly fading light. About 6 pm, he decided he couldn't see well enough any more and he gently washed out the last scoop of gravel and dirt back into the sack, then climbed back up to the ledge with his new pile of little red stones. He put up his tent, tying the lines to the bushes and under rocks, then started a fire. He sat beside it, eating noodles and veges straight from the pot. He could think of nothing but the red, glistening stones sitting beside him, lying inside the small, lined bag.

He figured he had made a thousand dollars at least and he hadn't washed all of the gravel in the bags yet. He decided he would stay another day or two and take as much material back as possible on this trip. He thought he might even hold some back from old Garth. He could always drip feed it to him over the next few weeks or months, so the old bugger wouldn't be any the wiser. He didn't know why, but he'd felt slightly uneasy ever since he'd shown him the little rubies at the shop. It was like a small fire had started somewhere deep inside the old man's eyes. Maybe it was his imagination, or probably it's that victim thing again …

Colin felt exhausted and his swollen ankle was giving him a little trouble, but he fell asleep that night easily enough. He dreamed he was travelling the world far and wide, pulling handfuls of rubies from his pockets to the delight of laughing, shouting children as they held out their small hands to him, calling his name, pleading with him for more. Their hands grabbed at him, getting more and more demanding, until suddenly, it was Brother Simon's hands all over him, touching him, calling his name, demanding he obey him, demanding he …

He woke up in a sweat, his hands shaky, and the inky darkness around him disoriented him. He thought he heard a crack from the bush further down the river, so he sat up, listening for any other strange sounds. There were hundreds of sounds all around him, but nothing that made him think anyone was out there. Eventually, he fell back into a fitful, uneasy sleep.

When he woke the next morning, the sun had filled the sky with dark crimson light. Red in the morning, sailor's warning, he reminded himself, as he boiled water for his coffee. After finishing his drink and struggling through two quick muesli bars for breakfast, he looked around. There were still bags of gravel to be washed from yesterday, so he dragged them down to the stream and slowly sluiced the muddy stones and grit in the icy, cold water. He gained some more of the little red seeds from the gravel. He decided to make himself a large brunch that would keep him going through the day. He washed it down with two cups of coffee, then wriggled his way down the hole again and into the first chamber. He made his way through to the second chamber and approached the pit. It was hard, slow work in the pit and it had been harder than he'd realised, hauling the heavy gravel sacks up the shaft to the surface. He wondered if there was a better way, but he knew the little stones wouldn't shift themselves, so he bent to it and started into the wet gravel. After a while, he had an idea. He looked over to the far end of the pit where he had seen more of the glints of red in the torchlight. He shook his head though at the thought of a body possibly buried there and so he threw his weight again behind the shovel. The little steel shovel clanged against something hard. He felt around, then he slowly levered out a long, white bone from the thick muck at his knees. He got out of the pit, wandered over and laid the bone down against the far wall, beside the skull he had found on the first dig. It still sat there, grinning silently in the gloom. He picked up the skull gently and examined it, brushing off the dirt and grime. There was a large crack that looked a bit like a lightning bolt leading to a wide split at the back of the skull. He put it back down again on the wet rock. He knew it was most probably a person who had found the pit and paid for the knowledge dearly. He climbed back down into the gravel and moved further to the right. He began digging again, the dim narrow light of the torch throwing long shadows across the walls as he worked. After five minutes, his blade struck something hard and he stopped again. He worked the roundish object up towards the surface and then slowly levered it out. It couldn't be … A small chill ran down his back. It was another skull. He picked it up and looked at it closely in the torch light. Its jaw bone was missing and there was a large, triangular-shaped gash in the right side of the skull, just behind the ear cavity. He looked at it, deep in thought. The sharp-edged hole signalled a fairly similar demise to the person that the first skull had belonged to. Another cold shiver ran down his spine as he realised it was obvious more than one man had died for the knowledge of this grotto. He instantly assumed the two skulls were very old, but he had no real idea, and slowly he realised the skulls might be more recent. Who would know? The noises in the grotto began to play tricks on him, the dripping water sounding like someone's footsteps behind him. He shook off his gloomy thoughts as he climbed out of the pit, walked over and placed the second skull on the wet rock, beside the first one. This time he moved further along in the pit and began to dig again. A cold chill tingled across his skin as his spade stopped with a hard clunk once again. He dug around and then carefully eased out another large, long white bone. *Looks like another femur,* he thought, as he reached up and placed it on the ledge behind him. He stared at the white bone. God, how many bodies are there in the pit? Two? Is that all?

The dank air shrank around him and the constant dripping noises kept his nerves on edge. He moved further down the pit, away from the bodies, and continued to work.

After an hour or so, as he was working in the pit, he thought he heard a noise in the chamber. He stopped, the sweat dripping from his forehead, as he listened carefully in the darkness. He heard nothing. He shone the torch around the chamber, but the beam just revealed glistening, wet walls. As he moved the torch he noticed the beam catching a bright little spark of red at the other end of the pit. He knew the other end contained more remains, but that little spark of red called out to him like a siren, crying his name. He put the torch on the edge, pulled himself from the pit and made his way to the other end, where he stepped into the gravel. He placed the torch behind him, with the beam concentrating on the area in front of him. The gravel seemed less wet and more solid at this end of the pit as he dug into it with the spade. On the second drive, a small, fiery stone caught the light as it tumbled down the scree and disappeared into the dark pool of water at his feet. He stopped and scrabbled around with his hand in the cold muck. Carefully he pulled up a handful of stones and held them in the torch beam. Nothing shone at all. He knelt down and felt around with his hand again and pulled up another handful. He shone the torch on the stones. There, sitting in the middle of the pile, was a rough, dark stone, about the size of his thumbnail. It gleamed a dull, red colour in the beam of the torch. He carefully picked it up with his fingers as adrenaline surged through his veins. It was definitely the largest stone he had found. He wondered how much it might possibly be worth. What did old Garth say? Two thousand dollars per carat? He had looked it up online. A carat weighed one fifth of a gram. He thought it might be worth a few thousand dollars at least. A dark shadow swept across the wet walls of the chamber and Colin ducked instinctively. A huge weight slammed into his shoulder. He fell forwards, the blow knocking the wind from his lungs and the little stone in his fingers flying from his grasp into the darkness. He rolled to one side, just as a heavy-handled spade smashed into the gravel beside him with a crash. He spun around and scrabbled frantically across the gravel pit, but this time the spade caught him flat across his cheek and sent him flying. He coughed once and lay still amongst the slick stones. A dark figure jumped into the gravel of the pit. He held the short-handled spade with one hand as he scrunched through the gravel, his boots sinking into the heavy wet stones. He stopped, standing over the top of Colin's still body, then slowly raised the heavy spade high above his head. He brought it down with all his force. At the last moment, the figure lying at his feet twisted to one side and the spade slammed into the stones, sending sparks flying from the metal edge. Colin drove upwards with his leg and smashed the figure backwards against the stone lip of the pit. The shadowy figure grunted in pain, bent over double and dropped the spade. The handle fell near Colin's left hand. He stood quickly, scooping up the spade as he did. He hesitated for just a second, then swung it in a vicious arc and heard a satisfying crack as the edge of the blade struck the figure's head. The person toppled to the ground in the darkness. The anger and bitterness of years of hardship, every bit of his abuse and even the pent-up frustration with Hayley, welled up inside him and he struck the figure lying on the stones with the back of the spade, again and again, as hard as he could. Colin stood there, gasping heavily in the gloom, his mind reeling from what he had just done. Where the hell had that come from? He regained his senses slowly and stepped over to where the torch had fallen. He picked it up, then stepped carefully back to the body. He took a breath and shone the beam into the face of the figure. It was too shocking for him to register and he looked away quickly. The blade had driven deeply into the head of the figure and the face was distorted and hideous, the eyes bulging out unnaturally, the face severely misshapen from his beating. He fell to his knees and began to dry retch. Slowly, he got his thoughts together and climbed out of the pit. He couldn't believe what had just happened. He made his way through the chambers, then scrambled up the entranceway into the bright light outside. He took some deep breaths. A small pack sat on the ground just outside the gorse bushes and frantically, he looked around in case someone else was there, already waiting for him. Again it took an age before his heart stopped racing and he could think properly. He sat down and put his head in his hands. He knew he had acted in self-defence in the cave, but the rage that had come over him truly terrified him. His hands shook. He knew if he notified the authorities, any chance of his getting the rubies from the pit would be gone forever. It took him a long time, but finally he shook off his fog of disbelief. He walked over and picked up the small pack on the ground and opened it. It had three tins of baked beans, a packet of tobacco with papers and a lighter inside, a small primus and a raincoat. He shook it out upside down and a set of keys fell from one of the pockets. He stared at the contents for a while, but there was nothing to tell him who they belonged to.

He waited for more than an hour before he could go back down the hole again. His hands shook uncontrollably as he moved through the darkness by torch light. He approached the still body. Fighting back waves of nausea, he used all his effort to pull the body over towards the pit. He simply couldn't bring himself to look at the hideous features again in the darkness, so he rolled the body over, towards the end of the pit where the two skulls had come from. He dug as deep a trench into the gravel as he could. He had to toss other bones he uncovered out of the way, then he dragged the body into the shallow trench. He scooped gravel over the top and left the chamber as soon as he'd finished. He squirmed out of the hole and took the small backpack he'd found and all its contents. He loaded it with stones and threw it into the river. He watched the pack sink swiftly to the bottom. With a feeling of disgust, he threw the bloodied spade as far into the middle as he could. The only thing he kept from the pack was the set of keys. He simply couldn't go back into the chamber again and as the night began to fall around him, he lit a fire and slowly cooked himself a meal. The dark night shrank in about him. Every sound made him jump and though he eventually drifted off to sleep that night, wild dreams of fighting black shapes leaping from the darkness and the old nightmares from the boys' home in Greymouth woke him constantly, leaving that old coppery taste in his mouth.

The next morning he summoned the courage to go back into the hole again. He clambered slowly through the dark, dripping chambers, then he stood and stared for some minutes at the slight mound at one end of the pit. Finally, he moved away to the other end and with an extreme effort, he began to dig slowly into the gravel again. He filled his bag and dragged it to the opening, stopping and listening every step of the way for strange noises. After four hours of work he felt he had enough. The cold, clammy conditions were playing tricks on his mind as shadows danced across the walls whenever he looked up from his work. He imagined bone-white faces grinning from the gloom, but whenever he shone the torch, there was nothing but cold, blank walls. His heart would race and pound in his ears at the tiniest sound behind him and finally he decided to drag his bags out into the light. He squirmed and wriggled out with his haul, pushing and pulling the bags, one by one, then he carried them down to the stream bed, where he washed and sifted the gravel. He sat there panning the dirt and pebbles, until the bags were finished. Finally, he looked down at the mound of dark beads piled in his small fabric bag. It was at least four times the size of the first haul he had managed and there were some larger pieces this time. He had even searched for the large stone that had been knocked from his hand. He'd given up after an hour of frustrating effort, feeling around in the cold pools of murky water in the far corner of the pit. There was only an hour or so of daylight left, so he made his decision and carefully packed his gear up, blocked the entranceway again and after a few minutes of checking there were no signs of his camp, he left.

He made about half a kilometre before the darkness came creeping through the trees all around him. He stopped and made a small fire near the river and cooked some stew, relieved to be away from the dark cave and the gruesome nest of bodies. He pulled the key ring from his pocket and studied the five little keys on it for the twentieth time. They still told him nothing about the figure who had attacked him. He slept fitfully that night, dark forms and ghostly-faced figures swimming in and out of his vision. Some yelled at him, some grabbed him and he attacked them all, the edge of a shiny spade singing through the air, again and again. He woke in the morning and poked his sweaty forehead out of the tent. The sight of thick, soupy clouds hanging low over the valley and the threat of rain in the air greeted him. He cooked a quick breakfast, then broke camp. The cut on his ankle had nearly healed and it was no longer swollen, but he still moved along fairly slowly, making sure of his every step. As he made his way along the river, the bag of little stones strung round his neck bounced heavily against his chest, reminding him of his responsibility to get himself and his precious haul back to Karamea. It began to rain, softly at first. He pulled his small, pocket raincoat from his pack, unrolled it and pulled it over his jacket. He continued along the river bank, heading vaguely towards the peaks of the Twins, hidden away amongst the dense clouds somewhere above him. The rain became heavy and he found the going much tougher in the cold, wet conditions. The bush around him turned into a glorious, glittering shower of mirrors, reflecting every single shade of green known to man, millions of tiny, crystal drops bringing a magical, silvery sparkle to every leaf or branch, which then unleashed a waterfall of droplets on him as he passed by. That night he stopped early and set up a small camp far below the ridgeline of the Twins. It was freezing cold even down in the lighter bush, away from the barren, windswept peaks.

He woke in the morning shivering and wet on one side, because his small tent had begun leaking down one seam. He had a coffee and three biscuits for breakfast. Then he set off in the light drizzle, slowly climbing up, then over the range. A little after 1 pm, he spotted the small suspension bridge below him in the mist. The drops of rain suddenly became larger and soon it began to pelt down furiously. He got to the bridge and slowly walked up the short track, which was turning to mud. He finally walked into the rest area just before 3 pm. He was completely soaked as he walked over to his car, then suddenly he stopped. A motorbike stood on its stand, hidden away in the bushes on the other side of the totara trees. He walked over to the bike and stared at it for a few seconds. He thought it looked like the bike that had been behind him on the road three days ago, but he wasn't sure. He slowly pulled the set of keys from his pocket in his jacket and tried them in the ignition. The third key slid into the ignition lock and turned the barrel. The ignition lights blinked on. He pulled the keys back out and looked around nervously. He realised then, it had to be the same bike that had been behind him on the Karamea road. The rider had overtaken him, but then he must have stopped somewhere to watch him. Then he must have followed him along the trail, all the way to his cave. He realised lighting his fires at night would have given his camp sites away to anyone else near him in the bush. He walked quickly over to his car. He climbed in, started the engine and drove out of the rest area. He headed down the road out of the mountains, back to Karamea. About fifteen minutes from Karamea, he made a decision. He tossed the keys out on a steep corner overlooking the river. He flung them out the window and they flew in a great arc, disappearing over the edge.

He cruised slowly into Karamea and parked the car outside Greenstone Heaven. He fingered the small bag of rubies around his neck with satisfaction. He got out and walked up the steps to the front door. He pushed on the handle, then rather slowly, he realised it was closed. A small, white sign saying 'Closed' sat on the ledge in the window. Colin peered through the glass, but it appeared there was no one at work inside. His luck was obviously out. He walked back to the car. He decided to head over to the hotel and get something hot to eat. It was nearly 4.30 pm and he figured old Garth must have closed the shop early.

He parked at the hotel and wandered into the restaurant. He ordered steak, eggs and chips and drained two beers with his meal. He had a third afterwards, contemplating whether Garth would be there early in the morning. He was about to get up and head for his flat when a tall, good-looking brunette sat down in the chair beside him.

'Hi, Colin, isn't it?'

'That's right, uh — do I know you?'

She smiled. 'It's Mandy, remember?'

Her eyes were large, hazel-coloured and mesmerising.

'You don't remember, do you? Shit, that's a bummer. I was here last week and there was a bit of a party going on in here and we had a drink then danced together a bit, then I turned around and suddenly you'd disappeared.'

He looked at her blankly, trying to remember the details of his drunken night last week.

'Oh, never mind, it shouldn't be that hard to remember, should it?'

She made to get up and leave.

'I-I'm sorry, I was really drunk that night,' he stammered. 'Terrible, I know … ah …' He managed a small smile — 'Buy you another drink?'

She paused, looking down at him with those brilliant orbs, studying him for a second.

'Oh, what the hell,' she said laughing. 'Why not?'

They talked while they sat there drinking and Colin found the conversation wide ranging, but fairly general. Mandy was very easy-going and he began to slowly relax more and more and enjoy himself. They got happily drunk together and finally left about 11 pm and he offered her a ride home.

'Sure, I'd appreciate that,' she said flashing her beautiful eyes, which had slowly become greener as he had steadily got drunker.

'What about your place, can we go there?' she suddenly asked him, just as they drove off from the pub car park.

'Ah sure, but it's only a small flat.'

'Should be warm then, with just two of us,' she giggled.

He smiled. Maybe his luck really was changing — after all.

The figures drifted in and out of his consciousness, different faces that swam closer and closer, then just as he thought he could recognise their features, the faces faded away back into the darkness again. Suddenly Brother Simon's white face leapt into view, his eyes protruding grossly from his sockets, a shovel blade embedded hideously, deep into the side of his skull.

Colin woke, shook his head to clear the pain, then instantly regretted it, as his brain began hammering back at him from inside his skull. It took him a few moments to realise where he was. He looked around in disbelief. His place was a total mess. His clothes were strewn everywhere across the floor and a bottle of wine he had opened when they got home last night lay on its side, a dribbled red stain under its neck. He felt terrible as he looked around and noticed there was no sign of Mandy. Then he realised the flat was in a worse state than normal and suddenly it hit him. He sat up quickly and reached for the small bag that was tied around his neck. No! It couldn't be ... No! The rubies were gone! He searched for the bag everywhere, making even more of a mess of the flat. Then afterwards, he sat morosely at the end of the bed with his aching head wedged between his hands. *How could I be so stupid?* he thought to himself angrily. He kicked the bottle at his feet and a thin dribble of wine ran in a line across the floor as the bottle spun away and clanked against the wall. His hands were shaking and he felt an anxiety attack coming on. He hadn't had one like this for years, not since ... He buried his face in his hands again and tried to block images of the long black frocks and the hands holding him down. The voices laughing ... He picked up the empty glass beside him and hurled it at the wall.

* * *

After he had cleaned up the flat, he sat there at the window thinking. His money from last week was almost all gone. He knew he needed to go back to the pit again, but he simply didn't want to go. The thought of the dead bodies in the pit and especially the one he had buried in the gravel made him nearly puke thinking of it. He wanted to head in any direction except back up that same road again. *Maybe I'll move to Christchurch,* he thought, *and be a burger flipper or something.* He'd always wanted to go deep-sea fishing; maybe he could try that. Whatever plan he came up with, he knew with an unsettling dread, deep in his heart, that he was heading back to the cave and down into that goddamned pit — again.

* * *

HE PARKED the car and his eyes couldn't help being drawn to the spot behind the totara trees where the motorbike had been parked. It wasn't sitting there any more, it was gone. There was only a campervan in the rest area, parked near the entranceway to the road. He wondered if he'd got it wrong about the bike. Maybe the key fitting the ignition was a coincidence. He'd heard some locks were so loose, almost any key would fit. He slung his pack over his shoulders, locked his car carefully and headed down the bush track. He walked quickly along the worn path. It meandered through majestic stands of tall nikau and giant ponga ferns. Speckled here and there were groups of tall, spindly cabbage trees poking up stubbornly through the canopy. Penny-grass and delicate moss covered the ground around the smaller trees, flanking the path, giving it a magical, fairyland-like feeling. The track followed the ridge for a few more minutes, then eventually led down the hill in winding curves to the foot of the swing bridge that stretched across the river. On the other side of the cable bridge, the path swung to the right, but he turned instead to the left, straight into thick bush. He made his way along the river bank, then after half an hour, he began to climb upwards towards the two peaks. He camped that night on a steep incline above the river, away from his previous sites. He did without a camp fire, heating his meal on the little primus, which he shielded in a hollowed-out spot beneath a fallen tree. He ate only half his meal. He kept a lookout from his vantage point, watching both up and down the river, but he saw no lights, or objects moving in the area. That night, he dreamed of finding a huge ruby, bigger than his fist, in the part of the pit where he'd found the bones and skulls. It was also the spot where he had buried the body — the man he had killed. The giant ruby shone before him in his dream, like a great lump of glowing coal, only to change somehow into a bloody face he couldn't seem to recognise. It was a twisted mess of bloodied features and it refused to go away, swinging constantly into view, but remaining out of focus.

He woke just before 5 am, his heart pumping and his breath short. It was still dark, so with the help of his torch, he got up, boiled some water for coffee, ate the other half of last night's meal, then packed his gear carefully and he left at first light. The pastel light filtered through the trees as he made his way down to the Roaring Lion River. He stayed deeper in the bush, forty or fifty metres from the edge of the burbling water. He had gone a short distance when a strange noise made him stop. The low rumbling noise grew until it was coming from the ground all around him and suddenly, everything began to shake wildly. He stumbled and fell as the violent seismic waves washed through the earth beneath him and tumbled him about, throwing him around from one side to the other as the ground twisted and jumped at him. Slowly, the rumbling and shaking decreased and with a final growl, it finished. He stood up and looked around. He saw boulders had come rolling down the steep hillsides all about him. He worried what damage the earthquake might have done to the cave ahead and he began to hurry forwards, scrambling over the jumbled boulders and rotting tree roots that had been exposed. He finally reached the area below the entranceway to the pit. He climbed up to the ledge and looked around carefully. He saw rocks had fallen down the cliff face and lay strewn around the small ledge. He pulled the pack from his shoulders, laid it down and quickly got to work pulling away the loose rocks around the entrance. He breathed a sigh of relief; the hole was still there, it seemed untouched. He retrieved his torch and the small shovel, then scrambled down the tunnel and wormed his way in. He emerged into the first chamber. He saw some large boulders above had cracked and massive triangular slabs had dropped into the first part of the grotto, mainly to one side, near the wettest wall of the chamber. They had left gaping, jagged holes in the ceiling. He shone the torch around, then made his way carefully forward, into the second part of the grotto. He saw piles of shingle and broken limestone rocks had fallen into the pit, mainly on the far side where he had dug up the skulls and hidden the dead body. Apart from the extra rubble, it seemed fairly intact. He breathed a long sigh of relief, rested the torch on the edge of the pit and jumped down into the stones.

* * *

THE WORK in the second chamber was going smoothly. He had figured out a proper method. He simply piled as much of the rough gravel on the ledge on one side of the pit as he could. It blocked his access through the chambers a bit, but he realised he'd be moving it again when he broke it down into bags, when he shifted them to the next chamber. Then he would carry the bags in relays up to the surface. It was much more work, but he'd be able to get a lot more product done in a shorter time this way. He was nearly finished the first stage of piling the gravel up on the ledge and sweat poured from his forehead, as he stood in the pit in a bright, white circle of light being thrown out by the new LED torch.

He was just about to drive his spade into the wet rocks, when a voice froze him to the spot.

'Don't move, Colin! Stay right where you are!'

He recognised the voice almost instantly.

'Mandy?' he said, the surprise obvious in his tone.

'Yes, it's Mandy, and if you value your health, turn around slowly and sit down, right where you are.'

He turned around, but he stood. He couldn't see her in the darkness. Then a torch clicked on beside her, the beam illuminating the hunting rifle with the telescopic sight, which she held steadily in her hands. The barrel was pointing straight at him.

'I told you to sit!'

Colin slowly shuffled about in the gravel, then sat down.

'That's better,' she said. 'Now, where's Garth?'

Colin was genuinely confused and shrugged his shoulders.

'Sorry?'

'Garth — you know, he followed you up here to find out where the rubies had come from.'

'Ah yes,' said Colin, sitting in the pit, 'the rubies, you definitely like those little stones, don't you?'

He couldn't see her smile, but he could hear the pleasure in her voice.

'I say you got a pretty good deal for your night of fun. Anyway, where's my goddam father, you prick. Come on, I asked you already — where the hell is Garth?'

Colin sat there, slightly stunned. The awful truth began to slowly dawn on him. Garth was obviously the biker who had followed him up the road and through the bush to see where the cave was. Garth was the figure that had come into the cave and swung the spade at him in the darkness.

Well, it was no mystery where Garth was. He was only a few metres away, lying under the slick, wet stones. Of course, he couldn't tell her that. *One mystery solved though,* he thought drily. Now he had a bigger problem. Mandy was Garth's daughter and she was standing in front of him with a loaded gun, demanding to know where her father was.

Colin tried desperately not to look at the mound in the pit to his right. He was thankful some of the fallen debris had collapsed over the raised pile of gravel.

'So, who's your friend?' he asked, pointing to the second torch.

A gruff voice spoke up.

'We're all partners and that's what you need to know. You should answer her question, which is — where the hell is Garth?'

Colin shook his head.

'I have no idea where he is. Why the hell would I know?'

There was a short silence.

'Shoot him in the leg, I don't believe a word he's saying,' hissed the voice angrily from Mandy's side.

Colin put his hands up in a vain gesture. He thought it was quite possible Mandy would shoot him, simply for the fun of it.

'Hey, hey … how would I know where Garth is? I turned up at his shop two days ago and the closed sign was in the window. I honestly have no idea where he's gone to.'

Again there was a lengthy silence.

'I don't believe him,' came the gruff voice from the darkness. Strangely, the voice seemed slightly familiar to him now.

'Shoot him in the damn leg, then he'll tell the truth.'

Colin braced himself, thinking he could leap to one side, though he knew it would be futile, when suddenly, a tremor rocked the chamber. It rumbled for ten or twelve seconds, then slowly faded away.

The voice rasped again, 'We gotta get out now, Mandy. Bugger his leg, shoot him in the head. Put him down like a damn dog, we gotta go.'

The shot suddenly rang out like a thunderclap in the small enclosed area and Colin was torn to his left. He felt a red-hot sensation in his leg and a deep guttural cry forced its way between his lips.

Mandy laughed from the darkness.

'I want to see him squirm some more.'

'Finish him off now, dammit, we gotta get out of here, right now,' spoke the gruff voice urgently.

Expecting the next shot from the darkness, Colin spun vainly to one side, just as the next tremor struck. It was much stronger and shook the chamber violently. It was as if the rock all around them was mounted on precision roller bearings, being whipped smoothly from side to side. Somewhere amongst the loud smashing and crunching of rock in the chamber, Colin heard the clatter of metal as Mandy dropped the gun. He was rolled and pitched along the gravel stones, eventually landing hard against the side of the ledge, in the bottom of the pit. He lay there, pinned amongst the murk and water at the bottom, as everything seemed to batter itself to pieces all around him. A huge crack, sounding like an explosion, shook the whole room and a giant block of limestone from the roof fell and smashed against the edge of the pit with a thunderous crash. Rocks rained down over Colin and he vainly curled up, trying to protect himself. The tremors rose in a violent crescendo, the noise inside the chamber becoming horrendous, and Colin found himself praying for the first time in years. Praying for the abomination to stop, please ... It continued, shaking the place to its core. Then suddenly, the vibrations began to fade and with a noisy rumble as a final threat, the shaking subsided into quiet, vague trembles. Colin lay there for a few seconds, then twisted out from the pile of rocks covering him, spitting dust and pieces from his mouth. His left leg ached and he'd been struck in quite a few places by the falling rocks. He could feel the warmth of his blood running down the side of his face — but he was alive. He realised he could see a small trickle of yellow light in front of him and he burrowed down into the loose rocks and water. *Thank God!* he thought, as he fished his torch from the cold muck. He was so grateful for the little device, but he was still worried about getting out as well as Mandy and her partner still in the cavern. He waited, then edged forward in the pit, listening for any noises. Thick dust billowed around him in the small cone of light from the torch as he slowly crawled forward. When he aimed it upwards from his position lying in the pit, he realised with a chilling shock that the entire cavern roof had fallen in. He was lucky he had been lying in the pit. Parts of the roof were only a metre above his head now and he couldn't stand up. He crawled along the small channel, under the ledge where the huge boulder above him lay flat against it. *The others wouldn't have stood a chance.* He was alive — but, was he buried alive? His little beam of light snaked through the thick dust in front of him. There were frightening cracks and groans coming from the rocks all around and he tried not to think how many thousands of tonnes of weight must be sitting on the boulder above his head. He crawled on through the rubble. Suddenly, he reached the end of the wall in the pit and he felt sick as his hands ran frantically around all the edges. There was no gap here, anywhere at all. He felt his heart race deep inside his chest. Check the other end, he told himself. Don't panic. Not yet anyway …, he heard a little voice way down deep inside him say. He scrambled around and began to worm his way back in the other direction. As he scrabbled along, spitting out the thick dust, he saw a flash of red amongst the darker rocks. He just couldn't help himself. He stopped and carefully dug at the gravel where he thought he saw the deep crimson glimmer. He felt something hard and immovable and he cleared stones away, then carefully shone the torch at it. A white, twisted face peered up at him and he jumped, swearing out loud. It was old Garth's head, he realised in disgust, and went to turn away, but again the sparkle of red caught his eye. He saw that sitting just below the ricked grin on the pale, distorted face was a dull gleam of red light caught in the beam. He dug frantically beneath Garth's head, which lolled backwards and forwards like it was ghoulishly laughing, and the red glow grew larger. He scrabbled at the stones beneath Garth in a frenzy and slowly revealed a large, lumpy piece of stone. It was bigger than his fist! He levered it from the wet gravel and shone the torch at it. His eyes filled with wonder as it gleamed blood-red deep inside the stone. He laughed out loud and the noise startled him. He remembered the dire trouble he was in. He stared at the dark lump in wonder for a few seconds, then thrust the rough jewel deep into his pocket and began to crawl onwards. It bounced and banged heavily against his ribs as he wormed along. There were rocks of all shapes and sizes fallen in the pit and some of them caught the light of the torch in weird ways. It looked like a seam of quartz had run through the boulder in the roof and it had shattered into thousands of pieces. The glass-like edges of the quartz segments scattered the light into wide, iridescent fans and patterns in the gloom. He kept inching forwards along the pit.

Please, please, let there be a way out, he thought desperately.

He finally reached the other end of the pit and peered forward hopefully, but thick, swirling clouds of dust stopped the torch beam reaching through. He stretched forward with his hand and felt a solid wall of rock. He panicked and felt madly around with his fingers. Was he entombed with his fantastic ruby? His heart began to thump wildly as he realised he could feel no gaps at all. Then suddenly, his hand was in space. He shone the beam into the small gap. It seemed too small for him, but he knew he would try. He had no choice.

He pushed his head and arms in, then wormed his way forward. He made a little headway, but was caught around his chest. He tried not to panic, but another tremble alarmed him and he struggled there vainly, unable to go forward or back. The large ruby caught in his clothes. The trembling stopped and he slowly breathed out as much as possible, took the large stone in his left hand, then wriggled as hard as he could. His head and shoulders were suddenly through! He squirmed his hips and legs and pushed through the gap, then shone the torch forward again. He couldn't see more than a metre into the dense, swirling dust. He edged along, feeling his way forward. It seemed to open up a little as he crawled, then the sounds of dripping water and strange echoes began to reach his ears. He shone the torch ahead … more stone, but yes, there was a gap up ahead. The stone he was crawling along was fairly flat and it disappeared invitingly into gloom ahead, beyond the swirling dust of the beam. He edged forward, turning on his back in the tight space, shining the torch up at the jagged face of rock sitting closely above him. In the middle of the rock, it had broken in a long, jagged line and there was an ugly, twisted triangle of shining quartz in the centre. It jutted out nastily, right where he needed to squeeze past. The point of the tip glinted and sparkled with a myriad of colours every time he shone the torch at it. He pushed forward, scraping across the rock on his back. His leg and head began throbbing with pain, so he stopped for a second. Suddenly, another large quake rocked the area. He tried to move forward, but the motion was too wild, so he clung there, horrified, as the boulder above him began swaying in the opposite direction to the one he was lying on. He watched in frozen terror as it swept backwards, then forwards, only half a metre above him. The jagged quartz where the seam had broken jutted down from above. There were several loud cracks, then a nasty ear-splitting screech and the boulder above dipped. A cloud of dust billowed out, blotting out the light. The jagged point he was trying to squeeze past swung wildly, brushing his chest, and he tried to flatten himself as much as possible. Another sudden crack deafened him and the whole face of the boulder above dropped with a quick jerk. Little puffs of dust and debris rained down. More strong tremors ... He shuffled the stone into his pocket again and as he did, he saw the iridescent point snake past in the gloom, just missing him. He froze in terror and hung on to the stone beneath him with all his might. The tremors increased and the rock he was on shifted. The rock above him swept sideways again, the wind of it brushing against his cheek this time and the jagged point of quartz sliced through the fabric of his jacket like a scalpel. He sucked in his chest as much as he could and tried to hold his breath. The small cavity shook and he saw the shining iridescent point swing away from him, then come knifing back again. Suddenly, the waves of motion tapered off and stopped with a huge, grating shudder. The jagged point of quartz ground to an agonising halt against his rib cage. He squirmed forward quickly, his fear giving him instant energy. The dark, dust-filled gap seemed smaller now and he could feel the rock was wedged only a few centimetres above him. He scraped forward, his heart still pounding with any small aftershock. Finally, he reached the edge of the gap. He dragged himself over the edge and collapsed on the jumble of rocks on the other side. He crawled forward, shining the torch in small circles ahead. He squirmed away from the gap, into the darkness. He felt sure he was somewhere in the first chamber. He got to his knees, then stopped to check the giant ruby in his jacket pocket. He pulled it out and it sat in the palm of his hand, still glowing that deep crimson colour in the beam of light. He could hardly believe it. It was magnificent. He placed it back into his pocket again. He was about to step forward when something stopped him. He noticed the beam of light he shone at the rock in front of his feet, through the roiling dust, disappeared in front of him. He waited for the dust to settle a bit and bent down closer. His beam shone straight down a huge hole. He could see the ceilings had not only fallen in, as he shone the torch around the first chamber in the grotto, but there was now a large, gaping black hole in the floor before him. The loud cracks he'd heard must have been the floor of the first chamber giving way in sections, as there were more holes everywhere he shone the torch. The holes seemed very deep, well beyond the light of the torch. He tossed a small rock over the edge of the hole in front of him. It was over five seconds before it hit other rocks way down below. He shone the torch along a small ledge to his right and began following it carefully. He thought it might carry him halfway across the broken chamber floor. He felt another tremble through the rock and dust poured from above. *He certainly didn't want any big shakes right now.* The ledge narrowed alarmingly. He got down onto his knees and was about to crawl forward when suddenly a hand shot from the darkness behind him and grabbed his foot. He whirled around and shone the torch behind him and in the beam he saw a bloody face that shocked him. The figure snarled with rage, then grabbed him with both arms and tried to drag him backwards. He struggled with the figure, then struck out with the torch, landing a solid blow. He felt the hands behind him let go. He shuffled back and spun the torch up again, into the face of Sergeant Ratherty. He stared incredulously into the bloody face a few feet in front of him. It took all his willpower not to move backwards, for fear of disappearing down one of the bloody great holes. It seemed strange; the man was trying to move forward to get at him, his arms snaking out, his mouth making foul snarling noises, but he seemed … stuck, or something. Colin shone the torch carefully behind the bloody face and saw in horror that the ledge had come down on the sergeant's lower body. The huge slab was covering him almost to his waist. Only his torso, head and arms protruded from the chunk of limestone that had completely crushed his legs to his hips. Unexpectedly, one of the man's flailing arms reached out and grabbed the torch in his hand and they both wrestled with it. Colin moved closer to pull the torch from the trapped man's hand, but he seemed incredibly strong. Then his other arm reached in and grabbed at the large ruby in his jacket pocket. Colin frantically grappled with his other hand. They wrestled for a few seconds, the torch in one hand and the ruby in the other, and Colin knew he needed both of them desperately. Suddenly, he realised he couldn't have both objects, but before he made a decision, something inside him relaxed and he simply dropped the torch. Ratherty fumbled with it and Colin saw it bounce away, then tumble into the darkness and disappear, its beam spiralling away into the gloom. A few seconds later the light disappeared and he heard the crash as it landed at the bottom of the hole. He fought madly for the ruby with both hands in the pitch black now, sheer anger driving him on in a fit, and in one great twist, he managed to wrench the stone from the man in the darkness. He moved back only half a step, breathing heavily.

'You little bastard!' cried the voice from the darkness in front of him.

Colin felt carefully backwards with his foot in the pitch black, making sure he didn't follow the torch straight down the deep hole.

'So what are you doing here, Sergeant Ratherty?' he asked, picturing the poor man just in front of him, with his legs crushed by the huge boulder.

There was a nasty laugh from the darkness, then a long silence.

'So it was you there, partners with Garth and Mandy, eh? Prepared to kill me and take the rubies for yourselves? Not normal police work, is it, sergeant?'

There was no answer at all from the blackness. Colin put the ruby back in his pocket. He felt the edge of the large hole near his feet, so he knelt down slowly and ran his fingers around the rocks.

'So, how's my case against Brother Simon and the boys' home coming along? I haven't heard anything about that for quite a while.'

There was a snarl from the darkness, then the rasping voice seemed to fill the whole cavern.

'You deserved everything you got. Brother Simon told me you were gay and seduced other boys, that was the real story, wasn't it, Colin?'

Colin fought back his anger and kept creeping very gently away from the voice, further out onto the thin ledges of rock in the darkness.

'You were just a little faggot, weren't you?' came the rasp from the pitch black.

'Brother Simon was a true man of God, a priest, and you were a dirty little homo just asking for it. A pervert! You know you don't deserve those rubies. We all agreed about that. Garth said you didn't know what you were doing up here in the bush, but somehow you'd found the cave with rubies. An old legend hardly anyone knows about.'

There was another small silence as Colin crept backwards.

'Garth's been looking for this place his whole life.'

Colin kept feeling around in the dark. His fingers scraped against a small ledge and he shuffled along it, balancing precariously.

A long cry suddenly issued from the dark.

'Oh God, please help me, don't leave me here … not like this.'

He nearly stopped, but something the sergeant had said hardened his resolve halfway across the ragged little ledge he was clinging to.

'God? You want help in God's name? Go ahead, go on, you ask him. See if he bloody listens to you. I bet you he won't. He never listened to me, you selfish arsehole. He never listened when I needed help, so talk to him all you want, see if he answers your special prayers right now, when you really need him.'

There was a whimper from the darkness and silence as Colin turned, feeling with his hands in front of him.

'You don't deserve that ruby, not a disgusting creature like you. You'll never deserve it!'

A sharp crack sounded beside Colin and rattled away in the dark. Ratherty had thrown a rock at him. He shuddered at the thought of it hitting him and toppling him into one of the dark holes. He tried to remember the layout of the floor, when he had shone the torch around the chamber, as he inched forward again.

'Please, please, don't leave me here to die!'

Colin inched forward, then stopped, his hands feeling air in front of him. He thought he must be halfway across the chamber by now.

Another long aftershock trembled through the cave and he held his breath and hung on desperately, swaying and balancing on the tiny ledge in the dark. It finally stopped and Colin breathed out.

'Arsehole!' came another cry from the dark.

It made Colin mad.

'By the way, your mate Garth, do you really want to know where he is?' he asked sarcastically.

He finally reached a solid spot where he could feel rock around him.

'He's not very far from you actually, in lots of ways. He's lying down there, quite near. I buried him in the pit. At least you'll have someone you can talk to — pretty soon ...'

He heard Ratherty swear at him and another crack sounded off to his left as a rock struck close to him and bounced away into the blackness.

'I put the spade right through the side of that nasty old head of his. I'm glad I did it now, it's what he deserved really, although I'd say there's going to be a much longer wait here in the darkness for you, isn't there, sergeant?'

A long whimper sounded from across the chamber.

Colin shifted slightly; he realised there was a great yawning hole just below him to his right. His left side ached and burned ominously. He continued searching with his fingers.

'The real funny thing is — the place where I buried him in the pit was a very special spot. Right underneath him was this great big ruby. Sitting right beside his head.'

Something made him stop for a second in the darkness. He'd heard this somewhere before. Betelgeuse — the shining red star. *It was located at Orion's shoulder,* he thought. It was even mentioned in the old letter. How strange was that ...?

'You'll never get to enjoy it,' the voice rasped nastily. 'Yours is coming, Davies. We've got our eye on you in town. You won't last long, not if you ever get out of here ...'

Colin shifted forward in the dark, feeling the cold, solid

stone around him, but there was nothing to his right, or now his left. He had crawled out onto a dead end, a pinnacle of rock surrounded by nothing. He would have to make his way back, back towards … He stopped, balancing there on the tiny ledge. He knew he couldn't go back, but there was simply no way forward.

A rock suddenly bounced off something beside him, the blow landing so close, tiny fragments of stone sprayed into his face, blinding his eyes and stinging his cheek. He hung on grimly with all his strength. If he slipped or fell, it would be straight down one of these gaping holes in the darkness … Another stone struck the rocks near him and bounced off into the darkness, then clattered to a stop somewhere on his left, ahead of him. He instantly wondered …

He knew the stone had landed on something solid, ahead and slightly to his left. Could he risk it? Could he jump across the gap — in the darkness? The thought of what might happen made him feel sick to the bottom of his stomach. *What should I do?* he wondered. He couldn't go forward or back now. Another trembling motion rolled through the chamber and he heard a whimper from the darkness across the room. Quickly, he decided. He gauged the position of the noise that had come to him in the darkness from the clatter of the stone, held his breath, then he jumped.

There was a long feeling of weightlessness as his heart hammered in his chest and thoughts raced through his head. Just as he feared he'd misjudged and was bound to hurtle to his death, he crashed into cold, hard rock, knocking the wind from him. He was dazed. He shook his head slowly and sat up. His elbow had taken a sharp crack, he'd banged his head and he felt bruised down the whole side of his body, but — he was across! An aftershock trembled for a few seconds, then slowed and finally stopped. He winced as he shuffled forward, the pain in his arm nearly making him cry out.

Suddenly, he touched a cold rock face right in front of him with his hands. He stopped and at the very same time, he felt a slight breeze on his cheek. Was this finally the chamber's wall? Was the entrance still here somewhere, still unblocked? He wondered, hoping with all his heart it might be true.

The ragged voice from the darkness started again, but it had a frantic, hysterical edge to it now.

'They're gonna get you, you little bastard, I promise you. You'll have to beg them to end it! They love to get little homos like you. Do you hear me? They'll play with you like a little girl! You'll be begging for the end when they get you, you useless little prick, Davies!'

He felt carefully along the wet, dripping wall. He felt the breeze stiffen slightly as he moved to his left. He shifted sideways, following the cold air, then he felt a small space where his left hand was. He shuffled a bit to the left, then stood very slowly, his head and shoulders entering the large gap. He could feel cold air streaming past his face. He pushed himself into the gap and began to scrabble painfully upwards as the rasping voice screamed out at him one last time.

'You dirty little bastard, you won't escape, they're gonna find you! They're gonna get you — you hear, Davies? They'll get you, you little baaastaaard …!'

Colin saw light ahead of him and he wormed forwards using all his energy as the high-pitched wail began to fade behind him. Finally, his head burst into open air and the bright light seemed blinding. He scrambled exhaustedly out of the hole, breathing heavily, sucking in the fresh, clean air. He forced himself to look down at his aching leg. His clothes were all covered in dirt, but a large, dark stain ran down one side of his trousers, from his hip to his foot. He undid his belt and checked his thigh. A dark red hole sat just below his hip bone, oozing thick blood that ran stickily down his leg. He twisted his head and saw another small hole at the back of his leg, also weeping blood. At least the bullet had gone right through.

A flesh wound, he told himself sternly.

He took a T-shirt from his pack and tore it into strips. He bound his leg as tightly as he could, then wrapped the rest of the T-shirt around it. A sharp spike of pain knifed through his side as he dragged his pack up and over his shoulders, then he slowly climbed down from the ledge and set off. He followed the river, trying to figure out what time of the day it was. The sun was almost behind the Twins. He had no idea how long he had been in the grotto, but it must have been many hours. He found it tough going, especially getting over the large boulders, as he struggled along the river bank. His left leg began to get stiff and very sore. He loosened the makeshift bandage off a little and kept moving. Halfway across a small stream, he tripped and fell heavily amongst the rocks in the shallow ice-cold water. He tried to stand up again, but his leg wouldn't work properly and the freezing water seemed to suck his energy from him. He lay there as the flowing stream moved and dragged him a little further. He let it carry him a few metres, but then the thought of the river made him panic. He stopped himself and tried to stand and his hands scrabbled at the bank. He fell, landing in a deeper section. Suddenly, it pushed him into a quicker section of the flow and he tumbled into some faster water near the mouth of the stream. The swiftly flowing stream entered the larger river itself. He heard a muted roar off in the distance and he remembered the great waterfall of the Roaring Lion River. He had seen it from a distance. It was a rock-strewn, sheer drop of over twenty metres. The fast-flowing water poured straight over an enormous granite ledge and fell into the river below. He'd seen the white spume from its thundering base rising high into the mountain air. A great rumbling noise steadily began to fill his ears.

He slammed against a large rock and took a mouthful of freezing water. He frantically tried to grab the slimy boulder, but it just slipped past him in the icy, cold flow. The current was strong and flowing fast now and it tumbled him over and around a couple of boulders as he neared the rushing edge. The roar increased, reached a great crescendo and suddenly, he felt completely weightless for a few achingly long seconds. With a crash that knocked him senseless, he was crushed through the frigid water at the bottom and pinned against the huge granite boulders right at the bottom of the fall. His consciousness slowly began to slip away as he was pounded mercilessly by the turbulence. He spun around and around, caught in a cycle by the tremendous flow of tonnes of water crashing from above. Like a cat playing with a mouse, there was no escape from the mighty river as it pinned him down with a great cold paw, spinning him round slowly in the hole, deep at the bottom of the falls. He never felt the large, red ruby slide from his jacket pocket into the icy water. It bounced slowly along the bottom, then rolled away, the crimson glimmer spinning on, whirling and tumbling through the endless waters of the Roaring Lion River.

* * *

In the back room of the church bookshop, the large box sat on the table, ready to be unpacked and sorted with the others. Simon pulled open the cardboard flaps and began pulling out books, stacking them in basic piles on the table. A large, dark covered book fell from a stack and landed awkwardly on the table. The pages splayed open and two pieces of paper slid across the table and fluttered gently to the floor. He knelt down and picked them up. One of the documents was an old letter. He opened it and stood there reading it slowly, vaguely interested. As he took in the old handwriting and its contents, his eyes began devouring the words that were scrawled across the battered old paper. He finished reading it and placed it down on the table carefully, his face impassive, but his eyes sparkled with genuine excitement. He unfolded the creased square of paper and studied the hand-drawn map with its marks and little squiggles. It seemed very old. He picked up the book from the table. It was a nice-looking leather Bible. He opened the cover. Written in small, backward-slanted letters at the top of the front page, it read:

Colin Davies,
47 Granity Creek Rd,
Granity,
West Coast.

He instantly recognised the handwriting of a left-hander, just like himself. He stuffed the two documents quickly into his pocket, and put the Bible in the good stack as Catherine walked in and placed another heavy box of books down with a thump.

'Anything interesting in that one?' she asked, wiping a stray lock from her face.

'No, nothing worthwhile at all in that box,' he said.

WAY OUT

THE GREY DUSTY ROAD TWISTED AND TURNED. IT SEEMED TO wind on forever through the thick bush. Glorious picturesque views opened out onto farmland stretching to the hills, then disappeared again as we descended the Waitakere Ranges towards the west coast beach. Finally, some brief glimpses of a turquoise sea emerged and began to beckon to us through gaps in the foliage. The road dropped so steeply, some inclines felt like being on a roller-coaster ride. As we got closer, the grey, purply-green fingers of dust-covered bush seemed to creep out from the fringes of the gravel road, brushing the car as we flew past. We crossed two small streams and suddenly the sharp, salty smell of the sea filled the car.

We had managed to get everyone into two cars. There'd be nine of us to camp the night out at the heads, past Huia. There were three guys — me, Mike, Dave and two of the girls, Danielle and Melanie, all piled into Dave's old Falcon wagon. The two couples, Eric and Janine and Steve and Amanda, were riding in Amanda's little Toyota. They'd stopped at the shops and were half an hour behind us.

We left the car in the little, sandy car park and began to walk. The bush petered out and soon we were trudging through sand dunes in the hot afternoon sun. Finally, we reached the black, purplish streaked sands of the Manukau Heads and looking across that constantly shifting, curling sea, we knew we'd left the city far behind. We were gonna have a great trip.

When I say trip, by the way, I mean LSD. We were obviously young and enthusiastic and in hindsight you could swap those words for 'desperate and foolish', though in our own minds, we were just searching for fun. Experience was a word we had no great understanding of back then. Experience made you old, and who would want that? With nothing really to fear in our own little worlds, we took a lot of risks without really thinking about it in those days.

The others had finally caught up with us and as we stood there on the beach talking and watching each other nervously, I remember looking down at the tiny square of coloured cardboard in my hand and being a little afraid of it. Of course, I wouldn't have admitted it to anybody else. The tiny little square had a miniature purple strawberry, with green bits at the top, printed on one side. You probably know all those stories of bad trips with LSD and people jumping off buildings, or going mad, but here there were no buildings and most of us were already a bit crazy and I reasoned it couldn't hurt me any more than a twisted knee or maybe a hangover would. I put it carefully in my mouth at the same time as everyone else and slowly chewed it until the sour taste was all that was left. They sometimes take a while to come on, so we drank a few beers and ran around in the soft sand amongst the bulrushes and flax bushes and those little plastic netting fences they put in to stop erosion. We burnt up a bit of energy pretty much just for the hell of it really. It was quite tiring running around in the sand, but we were full of nervous energy, knowing what was coming our way and you know — it's exactly like they say — once you've taken it, hey, you can't get off the bus.

* * *

It was about five-ish and still quite light when I first noticed things changing. It was weird; the colours seemed to merge together a bit and the faster you ran, the less you seemed able to focus on things. Small things appeared highly interesting in bizarre ways, like a piece of grass, or a shell, or a stick of driftwood that looked like a dragon and even big things would catch your eye. The subtle intricacy of nature mixed with LSD is pretty mind-blowing, to me anyway. Just lying there on your back in the sand, watching cotton wool clouds floating by in a great dome of blue sky, felt truly awesome. I remember Janine, who is pretty, with long brown hair and a great body, lying down beside me at one stage, which can always make me a little nervous, and she was telling me what the cloud shapes meant to her. I saw quite a few weird things in those clouds, but I truly couldn't see any of the things that she saw. Not a single thing … I remember one of the guys, it was definitely Eric, with his long, slightly reddish hair, draping a piece of old green plastic around his shoulders and standing at the edge of the water, the wind blowing the plastic out behind him like he was flying and pulling all these poses, which made all of us laugh hysterically. Strange things like that seem to stick in my mind. My face and cheeks ached for a while, because we laughed so hard for so long. Then, just when we got really thirsty, the beer was all gone. Dave and Eric had gone off together and got stuck talking. They had polished it all off. Danielle, who had been in the back with me, her little frame wedged tightly between me and Mike, had some pot in her bag and she'd already rolled a few joints up. She came up to me while we were arguing over who had drunk all the beer, quietly lit up a smoke and the next thing I knew we were somewhere else, doing something else and I couldn't remember what had actually happened in the meantime. My face felt really red for a while, I remember that. Then, Danielle suggested we should all search for firewood to have a fire and we all agreed. So we got stuck in, wandering round the beach, gathering a bloody great pile of driftwood, and just before the sun sank into the darkening, blue sea, we lit the fire and stood around, warming our hands.

I think it was while we were gathering up firewood that someone discovered the caves. I don't remember who it was. We all ran into the large entrance, then we found the smaller cave off the first one and explored this one to its end, which was split at the back into two pieces. One of the drifts went back to a flat wall and the other one tapered into a thin, narrowing shaft, then petered out with a sharp, jagged spine in the rock cleft right at the end. The jagged spine climbed straight upwards to the roof above us. It was only about a couple of metres up and we could touch it with our hands — well, some of us could. The first section of the cave was a big, round-shaped space with nothing in it except seaweed and rotten driftwood piled up the back. I'm sure we didn't see the little tunnel down by the floor then, not that I was aware of, anyway. There didn't seem to be very much to do in the main cave, with just the dark sand and its fairly smooth, glistening rock walls, so we ventured out again and ended up back at the fire. One of the girls brought out a wine cask and we quickly got stuck into that.

The last really good thing I remember was laughing at one of Steve's stupid jokes. He's the youngest of us, but his silly jokes are legendary. They go on for absolutely ages and when you think you can't take any more, he keeps on going until you finally just give in and listen to him. His biggish nose, square chin and jet-black hair seem slightly at odds with his bright blue eyes, but he sure tells a mean joke.

The fire was still burning when someone suggested we walk down to the water. By this time we were really starting to trip and everything was a bit of a chore, from talking properly to walking properly, but we were all happy. There was a bit of moonlight guiding us and when we reached the water, we looked out into the dark night, watching a great silvery sea monstering and raging through the heads. It looked formidable. It is the west coast, after all. We could see ugly-looking back currents and big, curved holes as the tide and waves came pumping in. Mike suggested we go for a swim, but most of us were wise enough to say no one should swim there. I'm sure it was Mike's bravado that was talking.

It was on the way back, heading for the fire again, that someone suggested we go to the caves. It might have been Melanie, who is the quiet one, but I honestly can't remember. I'm sure it was one of the girls, anyway. I remember walking there clumsily through the sand drifts because the moon had hidden itself again. Then we were there, stumbling into the first roundish cave in the pitch dark and someone was laughing and I couldn't believe how loud it echoed in the hollowed-out space. We were there for quite a while, when suddenly there was a scream that seemed to cut off the air in my lungs.

Now when I say a scream — I mean … a real scream. It was one of the girls, but I had no idea which one. Then there was a long moaning sound, so I crawled forward in the darkness and sure enough one of the girls was lying on her side in the sand. When I put my hand to her face, it was all warm and sticky. I couldn't see a single thing it was so dark. She was mumbling something, then she said four words quite clearly.

'There's something just outside.'

Then she collapsed, right in my arms, and I had no idea what to do next. My head was spinning pretty fast with everything and I think I froze for quite a few seconds. Then I half carried, half dragged her over to the back of the cave. As I bumped into the others in the dark, one of them screamed in my ear in sheer terror. The next thing I remember there were five or six of us crammed together at the back of the cave and someone was saying it was Melanie that was hurt and she was bleeding badly. When the commotion died down enough for us to work out what was happening, we did a quick head count. It was Melanie after all. Two of us were missing, because there were seven of us at the back of the cave. Steve and Dave were out there, somewhere. Then, another loud scream came from right at the entrance to the cave. We were all huddled together and it was dark and although I thought I couldn't see anything at all, some of us saw a large dark shape run suddenly across the front of the cave. It was big and it ran with a lopsided galloping motion on four legs. The girls screamed madly and I must admit I wanted to, but my heart was actually in my mouth somewhere, blocking it from working. The girls were crying and hanging on to each other and quite frankly, I felt like joining them. Then I heard a deep guttural sound, like something grunting, that I swear I have never heard before, coming from the entrance, then a horrific sound, just like bones snapping and another very long scream. The girls took off into the second part of the cave, carrying Melanie. Eric, Mike and I were left in the main cave. We had an urgent discussion. Eric and I decided to investigate and Mike snuck quietly after the girls. We both crawled forward down one wall of the cave to the entrance and there seemed to be no sound now except the wind and the distant thump of waves on the shoreline. When we finally got outside the entrance we saw there was a small slice of moon hazing through some light clouds and it looked like there was nothing at all outside the cave. We both stood up and searched all around the entranceway. There was a lot of sand kicked up, with a large, jagged line in the sand, running away and disappearing into the night towards the water. It looked as though something heavy had been dragged through the soft black sand. At the beginning of all the marks was a round, dark area and when I put my hand into it, it was sticky and warm to the touch. In the bad light I couldn't see colour, but I instantly felt sick from the rich, metallic smell there. I knew deep down it must be blood. I saw some lights going off all over the place and I thought at first someone must have been letting off fireworks or something, but when I closed my eyes, they were even brighter and more colourful, so I knew it was just the acid inside my head. I turned and looked at Eric, whom I had known for five or six years, and was shocked to see he had teeth like thin, little knives inside a large grinning mouth. They were dripping blood and his eyes shone red, like a cat's eyes in the dark. His face looked all distorted and he was grinning like a demon at me.

Honestly, the next thing I remember, I was lying in the sand and it was dark and I was all alone. Eric was gone. The wind was whipping around me like a mini storm, but the moon had shifted in the sky and it was lighting up the area down by the shoreline. I could see big white, iridescent waves flashing in the dark down there and I could hear the rumble through the sand at my feet as they crashed hard against the beach. I stumbled towards the moonlit scene in a strange kind of trance, wondering where the hell everyone was. I half expected them to come running out of the darkness from all around me, yelling 'Surprise!' As windswept and lonely as that place already is, standing there at night right then, it felt terrible, like I could have been all alone on a lifeless moon, on some distant planet.

I moved forward and I could swear there were shapes that moved with me just on the edge of my vision, but every time I turned to look, they simply merged into the shadows and disappeared. I got down near the beach and in the half-light I saw something that made my heart leap in my chest and thump against my rib cage. Down there in the soft, greying moonlight with the white surf dancing in the background was a great, dark creature and it was lunging up and down, grunting and growling like some kind of movie monster. I got quite close. I was looking, staring in a kind of disbelief, thinking it was my mind playing a trick on me, when it turned and looked straight at me. Its eyes locked onto mine and I froze and then I slowly lowered myself to the sand, hoping I was out of sight in the darkness. I was absolutely terrified. When I could bear to look up and over the little sand drift that I was hiding behind, the creature was gone, but there was something else lying there in the sand, not far from the silvery edge of the water. I crept forward, checking left and right, seeing nothing but leaping shadows in the night. I was sure they were my own imagination, but I decided to sprint down to whatever it was lying there in the sand, just in case. I ran, my lungs trying to get oxygen, because it seemed the air was thick and hard to breathe. When I got closer I began to worry because I thought it would disappear or turn into a piece of driftwood or something, but I could tell it was a human body. I crept up to it, bending low, hoping I wasn't being watched, then stopped at its feet, which were wearing a pair of Doc Martens boots, just like Steve's ones. It was Steve and he was all torn up terribly and when I touched his neck, he was still warm, but I knew he couldn't have been alive. His face was ripped up on one side horribly, right to the neck, but the worst of it was done to his torso and stomach. They were open to the wind and night, intestines and organs splayed out and covering the sand all around his body. I remember being sick beside him and then my legs wouldn't move as I heard another terrible scream in the black night from somewhere way off to my left, carried down to me by the wind. I checked Steve's neck again on the right-hand side; it was the only part of him that was untouched really, but he felt colder now and there was no sign of life at all. My heart began thumping wildly and I knew this part couldn't be a dream. I decided to head back to the fire we had lit and I bent over underneath the sandy ridge line and half ran, half collapsed, my legs stumbling along through the thick sand, back towards the bonfire. It was where I'd heard the other scream come from. It was definitely a human scream. It was low pitched and didn't sound female to me, but it sounded truly bloodcurdling in the dark, windy night. Bushes whipped my face, and my legs felt like lumps of concrete and I had to will them to work properly. When I reached our little campsite, I nearly stumbled over the dead and useless fire. Again, as I stood there I felt like somebody was watching, but every time I turned, there was no one there. I wanted to abandon our little adventure at the beach now and try to get help or, to tell the truth, to save myself and make a break for the cars, but I knew I couldn't abandon the girls. My last memory of them was back in the cave. It was the hardest thing I think I've ever done, but I turned back and headed for the cave. Every terrifying step seemed to ask all my energy as I staggered through the heavy dunes. I only just saw the rocky walls at the last second when I nearly stumbled straight into them in the dark and I had to work hard to get my bearings for a while. Finally, I recognised a spur coming out of the rock and I knew the cave was a little further to my right. As I approached it I heard a long, low moan come from inside, as though the cave had turned into some strange animal, and I admit I was deeply afraid of going in there. Right at that point, I'm sure I heard an engine somewhere off in the darkness, as I hesitated there, just outside the cave. It sounded like a fishing boat to me, or maybe someone going through the heads, because a few seconds later, the noise was gone again. Inside the cave was just like the blackest of all nights, so I crawled in, slithering along the floor by the right-hand wall, like a snake wriggling along in the dark. I came to the end of the main cavern where the seaweed and rotting driftwood was and I stopped there. There was no sound I could hear apart from a distant, soft booming sound of the surf in the night or maybe it was my own heart thumping in my chest. I felt my way slowly round to the right and found the gap leading to the other part of the cave. I banged my head and scraped my knuckles in the darkness. My fear was driving me on and also yelling at me to stop and run away. I searched on my hands and knees and finally at the back of the next grotto, I bumped into something soft and heavy on the sandy floor. I felt carefully — it was one of the girls, I was quite sure, but I had no idea which one. The whole upper body was covered in a heavy, gooey mess. I recognised the same smell as before and I was sick again, dry retching into the sand in the dark. A deep primal moan suddenly issued from the other little channel. It sent all my nerves jangling and I had to force myself to move forward and find the opening into the last, tiny grotto in the rock. Once again I had to feel my way around by bashing my fingers and my head to find the way in the blackness. Again the strange moan issued from somewhere in front of me. It was softer now, almost pleading. I crawled forward, the tension inside me going past all known places I'd ever been. I suddenly touched a leg in the darkness and stopped. I could feel the shape of a shoe and then a knee and then nothing more, just a wet stump. It was too much for me. There was a shifting sound in the darkness right before me and all my nerves screamed at me to get out of there. My breathing stopped and I physically had to count it in and out again for a few long seconds. Another moan came, right in front of me again, so I pushed on carefully, my heart waiting for terror to find me in the darkness. Then I bumped into something that moved slightly when I hit it. I felt around carefully for a few seconds and realised what I had nudged into. It was a pile of bodies, lifeless, heavy, stacked or jumbled one on top of the other, like some gruesome puzzle of death. This time I couldn't breathe and my mind simply left my head and raced off into the night somewhere as I reeled to make sense of everything that was happening. Then I heard the tiniest sound; it was the softest moan of the lot, like a very small whimper and it seemed to come from somewhere below me. My mind returned somehow and I felt forward through the horrific pile of twisted legs, arms, heads and torsos. As I touched something deep underneath that cold pile of tangled limbs, a wailing, piercing shriek of 'Noooooo…' erupted in the darkness and I felt the pile move and someone tried to shift away from me. At the very same time, I heard a bloodcurdling growl so deep, it put all the hairs up on me from one end of my body to the other. It came from right behind me in the darkness. The sound made me aware of its presence in a primeval way, that even now I cannot understand. I heard a shuffling noise, so I moved as silently as I could away from it, feeling for the cave walls. As I did so, I heard the soft scratching of something else moving to my right and I knew instantly that it was whatever, or whoever, I had touched in the darkness. I also knew whoever it was, was going the wrong way. Before I could do anything at all, there was a loud, bloodcurdling scream. Again it sounded like one of the girls, but there were shrieks and crunches and smacking noises I shall never, ever forget, as long as I live. I moved slowly and deliberately away to my left, even though I knew it was a dead end, my mind screaming along with the ear-splitting screams that were coming from right beside me. As I gradually felt my way around the wall, my hands moved into a little gap between the rock and the sand, a small cleft we hadn't found or noticed when we first wandered through the caves. It opened up a little as I felt further and in some sort of deep primal instinct, my head and shoulders edged into it and I crept and slid under that little edge of rock like a coward, deep into the tiny crevice between the wall and the sandy floor. It seemed to me like a tiny, little tunnel leading under the rock walls. The screaming suddenly stopped abruptly, in mid-scream, leaving just some wet smacking and crunching sounds that made my body shake uncontrollably in the tiny little, cramped space I was jammed in. The narrow rock roof had come down steadily, trapping my ribcage and giving me no chance even to breathe. My hands began to claw at the sand and before I knew what they were doing, I realised I had cleared a smaller, even tighter little space a tiny bit further into the crevice. I somehow edged in, the rock walls above me now pushing down on top of me like a giant metal vice. All the noises from across the little cave had stopped and I finally stopped too and froze, my mind screaming for this madness to stop. Then, my heart jumped as small noises started again, slowly moving closer. I dug at the soft sand, peeling away a fraction more space and wedged in further under the rock that was pushing heavily down on top of me, stopping my chest from filling, suffocating me. I don't know how far I had reached, but now my face was pushed into the thick sand and my mouth was full of dry, tiny grit as I vainly pushed myself harder into the narrow, dark cleft that simply went nowhere at all. There was no way out. My body was trapped by the rocks above me and the dense sand below me and now I could not fill my lungs at all. I wanted to keep going on but I knew now that I would suffocate in here … and die. My mind raced with thoughts, uncontrollable memories from my youth, flooded with pieces of scenes from tonight, faces rushing by. The girls laughed and screamed, my parents called me, I even cried inside my mind, sorry to my family, for not living a longer, better life. I could not bear the black engulfing tension much longer as my chest beat wildly; the great mass of rock above and the dense, just as solid sand below, wouldn't let my heart beat properly in its tiny, little cage. That's when I realised, this was finally it …

Then suddenly, my leg was grabbed in a vice-like grip and with extreme force and brutality, I was ripped out of my crawl space. There was an almighty roaring sound in my ears and something incredibly heavy came down and tore my leg completely off from the knee down with a disgustingly loud crack. Then, I remember no more …

* * *

WHEN I FINALLY CAME ROUND, I was sitting in a plastic-seated chair in a white-walled room with no windows. My hands were shackled behind me. A large-bodied, square-faced man with angry, tired eyes was staring at me across a small square table that was between us, with the kind of look a stone wall might return. I realised there was another man in the room. He was leaning against the wall, fiddling nonchalantly with one of his fingernails. Both men were dressed similarly, with rumpled whitish shirts and their sleeves rolled up, and the one leaning against the wall thrust his hands into the pockets of his long, dark pants and cleared his throat with a small cough. No one spoke still and they both just watched me, their eyes never leaving mine. Finally, the man leaning against the wall said something and the words hit me like a hammer.

'So, Jeremy, why did you kill your friends?'

The simple, direct nature of the question smashed me in the stomach like a boxer's title-winning body shot and I literally gagged for breath and could not speak. With the most effort I could summon, I stammered out a 'W-w-what?' as I sat there completely stunned.

I looked down, towards the floor. Incredulously, I saw two legs properly attached to the rest of my body, both shackled to the metal legs of the chair. The men still looked at me completely stone-faced, like there was a million years between us and no connection whatsoever.

I stammered out like a child, 'W-w-what do you mean?'

The man across the table didn't flinch one iota; his eyes were like a pair of old grey flints that had started far too many fires.

'It's simple,' he said slowly, and repeated the same question.

My eyes flicked around the room, desperate for some sort of recognition, and the awful dawning of reality began to bite home with a sickening crunch.

He sighed; his large, chunky forearms dragged across the table and his fleshy hands pushed down against the table top as he rose to his feet.

'Bloody waste of time, Steve,' he simply said and the other man nodded, then the two detectives left the room without another word, the door closing behind them with a bang.

I remembered thinking then, what the hell *had* happened? Did I kill all my friends? To my utter despair, looking down at my two legs, I realised, I simply didn't know.

* * *

The journalist switched off his small recorder lying alone on the prison table between us. His black-rimmed, clear glasses made his eyes look slightly larger. Those sharp brown eyes were like scalpels though, as they searched my face for signs of truth, or falsity.

'So you didn't lose your leg, Jeremy,' he said, almost casually.

I shook my head.

'No,' I said, the frustration clear in my voice. 'I don't understand it myself, but that's what I remember,' I finished defiantly, but I was thinking how lame it sounded.

'And the bodies,' he said, 'the five in the caves and the other one washed up on the beach down at Port Waikato, you didn't …,' he hesitated just slightly, 'you didn't have anything to do with any of those.'

I shook my head.

'Apart from everything I've told you, which is all I can remember, no.'

'You're sure?' he asked, his face a mask of calmness and serenity, but his eyes searched mine again for … something.

'The truth is, John,' I said, looking directly into his unblinking eyes, 'I really don't know. The acid we took, the darkness, the drinking, the drugs, it all felt like a bad dream at the time. Now it's my own personal nightmare and it haunts me every single day, especially when I'm alone.'

'The two bodies that were never found, uh, Mike Gallen and Eric Hardy, what do you think happened to them? Do you think they were involved, or maybe they were washed away by the tide?' he suggested.

The surnames of my friends hit me hard again, as once more I was reminded of their families.

'I have no idea,' I said. 'Eric was a longtime friend, from school, he was pretty close. Mike was in a band we used to go and watch. He was a pretty quiet guy, but he always seemed the life of the party to me.'

Those eyes studied me for a long while and so we both just sat there. The sun was pushing a small slant of light in a long thin triangle from a high window and I watched the dust particles swirl around and up and then fall again, inside the light.

'The animals you described, any idea what they were?'

I slowly shook my head.

'They seemed big,' I said, 'but you couldn't see enough to know anything other than a basic shape in the darkness.'

He looked at me for a while and scratched his face, his fingernails and the short stubble making a sound like sandpaper in the small room where he'd met me three times. The meeting room where the yellow paint slowly peeled and the dust swirled around and around and nothing ever happened, or would happen for years, or it may as well be centuries, or even millennia, as far as my life was concerned.

'Okay, mate,' he said, and I knew that it was over.

'You realise this is my last call.'

I nodded slowly. I knew. Another dead end. Another futile search for vanished memories, only to find ashes where things had once stood. This room was really just another place exactly like the little hole that I had crawled into, between the sand and the rock in the far back wall of the little cave. There was no way out of here either. He left after shaking my hand, wishing me well and I just sat there, waiting for the guard, waiting for the inevitable nothingness that my life had become. I heard the slamming of doors moving slowly through the old building as he left.

* * *

John Taylor, reporter for the *Tribute* and independent journalist, picked up the day's paper. He'd heard about a story, just a small one that had pricked his ears and, he had to admit, also his conscience. About the seventh page he finally found it. It was a small article consisting of just seventeen words, underneath an advertisement for Jack's Outdoor Furniture. It read:

> A prisoner, Jeremy Charles Hastings, was killed in a fight in Paremoremo Prison's notorious A wing yesterday.

There were no other details. No follow-up article, and he knew there wouldn't be. He closed the paper and went back to the piece he was working on.

* * *

THE THOUGHT HAD GROWN in his mind steadily and it had finally developed into a decision. It had been a long drive out here to the coast, but the scenery was truly spectacular.

He switched off the car's ignition in the sandy car park and wondered if the effort was really going to be worthwhile and whether he shouldn't just turn around and head back into the city, back to the office. It was a long drive for pretty much nothing otherwise, he told himself, so he opened the door and slowly stood up, straightening his back. He stood there for a second, staring out at the rolling, dark-coloured sand hills and the great blue dome of a sky stretching out above him.

The walk was a long one, but the day was warm and the turquoise sea to his left kept him company and finally he was there. He had found the cave without too much trouble and he wandered through, examining it and its two small companions. It seemed just like Jeremy had described, maybe a touch smaller than he had imagined. He walked out and the bright sunlight flooding through his glasses struck at his sensitive eyes and made him shield them with his hand. He wandered off to the right, the strong smell of the sea drawing him on, and just over a small rise in the dunes, it came into sight. He went all the way down to the water's edge and watched the waves as they caressed the shore in their random, timeless motion. It was hypnotic out here with not a soul around, just a few seabirds wheeling high in the sky. A slight clanking noise caught his attention, off to his right. Way down the beach, nearly a kilometre away, he could see a machine working earnestly in the dunes. It was a lone symbol of man in the vast, natural landscape. He hesitated and checked his watch. Two more hours to kill, he thought to himself — why not?

After twenty minutes of walking through the soft sand, his footsteps leaving a long, spotted, meandering trail behind him and the sweat of his efforts beginning to show, he reached the digger and its driver still patiently at work. He was rebuilding a protective wall of sand dunes between the great sea and the small army of rushes and flaxes that were protecting the dunes from the tireless battle of natural forces. The driver raised his hand in a short wave to him, then carried on his work, and after watching for five minutes, John decided to retrace his steps back to the car. Just as he was walking off, the digger's engine dropped in revs and the scene went suddenly quieter. He stopped and turned around. The bucket had caught at something. The driver had exited the cab and jumped down from the tracks to investigate what he'd uncovered. Being a journalist and naturally curious, it was too much of an opportunity to ignore for John, so he walked the short distance back to the digger. The driver was pulling at something from the darker mass of wet sand he'd been excavating. John wandered up as the driver dragged at it and finally pulled it free. He stood there, contemplating his find. John stopped beside him, caught his eye and they greeted again, both nodding in silence.

'Bloody rubbish people bury round here,' the digger driver's gruff voice grumbled, as he pointed at the mass at his feet.

John's eyes were suddenly transfixed. It was two pairs of jeans and two sweatshirts, with dark stains of blood and grime covering them both, and two animal suits. One was a gorilla suit and the other was a large cat outfit of some kind, complete with pairs of bright red, reflective eyes. The animal suits were also covered in large sticky, dark red patches that had congealed and the smell coming from them was like rotting meat. John looked up at the sky above him, the clouds drifting into symbolic shapes and back out again. He studied the birds wheeling about, their tiny shapes spiralling up in the great blue vault. He began to go through all the details in his mind — again. It was a long, lonely walk back to the car and all the way the gears in his mind whirred round, like the hands of a sped-up clock. By the time he finally got back to the car, he knew exactly which story he was going to write this week. It would be Jeremy's story.

ABOUT THE AUTHOR

Jeremy Brock is an author currently living in Auckland, New Zealand. He writes fiction and non-fiction and loves writing horror and murder mysteries. The short story format has always intrigued him but his greatest love is the sea and he has been living on his boat for more than a decade. One day he will return to the land…

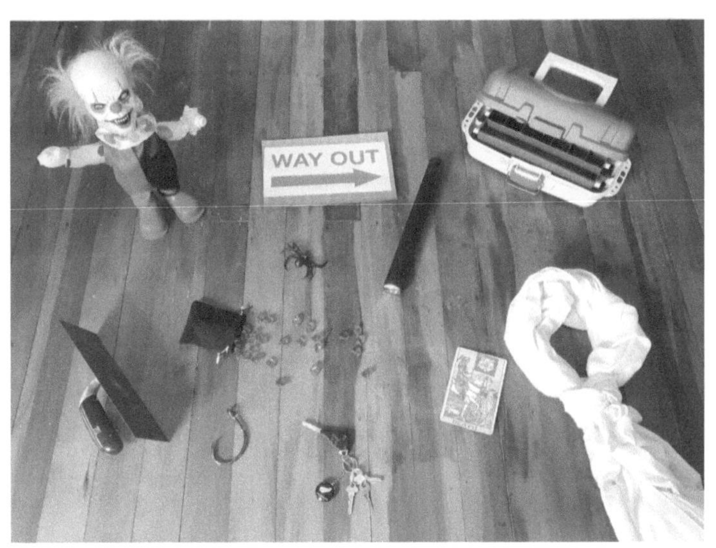
WAY OUT